STOLEN KISS

STOLEN KISS

by

Spencer Greene

2023

ISBN 13: 978-1-63679-364-1

This Trade Paperback Original Is Published By
Bold Strokes Books, Inc.
P.O. Box 249
Valley Falls, NY 12185

First Edition: March 2023

Credits
Editor: Cindy Cresap
Production Design: Susan Ramundo
Cover Design By Ink Spiral Design

Dedication

To NP, may our life together be slightly
less dramatic than *Stolen Kiss*.

CHAPTER ONE

Anna had been in her hometown twenty-six minutes, and she was already sitting on a barstool ordering a shot of whiskey. Twenty-six minutes was how long it took to become completely emotionally drained. What had she been thinking? Deciding to come home was clearly a mistake. She was without a car, without direction, and without a friend. Sitting at a no-name dive affectionately called "the Bar" by locals—the first place Anna had gotten drunk—on a Thursday afternoon, this was a new level of bleak. Not that Anna hadn't had her fair share of bleak moments over the last few months. It was actually those bleak moments that had propelled her into this less-than-ideal homecoming. Now she was three miles from her parents, the people least likely to be surprised by her current state of affairs—jobless, apartment-less, and preparing herself to ask for help.

Well, maybe not jobless and apartmentless quite yet.

It wasn't just her current situation or her desperation that brought Anna back to Trenton, it was an accumulation of everything. Her breakup with Beth six months ago had lead Anna to a realization. She was sick of feeling fragmented. She had already wasted too much energy avoiding her family. Ultimately, that's what ended things with Beth, her first "real" relationship, if you didn't count her many flings and one-night stands, which she didn't. Knowing her family didn't accept her made it so she couldn't envision a future.

Or at least that's how Beth put it when she left.

So there she was, single again. Her usual style of sleeping with different people and never getting too attached wasn't quite doing it anymore. She couldn't help but think how nice it would be to have someone to talk to, someone to share what she'd been going through. Anna didn't even know where to start. She had never *really* let anyone in before.

"You want another, Anna?" the bartender, George, asked.

"Actually, George, can I change to a beer?"

"Sure. Here, try this local brew. I'm sure you get all sorts of 'craft beer' in New York," he said with animated air quotes, "but I think Trenton is coming along. This one is from a small brewery owned by Josh Harris. I don't know if you remember, but he went to high school with us?"

Anna absolutely remembered Josh. Not only was his family close friends with her parents, but he was also her brother's best friend. They hadn't seen each other in a while, but she always heard about him from her mom who had a less-than-subtle setup agenda. Another frustrating facet of her parents' denial about her sexual orientation. Anna took a sip.

"Mmm, that's actually amazing."

"Yeah, I know. Josh is kind of legit!"

"I can see that," Anna said with genuine smile.

"So, George, how did you get this spot here at the Bar?"

"Ah yeah, it's weird right? Coming back and seeing me bartending and not off doing some post-whatever at wherever university."

George had been a stellar student when they were both in high school together.

"Well, my family owns the bar and when my mom got sick, I filled in and then I guess five years passed and here I am." George answered without the slightest bit of insecurity. Anna could tell he was in his element, and proud of his establishment.

Trenton was tiny, and Anna had known George since grade school. They hadn't been close friends at school, but they'd always gotten along. Looking back, it was probably because he wasn't quite the typical set in Trenton. The new blue streak in his hair didn't exactly scream *Antiques Roadshow*. Anna and George looked nothing like they had in high school. With George's blue hair and Anna's full sleeve tattoos, they could almost be members of the same indie band today.

Anna had been a bit of a loner growing up, with the exception of a select few. She couldn't help but think how hard it was to see who people really were under all that adolescent performance.

Like most of the people Anna knew from her childhood, she hadn't seen George in many years. Even the few high school friends she had were not a part of her life anymore. It was almost as if she knew growing up to pack light, that she'd be out of there as soon as humanly possible.

She lived in New York City now—*well, maybe not anymore*—and had new friends. She rarely came back to Virginia to visit and when she did, she made sure it was in and out.

"That's awesome, George, I always loved the Bar. It's nice to have a friendly face to go along with it."

"Yeah, I'm surprised to see you here. I've seen Clay a few times, but I don't think I've seen you since graduation."

Clay was Anna's brother, older than her by two years.

"What brought you back?" George asked.

Anna sighed and took a long drink.

"No pressure, I know this can be a rough time of year."

"No, it's okay." Anna took a deep breath and prepared herself. "I guess I'm here because I have to be," she said mysteriously.

George didn't press, but he didn't fill the silence either.

"It's been hard to visit regularly. My parents aren't really that easy to hang with. Lots of expectations, if you know what I mean."

"Yeah, I get it. Having Clay as a brother can't be easy. Harvard and then that weird scholarship he won?"

"A Rhodes Scholarship." Anna took another sip. "To top it all off, it probably doesn't help that I'm gay. Not ideal in the perfect Nelson house…" Anna looked up at George, letting what she said linger in the air. She had learned early on to come out as quickly as possible. It kept her from having to deal with someone saying something offensive. She didn't have the energy to endure the awkwardness of navigating that, especially not in Trenton.

George took her empty glass and filled it again.

"That's cool. I mean, not the parents being super judgy part… that sounds like it sucks, but the being gay part. I'm actually bi."

George grinned and pointed at a little rainbow sticker behind the bar. In Anna's opinion, it was a bit too small for anyone coming in to notice, but still, it was something. Anna felt some tension fall from her shoulders.

"Wow, George, I wouldn't have guessed."

"I mean, that's the thing, it's not really something to 'guess' right?"

"Totally, what am I even talking about. Sorry, that just came out. Wow, look at me, I can't even come out without my internalized biphobia showing." Anna grimaced at her tactlessness.

"It's fine. I get much worse here in town."

"Are you out here?"

"Yeah…or at least I don't hide it. I had a boyfriend for a while. We broke up a few months ago, but you know, people know. They obviously assume I'm gay. Which is I guess better than them assuming I'm straight, but…" He trailed off.

"I'm sorry about the breakup," Anna said earnestly.

"Thanks, it was hard but I'm doing better now. And it was good to get the coming out part out of the way."

"Well, I think it's awesome, George. And selfishly, it's really nice to know I have some 'fam' nearby," Anna said with a smile.

"We're everywhere!" he said with jazz hands. "The drinks are on the house. Family discount." He flashed her a wink. "I'll be right back. We're light on staff being it's a Thursday, so I've gotta do rounds at some of the tables out front. Enjoy!"

"Thanks, George," Anna said, hoping all her interactions on this trip would be that easy.

❖

Anna was, against her better judgment, picking at the slightly stale bar nuts when she noticed the sound of someone sitting on a stool a few seats down. She looked up and saw a woman she had never seen before. In her, albeit out-of-date, experience, only locals of a certain age would frequent the Bar on a Thursday at midday. Seeing someone her own age was a surprise.

Most people Anna knew would sit down and immediately take out their phone to escape the awkwardness of being alone, but this woman seemed to be completely at ease in her solitude. It was hard not to notice that she was beautiful. Even bundled up in her winter clothes, she stood out. It was like there was an extra outline around her, highlighted on the page. She had long dark hair under a rather goofy sheepskin winter hat, something more at home at an ugly sweater party or something. The look only endeared Anna more. She had dark arched eyebrows and the hint of a dimple in one cheek. Anna couldn't look away.

The woman peered up and caught Anna's eye. It was obvious Anna had been staring. The woman gave a half smile and looked behind the bar.

"The bartender just stepped out to serve the outside tables, but he'll be back in a minute."

The woman turned to her, seeming to take her in more fully.

"Thanks," she replied, before turning back toward the bar.

Anna noticed that the woman looked frazzled and her eyes were red.

Maybe she'd been crying?

Either way, it wasn't Anna's business and she definitely didn't come to the Bar to make a new friend. Based on the woman's body language, the feeling was mutual.

"Excuse me," the woman said softly. "Could you watch my coat? I'm just going to run to the restroom."

"Sure, but I don't think there'll be much competition for your seat," Anna joked, motioning to the almost completely empty bar. She'd replied without thinking. She would have said yes to anything this woman asked.

The woman smiled. "Thanks," she said and headed toward the back.

Isn't it weird that just meeting someone makes that person somehow trustworthy enough to watch your coat? This would never happen in New York.

❖

With the mysterious woman in the bathroom, Anna had the bar to herself again, or so she thought. She heard the now-familiar crinkle of a barstool and was reminded of the seat she said she would save. But this crinkle was directly next to her. Anna felt herself get hot. It was truly intolerable when someone chose the seat next to you when you were surrounded by empty chairs. This was another city thing. Sitting too close to someone was usually an indicator of some sort of danger or awkward situation. It was a social norm violation. Turns out, this sitter was of the dangerous type.

"Come here often?" a man with a stale whiskey stench and a southern drawl asked, putting his arm on the back of her chair. This was way too familiar.

"I don't." Anna avoided eye contact by taking a sip.

The man stayed seated.

"Actually, I was hoping to have some alone time," she said, hoping he would get the blatant hint. *More than hint.*

"Yeah, I know what you mean. Sometimes you just have to get out of the house. See some new people. I sure don't mind looking at you."

Was he not getting it or choosing to ignore her wishes? Anna took another breath and closed her eyes. Under normal circumstances, she was a pretty confrontational person. She had a very short bullshit tolerance, maybe to a fault. But Anna was out of practice. She hadn't spent much time in straight bars in the last five years. Not to mention she was in her hometown and was not feeling her normal "joie de vivre" so to speak.

"Listen, man, I'm not interested," Anna said firmly. She hoped this would be enough.

"Oh, don't tell me that. I'll just enjoy the chase more," he said with a smirk.

Anna could tell he thought he was charming, despite the obvious creepiness of his comment. He seemed to think it was normal to verbalize being into non-consent. This guy had her alarm bells going off and Anna was starting to go from nervous to actually scared. The guy was looking around for George when Anna noticed the woman at the end of the bar was back. She had definitely clocked the situation. The woman grabbed her jacket.

Great! Now I'll be the only person to witness my own murder. Anna began to prepare herself for a brawl when she heard the woman's voice very close to her.

"Excuse me, sir, you're in my seat." The woman was standing in front of the creepy guy with her stance wide and her eyes fervent.

The man moved his arm from the back of Anna's chair. "I don't see you sitting in it," he said, blustering.

It occurred to Anna at this point that this man was more than creepy, and was definitely pretty drunk, especially for someone just coming into the Bar. The woman did not move an inch.

"This is my friend. We came here to catch up. She's not interested in you, which I just heard her say, and if you don't back off right now, I am going to get the bartender and let him know that you are making us both uncomfortable."

The man puffed up at her words. "Hey, bitch, back off. Your friend was just warming up to me."

She didn't react. "I think you're very mistaken about your effect on women. And good luck getting served once I talk to the bartender. I'm sure being drunk is the only way you can live with yourself."

Anna was taken aback by the intensity of the woman's dress down. She was definitely not holding back.

The man seemed to hesitate. Possibly weighing his options, specifically in regard to getting another drink.

"Fine," he said. He got up as slowly as possible, getting in a final "*cunt*" under his breath as he moved toward a back booth.

When he was gone, the woman took a wet wipe from the side bar and wiped the seat and bar before putting her coat up.

She sat down and sighed. "Still no bartender?"

"Nope," Anna responded, trying to hold back her astonishment.

"Isn't the word cunt just so frustrating! I mean, there is nothing equivalent you could say to a man," the woman said with frustration. She flipped her hair to the side and began to get herself comfortable in her seat.

"Yeah, something tells me he uses it on the regular."

"Right? It came out so casually." The woman laughed with an eye roll.

Anna liked that the woman seemed to have a sense of humor about the situation, especially considering how serious it could have been. Anna was also like that. She didn't like to dwell too long on the inevitability of moments like that in her life.

"Thank you, by the way. He was just not getting it."

"No problem. Sometimes you need numbers to get the point across." The woman gave Anna a slight smile.

"Yeah, I wish you weren't right about that," Anna said, glowering a bit.

"Honestly, I'm not sure where that came from. I'm usually not so...vicious," the woman said, showing some trepidation. "It's been a long day I guess."

"Well, vicious or not, it was awesome."

The woman laughed freely. The sight was completely disarming for Anna. Maybe Anna was looking for a friend in Trenton after all.

At that moment, George came back in. They explained what happened, and George went over to the man and strongly persuaded him to move to another establishment. The guy left pretty quickly, considering the fuss he made with Anna and the woman, but

George was a big guy, and he did not look like someone you wanted to argue with. When he came back, he gave the woman a free beer as well.

"Fuck men!" she said, holding up her glass to Anna and George.

George made himself a shot. "I'll drink to that."

❖

Anna could not stop looking at the woman. She was even more captivating up close. Not to mention her display of force. For Anna, interest was very quickly becoming attraction. She was feeling that pull, the one that always got her in trouble. Women for Anna were often trouble. And the last thing she needed was to be attracted to some woman from Trenton.

Anna was definitely getting ahead of herself. She wasn't even sure if the woman was queer. Still, Anna was good at reading vibes, and she was not getting a strong "exclusively straight" vibe. The woman looked at her a little longer than was typical for a straight woman. Anna assumed it was because she had been staring first, but after seeing her talk to George and considering the woman in a more natural state, she was picking up on something. It was early, and it was subtle, but it was possible her attraction was not one-sided.

"So, what's your name?" the woman asked.

"Anna, you?"

"Louise."

"This is George, by the way."

"Nice to meet you, Louise." George grabbed some coasters and straws. "Hey, it's picking up outside so enjoy your drink and call me if you need me to get the bat," he said, puffing out his chest. Anna was sure George relied more on his size than his bite.

Anna resumed looking at Louise. She was already feeling that jittery feeling in her chest. If she were in New York, she would have gone straight to flirting. But she was in her hometown, and she was not feeling particularly confident considering the week she had ahead of her.

"So, are you from here?" Anna asked.

"No, I'm actually in town from Seattle."

"That's a long way away! What brings you to Trenton?"

Louise began to play with her cocktail napkin. "I'm meeting my boyfriend's family for the first time."

Anna deflated.

That settled that.

Ultimately, knowing Louise had a boyfriend was a good thing. It was the equivalent of an ice-cold shower.

"Wow, that's heavy. Traveling across the country for your boyfriend. I can't even imagine traveling to another borough for somebody I'm dating...But good for you!" Anna said, correcting herself. She didn't mean to reveal how jaded she was.

"Yeah, it's kind of a head trip," Louise said, feigning humor. The laughter didn't reach her eyes. Anna thought about when she'd first noticed Louise at the bar, red-eyed and flustered.

"Where is this boyfriend?" Anna asked. Anna hoped this idiot wasn't the reason she'd been crying.

"He's flying in this evening. I needed to burn a few hours before going to his family's place. Liquid courage!" she said, lifting her glass. "We're long distance right now, so we didn't fly together."

"Long distance? Must be difficult," Anna said, sort of wishing they could stop talking about the boyfriend while also trying to remind herself of his existence. It was taking effort to persuade herself not to flirt.

"I mean, it's really not. It works for me 'cause I'm in medical school. I'm always busy." Louise moved on to ripping small pieces off her cocktail napkin.

"Wow, medical school, that's pretty fancy," Anna said playfully.

"It's not quite as glamorous as it sounds."

"No really, that's amazing! I know firsthand how long of a process it is to become a doctor. You must be really dedicated."

"Are you in med school?"

"No! No, no no."

"Wow, that's a lot of 'nos' for something you were just praising me for," Louise teased.

"No, wait, not like that, sorry, um…" Anna took a pause and got her thoughts organized. "I have a doctor in my family is all. Incredibly admirable profession, it's just I'm not really math, science, school-y if you know what I mean. A bit more on the creative side, or at least I thought I was."

"So then 'secondhand knowledge' might be more accurate," Louise corrected her with a smirk.

"Yes, I guess it just feels like I went through it too!" Anna laughed.

Louise seemed to be considering something. Anna waited a moment, but Louise continued to contemplate.

"What made you want to be a doctor?" Anna asked.

Louise shifted in her seat and Anna could tell the air had changed a bit.

"I knew someone growing up who became very sick." Louise swallowed hard. "I just wanted to help."

Anna wished she had asked something that wasn't so painful.

"It was cancer. Ever since, I've been working to specialize in oncology."

Anna didn't know what to say. She wanted to ask more questions, but there was something foreboding about the conversation. The silence between them was heavy. Louise seemed to shift the air again. Her eyes lost that faraway look, and she turned back toward Anna.

"Sorry, I usually don't talk about that. I get asked that question a lot and I usually just say 'to help people.' Like I said before, it's been a long day." Her smile was half-hearted and clearly for Anna's comfort.

"Thank you for telling me."

Their eyes met, and for a moment, Anna stopped breathing. Louise looked away first and coughed softly.

"So, what do you do?"

Ugh. My favorite question.

"Honestly, at the moment, nothing." Anna could feel herself shrink at her own words. She'd been brighter since chatting with Louise, but with that question, her situation came tumbling back to the forefront of her mind.

"Sore subject?"

"It's fine. I'm just sort of at a low point. I'm a web designer and I started my own company that sort of catered to that community. Anyway, long story short I took a risk, and in just about"—Anna looked at her watch—"seventy-seven hours, the site I created will be shutting down for the foreseeable future."

"I'm sorry, that sucks." Louise looked genuinely upset.

"Yeah, I'm trying to come to terms with it. It's kind of why I'm here."

"At this bar drinking your sorrows away?" Louise joked.

Anna was relieved to have an opportunity to change the tone of the conversation.

"No...well, yes, here too," Anna said with the same lightness. "But I mean in Trenton. With family, for who knows how long..." Anna trailed off.

There was a pause in their conversation as Louise looked thoughtful.

"Maybe this is just a recharging moment, for your next adventure."

"That's a very optimistic way of seeing things."

"Optimistic yes, but you never know what you're on the precipice of. You can't know what's right over there." Louise gestured across the bar. "Endless possibilities." Louise's eyes twinkled.

It was nice for a moment to let some of that positivity seep in.

"Maybe," Anna said, reaching for another sip of her beer.

Louise reached for hers as well, holding it up in cheers. "To new beginnings!" Louise said with bravado.

"To recharging…" Anna returned reluctantly.

A calm set in between them. A feeling had been growing beneath the surface, and each second had Anna more aware of it. She tried to put it out of her mind.

"Hey, this might be personal so feel free to not answer, but you seemed upset when you came in," Anna said. She was conscious that the conversation had focused mainly on her, and she had been burning to know what had upset Louise.

Louise looked at Anna, studying her face for something. Anna tried to act normal, but her heart was beating so fast.

"Fuck it, I have no one else to talk to, might as well."

"Wow, that's flattering!" Anna said in mock indignation.

"No, you know what I mean," Louise said, laughing as well. She grew quiet and did that thing again where she looked a little too long. The attraction Anna was feeling was starting to become a problem, especially when she was trying hard to listen. Louise's mood seemed to shift again, giving Anna a feeling of whiplash.

"So my boyfriend's great, but I'm just not really sure I'm ready to be in a long-term relationship. I was trying to figure out how to tell him when he sprung this trip on me. Bought the tickets and everything. He was really excited, but I just feel a little… ambushed. Please stop me if this is too boring or personal."

"No, it's fine, I asked! That's a totally normal way to feel. I would hate if I had a trip to visit someone's parents sprung on me."

"Yeah, I guess you're right. We've been together about a year. I mean, this is the first time I've even had an opportunity to meet his family. It just feels so fast, you know?"

She continued to rip her napkin. The faraway look returned to her eyes.

George came in and got them refills. Anna realized she was really starting to feel the previous few drinks. This was her last for sure. She had to look at least somewhat put together when she saw her parents.

Louise began again. "It's just...I don't know." She seemed frustrated and nervous.

"Hey, listen, you're never going to see me again, I'm not going to say anything, what could it hurt talking it out with me?"

Louise gave Anna that searching look again. And Anna tried to remind herself to look normal while simultaneously forgetting to breathe again. Louise's expression was almost haunted. She pulled her eyes away from Anna's and looked back across the bar. She'd been clasping the barstool with both hands.

"I just don't think I'm in love with him," Louise blurted out. "Wow, I can't believe I just said that. Is that awful?"

Anna tried to calm her racing heart. She tried to quickly process what Louise said and all the many feelings it brought up in her. She tried to answer honestly.

"It's not awful if it's the truth. It's always a good thing to be honest."

"You think so?" Louise asked, failing to find any part of her napkin that she hadn't already ripped.

"What about when it hurts someone?" The haunted look was back. Anna wanted desperately to take that pain away from her.

"I think that's when the truth matters most, when it's hardest to say."

Anna wasn't sure where she was getting random wisdom from, but it just sort of poured out of her.

"People heal; life is too short to fake even a minute of it."

Louise seemed to be mulling over Anna's words.

"I mean, listen, I'm not an expert on honesty, but I'd bet on it being the right thing nine out of ten times at least."

George, who had just come back in, was cackling from the other end of the bar. Anna smiled a little thinking of the irony of this conversation.

Louise sat up straight. "What's so funny? Did I do something embarrassing?"

"No, no. Nothing like that."

George exclaimed from the other end of the bar, "I'm just laughing at Anna here. Before you came in, she was talking about her own little journey with *honesty*."

Louise looked at Anna puzzled.

Anna rolled her eyes.

"I'm gay, that's why he's laughing."

Louise seemed stunned for a moment. Anna realized she may have misread Louise.

"Did I just freak you out?" Anna asked.

Anna asked the question automatically, but she was already feeling vigilant about what the answer might be.

"No, I'm sorry. I was just surprised. Shit, that was dumb." Louise seemed to shift away slightly in her seat.

Is she trying to get away from me?

"I wasn't surprised. Never mind just…forget it. I promise I'm not some crazy homophobe," she finished lamely.

The comment was weird and her body language had Anna's walls up. There was another heavy pause in their conversation. This one was nothing like the ones from earlier that had this unspoken charge. Louise was avoiding Anna's eyes.

"Okay, whatever, that's just why George was laughing. Me, giving advice on honesty when my parents barely even acknowledge that part of my life," Anna said, trying to temper the ice in her voice.

Louise seemed to let her body relax and settle back into her cadence from before.

"Yeah, that is really tough. What's the deal with them? They know, right?"

"Well…" Anna decided to disregard the last few minutes and answer honestly.

"I've known I was gay since I was ten. I told them my freshman year in college, so when I was nineteen. Since then, no comment, no questions about my life, and just vague allusions to men I should meet because they think we would 'get along.'" Anna looked down at her feet. "Obviously, I could do more pushing, but it's just not something I ever enjoy doing. They're so set in their ways and want so badly to pretend it isn't happening. I guess I just let them pretend."

"Why? What's their deal? Are they Westboro Baptists or something?"

"No," Anna replied with a sigh. "Not that bad. They're just conservative. I live in New York and my life is so different from theirs. It's just another thing on the list of things they wish were different about me. My job, my tattoos, my clothes, my sexual orientation, basically...me." Anna could feel herself getting dark. "I'm sorry I'm being such a downer, hence the bar on a Thursday afternoon look," she said with self-deprecating laugh and a hand twirl.

"No, it's fine. I'm clearly not one to talk." Louise mimicked the hand twirl.

Anna smiled, finally feeling the tension from earlier start to melt away.

"And for the record," Louise said, "I love your tattoos." The comment could have been innocent, but it wasn't. The way Louise looked at her was impossible to mistake. She was flirting. Anna couldn't think of what to say. One second, Louise was acting like Anna had leprosy and the next she was blatantly flirting.

"I can relate to expectations and pressure," Louise added. "I hate hearing that they treat you like that." Louise had a genuine scowl on her face. "Anyone who can't see how wonderful you are doesn't deserve you in their life."

Anna froze, shocked by Louise's words and how they lifted her up.

"That's sweet of you to say, but you don't really know me," Anna responded. Her words came out harsh, but she only meant that she didn't want Louise to be kind just for the sake of it.

Louise gave her that look Anna had been curious about all afternoon.

"I can just tell."

The comment lingered in the air. Their eyes met again. Anna could feel Louise's thigh lightly touch hers. A random movement, maybe, but she was acutely aware of the sensation.

They continued to chat about Seattle and New York, both fans of each city, and realized they had very similar interests. They both liked pretentious movies and bad pop music. Anna could see that Louise's spirits had lifted and her own dismal mood had changed. The more they talked, the more the air seemed to crackle. At one point, Louise was laughing and she put her hand on Anna's thigh. Again, it could have been unconscious, but Anna knew something was happening. Maybe Louise wasn't aware, sometimes people weren't aware of how their bodies betrayed their true feelings.

Was this mutual?

Looking into Louise's eyes, Anna was slowly convincing herself it was.

❖

It was getting late, and Anna needed to start moving toward going to see her parents. She'd been dragging her feet for the better part of thirty minutes. George was already wiping down the booths as the weird Christmas crowd was petering out.

"I should probably get going," Anna said, her words heavy.

Anna could already feel a sadness begin to take over; she didn't want this conversation to end. Louise looked at her watch with shock.

"Oh my God, yeah, I am way late. I was supposed to text my boyfriend thirty minutes ago. I just totally lost track of time."

The word "boyfriend" rung sharply in Anna's ears. They each packed their stuff and left a big tip, compensating for all the freebies. They walked out together only to stand awkwardly in the street. The night was chilly, or was it the sudden distance between them?

"Well…" Anna said, searching for the words. "It was… unexpected…meeting you. I mean…it's been nice."

Why was she being so weird? Anna was usually pretty able to converse, and they had been so connected inside. There was something about the shift in location that had brought a certain reality to the forefront. Anna decided it would be best to escape as quickly as possible.

"I'm going to walk over to the store to get flowers for my mom before I grab a cab." She gestured vaguely toward the alleyway next to the bar that led to a nearby shopping center. She meant to walk away as soon as possible, but she found that her legs weren't working properly. A lull formed and hung in the air.

Louise spoke. "Okay, are you sure you don't need a ride?" Her tone seemed artificial. "My boyfriend has a rental. He won't mind. I just texted him. He'll be here in five."

Anna was thrown off by the tone and the offer for a ride, with the boyfriend of all people. Maybe they hadn't been on the same page after all. It was jarring to shift from a comfortable connection to awareness that they were strangers.

Anna was never going to see Louise again, so she decided to take a risk, one just like the many risks that had led to her recent downfall.

Anna stepped closer to Louise, never letting go of her eyes. Louise was giving her the same gaze she'd been seeing across the bar all night.

"I'm good," she said. "I'd rather not sit in a car with the guy whose girlfriend I've been flirting with all night."

Louise looked stunned, her eyes growing large. Anna held her stare. Having said it out loud felt like electricity. The connection traveled between them, permeating everything. Anna had gone as far as she could. She wasn't pushy; not everyone was comfortable looking at the subtext.

"It was nice meeting you, Louise, have a good…life I guess," she said with finality. Speaking the truth had left her with a feeling of closure.

Anna turned away from Louise and walked down the alley. Putting her hands in her pockets, she let out a regretful sigh.

Good-bye forever, Louise.

She tried to ignore the desire for another minute with Louise. Suddenly, she recognized the sound of footsteps behind her. She looked back hopefully.

"Wait!" Louise said, slowing down as she approached.

Anna stayed in her spot, obedient to Louise's words. She waited to hear more, but Louise didn't speak. She was breathing hard, her cheeks and lips flushed red. Louise didn't need to speak, it was already in the atmosphere.

Louise and Anna moved toward each other purposefully, stopping within a hair's breadth of each other. Anna's heart pounded. Louise's hands were on Anna's waist, Anna could feel the magnetism. They stood for the longest moment with their foreheads touching, not in hesitation, but in anticipation. Anna reached up to touch Louise's face, her eyes never leaving Louise's lips. Before Anna could process what was happening, Louise kissed her fiercely with warm, soft lips. Anna's body vibrated with excitement, and she kissed back, deepening it more. Anna was completely suspended in the feeling, in the moment. She felt Louise's tongue begin to explore her own as they melted together. A moan escaped Louise and their kiss deepened again. Anna felt she only existed at the points in her body that were touching Louise. She felt untethered. She let herself feel Louise, not thinking for a moment about the consequences. Anna couldn't remember who pulled away first, but their lips separated. Their foreheads still touched, tied together by an imaginary string, as Anna tried to calm her breathing.

"I've been wanting to do that all night," Louise said, as if she had been holding back the words as well as the kiss. She was smiling wistfully and Anna couldn't help but smile back. As their breathing slowed, reality began to set in. Louise began to untie the string. Somehow, Anna resisted the urge to pull her close again.

"I—" Anna started, but Louise put a finger up to her lips.

"Let's just leave it at this," she said with finality.

Anna felt the excruciating loss of Louise's hands on her body as Louise started to back away. She wanted to be covered in Louise, anything to stop the moment from ending.

"Good-bye, Anna," Louise said.

Anna searched for something to say, something to prolong their interlude, but she heard what was under Louise's words, a request to let her go, and so she held back her protests.

"Bye, Louise," Anna said, the words like razor blades in her throat.

They both walked their separate ways. Anna looked back. Louise did not.

On Anna's journey home, she replayed the kiss on repeat. She reveled in it from the grocery store to the cab. Her movements felt strange; she felt altered from the Anna who first came to Trenton a few hours ago.

It was just a moment, with a beautiful person. Leave it at that.

But Anna couldn't help but think, in a different place, at a different time, what could have been.

CHAPTER TWO

L ouise stood on the corner outside the unnamed bar where she had just spent the last few hours. She could still feel adrenaline pumping through her body. Louise had just kissed a stranger. A beautiful, interesting stranger but still, a stranger. The whole thing was so impulsive, so unlike her. But then again, everything she'd done since meeting Anna felt unlike her. At least, not like who she had been lately. Perhaps another version of her could have fantasized all afternoon about Anna's hands, her mischievous smile, the taste of her lips, but not this Louise. Not the Louise she had so painstakingly cultivated over the last few years. She'd been doing what was expected of her for so long that she couldn't even remember the last time she had felt so…

What was it she was feeling?

Alive.

This version of Louise was supposed to be gone, buried in the ground.

Buried with Gwen.

Louise shook her head. She couldn't think about Gwen right now. She wanted to hold onto the happiness that was filling her for as long as possible, not consider what her actions meant or who they affected. She wanted to exist here, now.

Her euphoria was short-lived. A black Nissan rental pulled up in front of her and cut the ignition. Clay was here. Clay, her boyfriend.

Clay, who she just cheated on.

He stepped out of the car looking very at home on the street corner with his long coat and his boyish smile. He came around to her side of the car, greeting her with a deep hug. The electricity left her body, and a slow drizzle of guilt started to ease in to replace it. Clay's hug was so comforting and safe that the guilt only intensified.

"I'm so happy you're here," Clay said into her neck, holding Louise tighter.

He pulled away and looked into her eyes. Clay was handsome, with a square jaw and bristly five o'clock shadow. His eyes were kind, something rare for men as attractive as him. He looked at her with affection.

"I've missed you," he said with sincerity. The comment reminded Louise that he could be open about his emotions in a way Louise could not.

"I know, I can't believe I'm here!" Louise hoped her lack of vulnerability would go unnoticed.

The awful feeling of guilt continued to grow. It had been a month since she last saw Clay. He had visited her in Seattle, but she'd been so preoccupied with exams at the time that now she could hardly remember it.

"Come on," he said, rubbing her arms to keep her warm. "Let's get in the car so you don't freeze out here."

Louise was anything but cold, but she did want to get some much-needed space to gather her thoughts. It felt like the mess of emotions she was feeling was all over her face. They got into the car and Clay started the engine. He paused for a moment and turned to her.

"You know what, I feel like I haven't talked to you in forever and I don't really want to go straight into 'parents mode.' Want to get a coffee first?"

Louise was conflicted. She wasn't sure if she was ready for a big long talk with Clay, but she also wasn't looking forward to parent-meeting stress. The parent stress won out.

"Coffee sounds good," Louise said with a smile. Thankfully, she was starting to regain the ability to speak.

Clay reached over the console and put his hand on her cheek, similar to the way Anna had just a few minutes ago.

Then again, it wasn't similar at all.

"Have I said yet how much I've missed you?"

"You have," Louise said, giving Clay another smile.

Clay leaned over and kissed her on her already bruised lips. His kiss was sweet and tender—so different from the one with Anna. Louise felt hyper-aware of the contrast between his rough, stubbly face and Anna's soft, incredible skin. And there was such a stark difference in the intensity of kissing someone for the first time versus someone so familiar. Finally, Clay settled back in his seat and put the car into drive.

"There's really only one coffee shop in a place this small, but I think you'll love Delilah's." Clay pulled out, turning the radio up.

Louise looked out her window as they passed the Bar. She was trying her hardest to leave the version of herself that was still pulsing with desire in the alley with that kiss.

❖

Louise and Clay pulled up in front of a cute coffee shop in the center of Trenton's main square. Louise continued to be surprised by how small Trenton was, but she could still see the appeal. Delilah's was charming and eclectic, with none of the franchise modernity or hipster-chic style so common in Seattle. It felt more like an auntie's living room, but with a strong roasted coffee bean smell. Louise and Clay ordered at the counter and sat down. Clay checked his phone and Louise used the opportunity to excuse herself to use the restroom.

She was washing her hands when she noticed her reflection in the mirror above the sink. She didn't look any different, which was shocking to her. It felt like her face should have been marked with some kind of evidence of her misdeed, maybe a scarlet "A" across her forehead, but there was nothing of the sort. She wasn't possessed by some spirit; her actions were her own.

Earlier that week, Louise had finished her semester and was hit with a heavy exhaustion. The feeling was deep in her bones. She thought completing the semester would be a relief, but instead she felt untethered. That morning, she had woken up early to get on a plane, only to learn upon arriving in Virginia that her rental car reservation had been canceled without her knowledge. It was only after she'd spoken to basically everyone at the rental place and confirmed that not even a moving van was available that someone suggested she could take a shuttle to Trenton.

She'd made it just in time to squeeze onto the small bus, only to sit for four hours on what should have been a two-hour drive. When she finally arrived in Trenton, not only was she exhausted from her studies, lack of sleep, and the stress of traveling, but she couldn't stop wondering if this trip was even worth it. Clay had bought tickets for them both and enthusiastically insisted she come meet his family. Louise tended to default to "yes" if she was asked a question while stressed or distracted, which had caused problems for her both personally and professionally. In this instance, it meant that her relationship with Clay was moving to the next level without Louise being in the driver's seat.

At least Louise tended to be good with parents generally. It didn't hurt that she was an overachiever on the road to becoming a doctor. Older people always liked that sort of thing. Louise knew she could get through the week, but she wasn't looking forward to the conversation about slowing down that she'd probably need to have with Clay when she got back to Seattle.

All of this had come to a head as she found herself on a random street in Trenton with hours to burn, staring at a neon sign that said simply "Bar." Usually, a sign like that meant whatever was inside was a nice, no-frills dive bar, and this was no exception.

Before she'd even sat down, Louise had noticed Anna. She'd been holding a beer glass, a bit hunched over, looking despondently at the wall of pictures behind the bar. Her clothes matched her dark demeanor—slightly distressed jeans, black-on-black Converses, and a black Breeders T-shirt. Louise couldn't help but admire what appeared to be a full sleeve tattoo covering Anna's right arm. Unable to help herself and completely out of character, Louise blatantly checked her out.

What was the hurt? She was just looking.

Anna's hair was dark like her own and shoulder length. The messy-on-purpose cut was cool in a way Louise was sure she could never pull off. And something about her moody demeanor made the whole look incredibly sexy.

Anna seemed out of place. Not so much her aesthetic, as the bar was kind of a match, but there was a separateness about her. Maybe it was just the weirdness Louise was feeling, her dissociative state post-semester. Still, Anna was intriguing, and Louise had become well practiced at avoiding intriguing people.

She'd intentionally opted for a seat as far as possible from Anna. But she was secretly pleased that the distance didn't keep Anna from talking to her. Louise remembered thinking how strange it was to hear Anna's voice that first time, how almost familiar it sounded even though she was sure she'd never heard it before.

Perhaps it was from a past life or a dream.

Louise wasn't a particularly spiritual person, so even that thought was suspect.

When Louise returned from the bathroom and saw the heavy harassment taking place, she found herself stepping in to help without thinking. She was often in rooms with men who needed to be heard. But her usual tactic was to lay low and navigate those situations indirectly. She was surprised that she had instead taken an overtly offensive position.

Hours later, staring in the bathroom mirror, Louise wondered if she'd really needed to move to the seat next to Anna. Had she just been creating circumstances to force herself into the place she'd wanted to be all along? It was hard to know for sure.

So there Louise was, sitting next to the beautiful woman who she found interesting, and who became more and more beautiful and interesting the more the afternoon progressed. Louise couldn't help but think about all the things she liked about this woman. When Anna spoke, she took her time; she brought Louise with her through hand gestures and playful smiles. When she looked at Louise, her gaze never wavered. Louise couldn't do anything but look right back.

The tension between them was palpable. Louise felt the prickling of goose bumps each time their eyes met. Then Anna said she was gay and everything stopped for Louise.

Shit.

All of a sudden, every look, every gesture, every laugh had new meaning. In that moment, Louise became unavoidably aware that she was intensely attracted to Anna. Everything clicked into place. It seemed ridiculous looking back that someone saying they were gay could have such an effect, but that's how Louise was. How she'd made herself.

Louise had known for a long time that she was attracted to men and women. But it was something she tended to avoid thinking about, mostly because so much of her sexuality had for so long been wrapped up in Gwen. Gwen had been her first kiss, her first love, her first everything. Mostly, she just didn't want to think about Gwen.

Louise and Gwen had met in kindergarten and grown up together. Gwen was smart and adventurous. She had a dark sense of humor that always managed to make Louise laugh. Having a friend like Gwen meant that Louise went through life with someone always in her corner, someone always there to hold her up. She tried to be the same for Gwen as well. Sometime in high school though, their friendship changed.

Gwen knew before Louise, and had started to pull away. At first, Louise was confused. That support and love that she had always felt was suddenly gone and she didn't understand why. Even now, Louise could remember that feeling of devastation. She racked her brain for weeks, trying to figure out why Gwen had gone silent. Later she would learn that Gwen was trying to give her space, that she didn't believe Louise could possibly feel the same. But as Louise examined the wound within her, she discovered the truth as well. She had fallen in love with Gwen.

When she got up the courage to tell Gwen, their time apart immediately ended. The new beginning had been scary and exhilarating. When Louise's fear threatened to overwhelm her, Gwen had been brave as always, and being with Gwen helped make Louise brave as well. Louise couldn't help herself when it came to Gwen, it was like she was caught in a current.

As they grew older, their love matured. It wasn't always easy and they weren't always sure their relationship would survive, but they fought fiercely for each other. If it wasn't coming out to their families and friends, it was deciding what to do after graduation. They were young and inexperienced, not yet jaded by the world, and they still believed love could conquer all.

And then Gwen got sick. And then she was gone. And Louise was left alone to pick up the pieces of her shattered heart.

There aren't words for what Louise went through. Even after a two-year hiatus from school—one year watching the love of her life wither away, one year unable to get out of bed—she still couldn't do anything but feel the intense, irreparable pain of her loss. But eventually, Louise realized her life was starting to pass her by. She knew Gwen would have never forgiven her if she'd let that happen. Resolutely, she decided to get organized, turning her attention toward routine, goals, growth. Anything to distract her from the loneliness of losing someone who was so much a part of her. Louise decided then and there that she couldn't, wouldn't be a mess of emotions anymore, not the good or the bad. No, she would dedicate her life to helping to cure the disease that took her love. Outside of that, there wasn't much more she wanted for herself.

The people she dated next all fit nicely into the new framework she had built for herself. Sometimes a person would cross her path who had that same pull, an echo of Gwen, but she would just turn to what had become her mantra: routine, structure, stability. She didn't want to love like that again because she didn't want to hurt like that again. It was that simple.

Louise knew, at least on a subconscious level, that Anna was dangerous the moment she saw her across the room. It felt so frustrating to want someone like Anna, someone so explicitly off limits in the world she built for herself. But her usual avoidance tactics didn't seem to work. Louise had considered ending their conversation and moving back to her seat, but time passed and she just...didn't. She found herself opening up to Anna, moving closer, a light touch, a flirty smile. Most of all, she found herself unable to look away from Anna's lips. At one point, she forgot to listen she was so distracted by what they might taste like.

Looking back, she was shocked by how honest she had been with Anna. Even alluding to Gwen, a subject she never spoke about to anyone except her mom who had watched them both grow up, and who had grieved as well. Louise could feel herself backsliding with Anna, losing control over the conversation. Finally, when she admitted that she wasn't in love with Clay, she felt she could not unring that bell. When Anna mentioned that they both needed to get going, Louise began the process of organizing her feelings and thoughts into nice little compartments in her head.

Connections like this happen all the time. Just because she's gay doesn't mean she's into you. You're about to meet your boyfriend's parents!

All of this rattled around in her head as she waited for Clay outside. When she asked if Anna wanted a ride, it wasn't because she wanted Anna to say yes, but because she thought pretending there was nothing happening between them might absolve her of her feelings of guilt. She didn't have an insane attraction to a stranger at a bar while waiting for her boyfriend. She was not dreading the feeling of watching Anna walk away. But when Anna showed her cards, saying quite openly that she had been flirting, Louise could no longer fight it.

Louise didn't know why she did it. Was it some sort of self-sabotage cheating thing? Was it a sudden fugue state brought on by alcohol and air travel? She didn't know. But she did know she couldn't stop herself. She didn't want to stop herself. Louise and

Anna had had a connection. She just couldn't let Anna leave and always wonder what being with her would've felt like, what her lips tasted like. Now she knew.

Louise walked away imagining the memory of that evening as something she could always have, a reminder that her desire wasn't really gone, that a person could still affect her, even in the most unexpected moments.

Looking in the mirror at Delilah's, Louise tried again to sort the increasingly messy situation into its right place. She would walk out of this room as if that kiss, that conversation, that connection had never happened. And later, when she was alone, maybe she could allow herself to remember.

❖

Louise sat back down in her chair, allowing everything to settle back into its rightful place: her tea, her boyfriend, her feelings.

"It's just so weird seeing you here where I grew up. What do you think of Trenton so far?" Clay asked her.

Louise considered her response. So far, all she'd seen was a dive bar and a coffee shop.

And Anna's lips.

She tried not to react as she again shoved the intrusive thought away.

"It's small, but sweet." She cleared her throat. "I'm mostly just nervous about meeting your family."

"What! Don't be. They'll love you, I promise."

"Tell me about them again? I want a recap so I'm prepared."

Clay laughed. "I should have made you flash cards, I know how much you love to study."

Louise rolled her eyes but smiled. She was starting to fall back into her groove with Clay. He was kind and stable. She repeated it to herself, her mantra.

"Well, my mom is intense, sort of what you'd expect from someone so accomplished."

"Yeah, I've heard you say that. She must be proud of you, working on your PhD and all in England."

"She is, I mean, of course she is. She's just sort of not into the verbal affirmation stuff. It's fine though. Really, my sister has it a lot harder."

"Tell me about her. You don't bring her up very often."

"Honestly, we don't talk much. We don't have a lot in common. Belle lives in New York City and sort of has a more 'artistic' lifestyle, if you know what I mean. It's all fine, but I think she thinks I'm a yuppie, and I just don't really know what to talk about with her."

Clay did sort of dress like a yuppie, but he was totally different on the inside.

"What about your parents, how are they with her?"

"I mean, I'd say they're a bit similar to me as far as connecting. It's not really easy for all of us to relate to her. They're a lot more vocal about it though. I think they just want her to be more ambitious, to commit more. I get it, but it's also sort of intense."

"You use that word a lot with them, 'intense.'"

"Yeah, it's hard to describe. I love them, and they're really supportive, but they don't exactly hide how they feel about your choices or decisions much. I mean, you'll see!" he said with a playful wink.

With a sudden lurch, Louise's mind dumped her unwillingly back into her chair at the dive bar, watching Anna flash her own impish wink in Louise's direction.

Kind and stable. Kind and stable.

"What about your dad?"

"My dad is quiet at first, but just as intense about school and work. Super strict. He's got his routines, his opinions. He was a political lawyer, used to be pretty big in the Republican Party. He's actually considering a run for the House in a few years."

"Wow. I'd be more impressed if it wasn't the wrong party. They both sound so accomplished."

"Exactly. But don't worry, you'll fit right in, except for the Republican part," he said with a smile.

"I kind of get why your sister is a bit of a black sheep. Anyone would be in a family with so many…credentials."

"Yeah, I agree, but she kind of brings some of it on herself."

"What do you mean?"

"I just feel like sometimes she's almost *trying* to be the opposite of what they want."

"I imagine it would make it harder having a brother who is so clearly meeting their expectations."

Clay thought for a moment. "Yeah, you're right. I guess that's probably why she and I haven't connected much. See, this is why I'm glad you're here! You totally challenge me to see things I wouldn't usually look for."

Clay reached across the table for her hand and kissed it sweetly.

Kind and stable.

Louise tried to return his smile.

"I'm glad to be of service. It's always easier to look at other people's families and not your own."

"Yours next year then!" Clay said with a playful wink again.

Louise wondered if there would be a next year. She sipped her tea and tried to remind herself one more time how much she liked kind and stable.

❖

Louise and Clay pulled up to a beautiful turn-of-the-century colonial looking…*mansion?* That was the only way Louise could describe it. She knew Clay was rich, but she hadn't really conceptualized what that meant in reality. Louise grew up with a single mom in a two-bedroom apartment. She was not used to space, especially not this much space. Clay walked around the car and opened her door. He had a chivalry thing that Louise tried not to hate, but it usually grated on her. She kept this to herself, feeling it was best to pick her battles. Not to mention, this was his family's house. It might be better to let him set the tone. His family could be watching him to make sure he was using his manners.

They walked toward the house and Clay took her hand in his. Louise found she was comforted by the gesture. It was nice to have a partner, someone in your corner when going into stressful situations. Even if that stressful situation had been orchestrated by that partner…No matter.

She was nervous, but she'd left a lot of her anxiety back at the coffee shop with her stranger-kissing alter ego. She was Louise Tanner. She was accomplished, she was charming, she was caffeinated, and she was going to make a good impression. Clay rang the doorbell.

"Ready?" Clay asked, a bit more geared up than Louise expected.

She nodded, and the door opened.

A woman with gray hair styled in a perfectly quaffed shoulder-length bob answered. She was beautiful and statuesque. Louise recognized her as Clay's mother, not just from the resemblance, but from the way she carried herself. She had a presence.

"Clay darling, welcome!" she said, letting him into the foyer and lightly kissing his cheek.

The greeting was more formal than what Louise was used to at her home.

She turned to Louise who had come in behind Clay.

"And you must be Louise."

She gave Louise a brief smile and reached out to shake her hand, putting her other hand on top with implied warmth.

"Dr. Cecilia Nelson," she said formally. "I have heard so much about you. I must admit, I'm happy to have Clay consorting with a fellow member of the medical community." She flashed a conspiratorial wink.

What's with this town and their winking culture?

Louise returned the pleasantries.

"Thank you, I'm sure he has given you too high of an impression of me. It is a pleasure to meet you as well."

"Ah, modesty. That *is* a virtue." She looked over Louise as if appraising her. "But no need for that here. I am impressed."

Dr. Nelson looked around as if just realizing they were still in the foyer.

"How rude of me. Please come in. We were just getting ready to start pre-dinner cocktails. Let me take your coats. Clay, show Louise into the parlor and make sure she is comfortable."

"Thank you, Mom," Clay replied. "This way," he said, grabbing Louise's hand again.

They walked past a wall full of family portraits. It looked like the Nelsons had a long history in Virginia. Louise couldn't help but think again how different Clay's life experience was from hers.

When they got to the parlor, she was met by a distinguished looking man, with a noticeably great hairline, sitting with a tumbler of something brown and a copy of the *Wall Street Journal*. He put down his glass and stood up to greet them.

"Clay, welcome home, son." Mr. Nelson shook Clay's hand rather professionally. Louise glanced at Clay and noticed his posture had changed entirely. He was like a soldier in front of his commander.

"Thank you, Father, and let me introduce my girlfriend, Louise Tanner."

Mr. Nelson turned his focus to Louise.

"Yes, Louise, nice to meet you. William Nelson." He held his hand out to her. His body language was less stiff, and his handshake was firm but considerably warmer than what she saw with Clay.

"Thank you, your home is beautiful. I feel so honored to be invited to someplace so...historic."

"Yes, it has been in our family for many generations." Mr. Nelson began to discuss some of their family history, and she continued to smile and act interested. Truth was, she was not really a big fan of house history, especially from a multigenerational southerner who was most likely leaving out at least half of that history. White people living in the South for generations did not get rich like this without some connection to slavery. Louise hadn't thought too much about it before just because she had spent so long in the Pacific Northwest. Not that the Pacific Northwest wasn't super racist as well—this was America, after all—but you were less likely to be confronted so directly with this level of omission.

She let the conversation die off, just to get her mind to stop asking questions about Clay's family.

Clay and his father began to discuss Clay's flight in, traffic, and other banal logistics, giving Louise a chance to look around the room. She zeroed in pretty quickly on a bookshelf.

"I notice you have a pretty incredible collection of books. Is that a first edition *On the Road*?" Louise asked during a lull in the conversation.

Mr. Nelson looked over and changed gears.

"Yes, it is. I'm not a big fiction reader, especially not Kerouac—really, I'm more of a history biography type, as you can imagine—but we grew our library collection when Belle was a teen. My daughter is a ferocious reader. Unfortunately, the collection at the time was not quite as interesting to her. She always ended up with secondhand and paperbacks somehow. She didn't seem to understand the investment aspect." He sighed, sounding exasperated.

Louise felt a pause and realized she was expected to agree.

"It's wonderful that you try so hard to support your children's interests." She hoped the statement was sufficiently non-controversial.

"Yes, well, it has always been somewhat easier with Clay than with Belle."

Louise was a bit shocked to see Mr. Nelson's favoritism so blatantly and so quickly expressed.

"Speaking of Belle, is she here yet?" Clay asked. Louise couldn't tell if he was truly curious or if he was trying to change the subject from something that seemed a little tense.

Mr. Nelson sighed again. "She got here about an hour ago, said she needed to make a 'work call,'" he emphasized the phrase with air quotes, "and has been hiding in her bedroom for the last twenty minutes." He said it with an odd amount of irritation. Louise was already feeling her family drama senses tingling.

It was at that moment that Louise heard footsteps on the staircase.

"Speaking of Annabelle, there she is." Mr. Nelson turned toward the sound.

Following his gaze, Louise watched as a pair of black-on-black Chuck Taylors descended the stairs. It took Louise a good few seconds to process the scene. It was a feeling first, foreboding, then she noticed something oddly familiar about the shoes, and then about the wearer's gait. The unmistakable and completely out of place tattoos crystallized into Louise's worst nightmare. Her eyes shot up to meet the same hazel eyes she had fallen into just a few hours ago.

Oh my God.

Realization crashed into Louise with the force of a freight train. It was Anna. Anna, the person she'd spilled her guts to in the bar. Anna, the person who'd felt so special to her just hours ago. Anna, the stranger she'd kissed in an alley. Anna, Clay's sister?

Fuck.

Louise saw her emotions reflected identically on Anna's face. *Annabelle's face?* Louise needed to get herself together quickly.

Compartmentalize, put this away, deal with it later. This is Clay's sister, someone you've never met before.

Clay seemed to sense the awkward tension in the room. He was clearly used to it. He grabbed Louise's hand and pulled her over toward Anna, who had stopped short at the bottom of the stairs. She was being pulled due to her legs not quite working properly anymore.

"Belle, I'm so happy to see you," Clay said warmly, reaching out for a hug.

Anna's eyes finally shifted to Clay, which must have helped her come to her senses a bit, as she quickly hugged him back.

"Me too," she said, stealing a look into Louise's eyes over his shoulder. Nobody winked.

This is Clay's sister, someone you've never met before.

Clay stepped away. "I want to introduce you to my girlfriend, Louise." He presented Louise, who became acutely aware of how much she felt like an object he was showing off.

"Nice to meet you. I'm Louise," she repeated unnecessarily. She was suddenly gripped with indecision. She couldn't decide if she should hug Anna, like she usually would've upon meeting Clay's sister. She felt so aware of her body and she just couldn't imagine touching Anna like that, right now, in front of Clay's family, Anna's...Belle's family.

Anna saved her by holding out her hand. It was awkward for sure, but it really was the best option, considering.

Louise reached for Anna's hand. It felt soft and warm. She let go as soon as she could, trying her best not to react like she'd been burned. They were looking at each other, but not like they had been earlier, not fearlessly. It was all shifty gazes, avoiding what couldn't be said. Their bodies recognized their guilt and shame even before their minds could fully comprehend the situation.

Thankfully, at that moment, Clay's mother reappeared with a pitcher of some sort of derby-looking cocktail and five crystal glasses.

Louise managed to arrange herself farther from Anna, with Clay in between them. Anna, clearly on the same page, moved farther into the room toward her father, and toward the chair farthest from Louise. They all sat down. Incredibly, the family seemed to miss the potent uneasiness that was so clearly emanating from Louise and Anna. Louise felt trapped under its weight. But Clay and his parents launched into an easy conversation as she squirmed. Louise tried to follow the conversation, but the exchange sounded both muffled and exceedingly loud. It was as if she was watching everything from the corner of the room. It was all too hard to understand.

"So, Louise, what do you think of Trenton so far?" Dr. Nelson asked, sipping her drink deeply. Louise's name cut sharply through the air and rocketed Louise back into the somewhat stiff parlor chair. She could feel the brocade under her fingers.

Louise took an imperceptibly small sip as well, buying herself some time. All her compartmentalizing was thrown out the window, now that the one person her mind had assiduously been avoiding was sitting just across the room from her.

"I haven't seen too much yet," she said, stuttering a bit to start, "but what I have seen, I've liked." Anna—*no, Belle*—raised an eyebrow. Louise was trying not to look at Anna, but somehow that had made her more aware of her. They locked eyes again. Louise was struck by the double meaning of her words. She definitely wasn't trying to speak to their time together.

This is Clay's sister, someone you have never met before.

"Yes, she had a bite at the Bar earlier, and then went to Delilah's with me. Basically, she's seen everything," Clay said with a laugh.

"Don't say that, Clay. Louise my dear, small towns have a lot to offer. Don't worry, we'll make sure you are thoroughly charmed by Trenton by the end of your stay." Dr. Nelson gave her a pert smile. "Although not everyone can see its charm, preferring the smog and noise of a big city."

The comment was clearly pointed. Louise assumed it was a dig at Anna, knowing she lived in New York City, but it was odd because Clay had been the one poking fun at Trenton.

"The Bar isn't such an awful first impression of Trenton."

The words came from the direction of the off-limits part of the room.

"It has a lot of that local charm, don't you think?" Anna asked. The question was directed toward Louise. It was unnerving having Anna address her like this. It was clear already that Anna was better at pretending than she was.

"Yes, it definitely has a certain charm."

Louise cleared her throat and changed the subject.

"Dr. Nelson, how do you find practicing medicine in a town like Trenton?"

Louise congratulated herself on the seamlessness of her redirect. Clearly in love with talking about her work, Dr. Nelson took the opportunity to wax poetic about small towns and her large presence in the lives of the locals. Like many doctors Louise knew, Cecilia seemed most comfortable talking about herself. Conveniently, the diatribe gave Louise a bit of breathing room and she tried to calm down, focusing again on the texture of the brocade under her fingertips. She couldn't help but wonder what Anna was feeling. Was the comment about the Bar just a way to fake polite conversation with Louise? Was it a deflection from her mom's weird dig? Was it an insinuation about what had happened between them?

There was a lull in Cecilia's monologue, and Louise realized she'd missed the last thing said.

"That is interesting, Dr. Nelson," Louise recovered.

Whew.

She could feel that it was an appropriate thing to say as the conversation rhythm continued.

"Would you mind letting me know where the restroom is?" Louise broke in.

"Of course, darling, it's through the door over to your left at the end of the hall." Dr. Nelson pointed her in the right direction.

"Thank you, excuse me." She got up somewhat unsteadily from her chair and moved toward the appointed door, shocked she was able to walk normally. When she got to the bathroom, she locked the door and let herself fall against it, barricading what was beyond the confines of her hiding place. She caught a glimpse of herself in yet another bathroom mirror, this one large, ornate, and framed in gold. This was the second time today she felt compelled to talk to herself. She pressed her head back against the smooth wood of the bathroom door.

This is why I don't talk to interesting women.

CHAPTER THREE

When Anna saw Louise in the parlor, she felt a jolt of excitement. She had spent the last twenty minutes preparing herself to never see Louise again and there she was.

Wait, why is Louise here?

Then she took in the room, her brother standing proudly next to Louise, holding her hand. Putting two and two together, her heart sank.

This can't be happening.

Anna resisted the urge to pinch herself, anything to wake from what had to be some kind of sick nightmare. Since leaving the Bar, she'd been replaying their conversation and alleyway kiss on a loop. It had felt so good, and she'd counted on riding that good feeling all the way through dinner with her parents, and maybe even through the week. But now she was face-to-face with the woman who had built up her confidence, suddenly experiencing one of lowest feelings she'd ever had. The easily forgotten "boyfriend" was no longer some random James Spader look-alike jerk she'd built in her head, it was her brother, Clay. Clay, who was looking at Louise, *his girlfriend*, like she was the only person on the planet. Seeing his face, a pang of guilt hit Anna in the gut.

And then there was Louise. She was beautiful, just like before, but this time her face was white as a sheet and her eyes were wide with panic. She clearly had not been expecting to see Anna here, or possibly ever again. How ironic that Anna had wished so hard the kiss they shared had not been good-bye, only to have her wish granted in the absolute worst way possible.

Thankfully, Anna somehow had been able to get control of her body by the time she'd descended the stairs and was able to reach out her hand to Louise in a passably normal greeting. But when she'd felt that hand in hers, the same one that had held her so tightly, Anna's composure slipped. Senses heightened, she'd smelled a fragrance on Louise that she hadn't noticed at the Bar, but that she now realized had been imprinted in her memory. Anna's complete focus was on keeping space from Louise.

For once, Anna was relieved that her parents rarely asked her questions. She'd been able to observe the scene without interruption. For his part, Clay was clearly proud to be bringing somebody home, and Louise was the perfect fit in this hard to please group. Clay reached out to hold Louise's hand. Watching made Anna feel itchy. Louise and Clay looked good together. Something Anna could never achieve with anyone she brought home—in her parents' eyes at least. It sunk in even deeper knowing that the person her family was so interested in had two hours ago had her tongue down Anna's throat.

Thinking about that kiss brought another jolt to Anna's system as she listened to Louise describe her first impression of the town. Thank goodness she'd chosen a seat as far away from Louise as possible. She felt caught between her desire to listen to anything Louise had to say and wanting to run from this room, this house, this state.

Unable to handle the mess of emotions roiling through her, Anna's natural defense mechanism—detached resentment—eased its way into her thoughts. Anna wasn't in a relationship; she hadn't done anything wrong. She was just going with the flow. Other people's situations were not her problem, and this particular "situation" was no different. Yes, the fact that the other party had been her brother made it worse, but she hadn't known. Louise was the one in the wrong here. Sufficiently reassured for the moment,

Anna began to relax into her seat. She'd tuned back in to the conversation just as Louise was speaking about her time at the Bar. Anna couldn't help but feel the subtext. She wasn't trying to play with fire, but watching Clay and Louise perform, listening to her mom's passive-aggressive comments, all of it was messing with her head. Maybe it wasn't a performance? Maybe she had got it wrong that they really were the perfect couple. Did the kiss really happen?

"The Bar isn't such an awful first impression of Trenton. It has a lot of that local charm, don't you think?"

Louise's pallor was replaced with a flush of crimson in her cheeks. She'd abruptly changed the subject.

Bingo. This wasn't so easy for her either.

Anna didn't want to make Louise uncomfortable, exactly, but there were more things warring inside of her than just her indiscretion with Louise. Being in this home, in front of her family, brought to the surface all the ways she was invisible, all the ways she was unacceptable, and something instinctual was fighting to be seen. Louise's ease in erasing her, even under these circumstances, twisted a knife pushed inside her long ago.

Anna could tell no one else was picking up on the underlying tension, but it was comforting to know she wasn't alone. This was obviously uncomfortable, but there was also a part of Anna that was grateful Louise was in the room. Just knowing somebody was there, who had seen Anna in a different context, as her more authentic self for a couple of hours, mattered. She wasn't going to dwell on how much they knew about each other, that was beside the point. She could only process so much of this roller coaster of feelings at once.

Anna watched Louise excuse herself to use the restroom. Was she just trying to avoid the awkwardness?

"Clay, she is just wonderful," Anna's mom said, clearly impressed.

It seemed irrelevant that Louise hadn't said more than a handful of noncommittal sentences. *Must be nice to rest on those doctor credentials.*

Somehow, her mother's obvious double standard didn't seem to bother her as much as it usually did.

That radiant smile probably didn't hurt either.

Anna felt her face grow warm thinking about Louise's mouth.

Clay beamed with pride. "Thank you, and yes, she's very special."

Anna's stomach turned as she heard what wasn't being said. This relationship was serious for Clay, and the family wholeheartedly approved.

Another pang of guilt. Anna and Clay weren't exactly close, but she would never want to hurt him like this. He clearly loved this woman and even just knowing that Louise didn't feel the same made Anna feel defensive of him, and ashamed of herself.

"I'm going to step out for a moment, last work thing I promise," Anna said, getting up from her chair.

"Please, Belle, try to be more polite when Louise comes back. This is family week. No social calls during dinner."

Anna bit her tongue, resenting the choice of name and the insinuation that her job wasn't real work. In fairness, she was technically lying about a work call. And kind of about having a job at the moment. But still, the comment stung.

"I know, Mom." She stalked out of the room toward the same hall Louise had just passed through, but still managed to catch her father's irritated mutter as she left.

"Ridiculous! There are no real emergencies in her line of work."

Her mother agreed. Anna didn't get to hear if Clay responded, but either way, she was acutely reminded of how much happier they all were without her.

Fuck them! She tried not to let their words sink in.

But they obviously did. Family did that. Anna knew, *hoped*, that her family was wrong about her, but still—it was hard to not be hurt that they didn't feel she was good enough.

Anna was passing the bathroom when she heard a light thump against the door. She paused and heard another thump. Louise was in there and she didn't want to interrupt her if she was really using the restroom, but the door was quite a distance from the toilet. Anna surmised that her intuition had been right. Louise was escaping.

After a brief hesitation, Anna lightly tapped on the door. There was a pause, and then "Occupied!" Louise said the word in a slightly singsong voice. It was kind of cute.

"Yeah, obviously. It's me," Anna whispered into the crack of the door. "Can I talk to you a second?"

"Um…yeah…what's up?"

Anna hesitated a moment, trying to collect her words.

"Um, actually, can you open up so I can come in?"

Another long pause. The lock clicked. Anna reached for the handle and entered. Louise had moved to the farthest corner of the room, plainly trying to stretch the physical gulf between them as far as possible. Anna quietly closed the door behind her. They stood in silence looking at each other. Then Louise abruptly looked down at her feet. She was clearly upset.

"I'm not gonna bite. You don't have to look so scared." Anna's light tease fell flat.

Louise looked up, her eyes fierce.

"I think you know why I look scared. This is obviously not an ideal situation."

"What do you mean?" Anna replied, playing ignorant.

"Please don't. I'm flipping out here."

"I wasn't sure if you wanted to acknowledge what happened earlier, is all…"

Anna saw Louise's eyes change at Anna's words. Was she thinking about the kiss? Louise cleared her throat.

"Honestly, I don't want to talk about it. Obviously, from this point forward, nothing happened. You're Clay's sister and we just met."

She looked down to pick an imaginary piece of lint off her top.

"If you say so…" Anna was surprised at her own somewhat petulant tone.

Louise's panicked eyes flashed back up at Anna's face.

"Please, you have to understand how serious this is for me," she whispered frantically.

"Of course I'm taking this seriously." Anna took a deep breath. "Listen, I'm not going to make this hard for you. Yes, of course, 'we just met' and I'm not going to 'out' you."

Louise's eyes threatened to burst from her head.

"Sorry, wrong choice of words!" Anna quickly explained, waving her hands in the air.

"I meant outing the fact that we've met before. Or anything like that. Please don't stress. I'm in the same boat."

Well, kind of...

Anna could see the tension in Louise's shoulders ease as they fell to a more normal level below her ears.

"Thank you." Louise let out a long breath.

Anna realized how long they'd been holding each other's gaze. Time was passing and there was nothing more to say and only more reminders of the precarious situation.

"Okay, let me get out of here before we get caught together or something," Anna joked, trying to make light of the situation.

Louise's face showed that she was not laughing.

"Sorry, sorry! I really won't bring it up again!" Anna said, holding her hands up in mock surrender. She feigned zipping her lips and softly slipped out of the room.

This Louise was not the same woman from the bar. She seemed completely rigid, almost angry at Anna. Anna shook her head for a moment, reminding herself she wasn't the one in the wrong here.

If she wants to blame me or whatever, she can go right ahead.

Anna felt herself getting riled up. Whoever it was she'd connected with just a few hours ago, that person was not here anymore. But she could deal with that regret later. Anna did not go directly back to the parlor, instead ducking into the kitchen to sneak in a quick text to Rachel, her best friend back in New York City.

Anna: *SOS! Please tell me you have time to talk today?*
Rachel: *Can't I'm with the fam. Doc & co. cutting you down as usual?*
Anna: *No. Well, I mean yes...but worse! I have a situation*
Rachel: *?*
Anna: *I accidentally made out with Clay's girlfriend...*

Anna could see the three dots showing Rachel typing. They vanished, reappeared, vanished again. Finally, her phone rang, with "Rach" showing up as the caller ID.

"Oh my fucking God, what? How? You've been there like five minutes! I mean, I know you work fast, but jeez!"

Anna tried to shush Rachel, frantically lowering the volume on her phone.

"Rachel, please, honestly, I can't even begin to explain. I'll have to call you later with the whole story."

"Okay yeah, obviously! You can't just text me a bombshell like that without all the juicy deets." Even with the volume all the way down, Anna was sure the whole neighborhood could hear Rachel's mirthful shrieks.

"Rachel, this is seriously not funny. This is a huge problem and really not a fun or cool situation."

Rachel finally lowered their voice a decibel. "I totally hear you, really I do. But you have to understand from my perspective, this is seriously like the most interesting thing I have going on right now. I mean my mom just made us all try three different types of to-fur-key."

Anna had forgotten Rachel was at their family's for the holiday this week too.

"But I hear you, friend in trouble, not funny, here for you." Anna could hear the humor in Rachel's voice, but she knew her friend. They were making light of the situation, not because they didn't take it seriously, but because they were just trying to calm Anna down a bit. Anna smiled, remembering why she'd texted Rachel in the first place.

"Okay, listen, I've gotta go, we're about to have family dinner. But seriously, please pick up later."

"Got it, babe. Try not to mac too hard at dinner, okay?" Rachel got in a final barb.

Anna grinned. "Fuck you, bye."

She hung up feeling a bit more stable. Calling Rachel had been a consistent and important part of any trip home. Being in a place that was so incongruous with her soul lent itself to a sort of gaslighting effect. She needed an anchor in reality. Anna took a deep breath and readied herself to reenter the proverbial lion's den. If only she could have Rachel at that dinner table, something to help keep her family, and now Louise, from messing with her head.

❖

The dinner began like many others. Anna's mother ushered them all into the dining room, and they each sat in their designated established places. Luckily, Anna was not seated next to Louise. Unluckily, she was seated directly across from her, with a perfect view of Louise's annoyingly symmetrical face. The seating arrangement made looking at Louise unavoidable, at least peripherally, in any conversation. Anna tried her best to get used to it.

Once they were all sitting around the table, Sebastian, the Nelson family cook, brought out the first course. It was Waldorf salad, plated like an Instagram meal.

The conversation flowed easily between Clay, her mother, and her father. There was a comfortable groove in their relationship, established by what Anna imagined had to be weekly phone calls and texts. Anna was at more of a once-every-six-months check-in level with her family. She kept quiet, aiming to keep the attention away from herself as long as possible.

Usually, she would've hoped for them to ask about her life, an indication that things might be shifting toward accepting her more, but not tonight. Tonight, she just wanted to be part of the fabric of her over-designed golden chair. And not just because of the elephant in the room that was Louise, but also because of the current state of her life in general. She was here because she had failed. She thought she had something unique, something special to offer the world, but it turned out nobody wanted it. Looking around the table, Anna couldn't help but wonder if anyone there would have bet on this dismal outcome.

Anna forced herself to take a bite of her salad. The fresh greens felt rubbery in her mouth. It was hard to have an appetite with so much on her mind.

"So, Louise," her mother asked, shifting the conversation toward their new guest.

"Tell us about yourself. Where are you from, and what do your parents do?"

Typical. Anna barely suppressed an eye roll.

Louise seemed to adjust the napkin on her lap and cleared her throat. Anna remembered the ripped up napkin at the Bar. The conversation was making Louise nervous. But then again, of course getting grilled about your parents' jobs would be nerve-racking for anyone.

"I'm from a small town in Oregon. I lived there until I was eighteen. Then I moved to California for undergrad and then Seattle for the past few years for medical school." She paused and sat up straighter in her chair before saying, "I was raised by my mom. She works in hospitality."

"Hospitality? That's interesting." Anna knew her mother was not interested. The only thing that interested her mother were the letters at the end of someone's name.

"So, when you say hospitality, do you mean hotels? Would I have been to one of hers?"

Louise paused a beat too long.

"Yes, she works in a hotel. I'm not sure, I imagine not, since it isn't in a frequently traveled part of Oregon."

Next to her, Clay shifted uncomfortably in his chair, his eyes on his salad.

"You never know, I might be in Portland in a few months for a conference," her mother said breezily. "Perhaps I can work out a deal with her and get some lodging for some of the doctors in her establishment."

Anna found the offhand request for a discount a bit audacious, even for her mother. Louise somehow managed to sit up even straighter. Anna wondered if there was an actual iron rod in her back.

"My mom doesn't have much say in the room rates at her hotel. She manages the housekeeping staff," she replied evenly.

Another lull.

"Well, that is quite admirable," her mother finally offered. Another pause. "How lucky that you were able to go so far in your medical studies with such humble roots." Each word seemed to stick in her mother's throat. She smiled flatly.

Anna was beyond embarrassed. Not for Louise, but for her family. It was incredibly obvious how out of touch and elitist her family was, and how uncomfortable they were discussing lives they chose not to think about. Louise did not fidget.

"My mother is very accomplished, both in her career and personally. She works hard and she's a loving person. She's an incredible artist when she isn't working and she did all of that while raising me single-handedly." Her tone light and generous, Louise had managed to put everyone at the table both at ease and in their places with just a few sentences. Anna was impressed.

Clay reached for Louise's hand under the table. Anna began to itch again.

"She sounds wonderful," her mother responded casually.

Anna knew her mother was saying the expected thing in the moment but would most likely give her real opinion once Louise was gone. Having a new person in the house had her on her best behavior, which was still pretty cringeworthy.

"So, you two." Her mother shifted gears and directed her attention to Clay and Louise as a unit. "How did you meet? I haven't heard many details."

Finally looking up from his plate, Clay began to smile and puff out his chest a bit. Louise looked over at him with a small smile on her lips. They began to describe their nauseatingly sweet meet-cute, when Clay had done a semester in Seattle for a fellowship last year. The story involved hijinks and laughter, each of them telling parts of it and correcting each other playfully when one felt the narrative was slightly inaccurate. All of this was typical for couples, but Anna found it extra saccharine, coming from two overachievers who were "a perfect fit" if you went by their story.

Anna watched Louise during the retelling. There was no sign of the doubts or ambivalence she'd seen at the bar when they discussed her nameless, faceless boyfriend. Anna could tell her parents were enjoying the story as well. They loved really basic, boring narratives, especially ones that reinforced heterosexuality.

Anna could feel herself getting more and more irritated. The laughter and the touches all grated on her. It wasn't just the ridiculousness of the story, it was also the utter fakeness of it all. This couple was not perfect—far from it. She knew it and Louise knew it, but everyone in the room just ate up the fantasy and reinforced the lie with every moment that went by. Not to mention, Anna knew how foolish Clay would feel, how foolish he might look, if he ever learned how Louise really felt. She distracted herself with the new dishes Sebastian periodically brought out from the kitchen. They were in fact quite tasty.

The conversation continued to flow between the four of them. Her father said very little, but that was more than usual. He must have liked Louise. Clay obviously had heart eyes for Louise, but it was more than that—he also seemed genuinely happy, bordering on relieved, to be in his parents' good graces. Anna couldn't understand it. What was there to be relieved about? Wasn't he always the golden child?

Anna was thinking down these lines and looking nowhere in particular when she heard her name. It was Louise, who was looking right at her. Anna realized she'd just been asked a question.

"I'm sorry, what did you say?" Anna asked, returning her gaze.

"I was just asking, where you live and what you do? I realized we had been focusing so much on me and Clay, it occurred to me that I don't know much about you."

That's a bit rich.

She needed to keep her irritation in check. It wasn't Louise's fault her parents saw her and Clay as the perfect picture of hetero bliss.

On second thought, maybe it was her fault.

"I live in New York and I run a tech startup for queer creatives."

At least for the next few days that was true.

Anna's father cleared his throat. She looked over to her parents knowing they were holding back a comment or worse, an eye roll.

"I didn't know that," Clay said. "I thought you were doing graphic design, or I guess that's the last I heard after art school..." He trailed off.

"Yeah, I did, for a while," Anna agreed. "But while I was doing contract work, I kept meeting other queer creatives who were doing similar short-term work. We all kept referring each other out to various clients, and eventually, I figured it would be easier to just create a platform where clients can come specifically to us, especially other queer clients who want to support their community. I still get to use graphic design for the platform, it's just I do a bunch of other stuff now too."

Clay and Louise seemed to be listening with head nods showing interest and follow-up questions and comments. Her parents, however, began asking for more wine, refilling plates, rearranging themselves. Anything but giving Anna their full attention.

"It's not a big deal." Anna began to minimize.

"It sounds like a pretty incredible idea," Louise said.

Louise's eyes were warm. And for a moment, she and Anna seemed to see each other again.

Her father interjected. "If you ask me, all of this 'identity politics' nonsense is ruining America."

No one was asking him.

"Reducing everyone to a bunch of categories. We're all humans, aren't we? Not a bunch of l-g-t-x-s letters. The other day I had to listen to someone call me a 'sissy white man' or something in a meeting. I don't even know what anyone is talking about anymore." This was the most her father had ever said at a dinner, and of course it was to argue with Anna.

"Categories can help people find community. Especially when society as a whole is so used to bending to 'cis' white men hegemony." Anna tried to speak slowly and calmly, but she could feel the mood of the room had shifted.

"This is what I'm talking about. Always trying to blame somebody else for your problems. Now you're even trying to create a society without us! Look at your site. It's discrimination, if you ask me."

There was another silence at the table. Anna was trying as hard as she could not to explode. She stole a glance at Louise, who seemed to be looking at her plate, her napkin, anything but Anna or her parents. Even Clay was avoiding eye contact. A sense of betrayal washed over her. It's not like she expected Louise or Clay to jump in and fight her parents with her, but the incredible hypocrisy in the room was too hard to ignore.

"You know what, Dad, I don't really care if you're so against my site. You don't have to use it. Some people do and more will. If you want to hide away in the past, in the way you wish the world still was, be my guest. What does it matter what I choose to do with my company?" Despite her best efforts, Anna's volume had risen to near shouting by the end of her statement.

Her mother responded in the gap left by her father's stunned silence.

"Because you are wasting your life."

She spat the words out as though she had been holding them in all night, maybe her whole life.

"You live in a hole, with roommates. You are constantly changing direction. You surround yourself with derelicts and weirdos. For God's sake, you have a new tattoo every time I see you. And then you waste all your energy, unpaid energy might I add, on something ridiculous that no one needs." The words came flying at Anna like missiles.

"Mother—" Clay tried to break in.

Her mother ignored him, continuing the tirade against Anna.

"Look at Louise. She is your age and she is saving lives every day. We gave you and your brother all the opportunities in the world, every door is open to you, but you've ignored everything we do for you. Not to mention, this lifestyle you live. It's one thing to be discreet, but to advertise it all over the internet, stamping your name all over. some *gay* website? How do you think that affects your father's political career?"

Another silence.

Anna looked down at her hands in her lap. She couldn't spend another moment listening to this. Their disappointment, their irritation, their dislike for her—it was all too much. Anna could feel eyes on her again. She looked up and saw sympathy. It was Louise. Anna burned with humiliation.

Fuck sympathy. She didn't need to be pitied. This whole charade was what should be pitied. Every person at this table was lying to themselves. Her mom about her father and his secrets. Her father about feeling emasculated by her mother. Clay about his girlfriend who didn't love him. And Louise...well, Louise she didn't even know.

"I'm feeling a bit tired from my flight, I think I'll excuse myself." Anna's voice was nearly shaking with anger.

"Oh, come on, Belle," her father said. "You can dish it out to us when you feel like it, but you can't take a little constructive criticism? This is why your site hasn't gone anywhere." This was the final twist of the knife. Not only because it was unnecessarily cruel, but because it was also sort of true. At least about the website failing. Anna stood up.

"Good night, everyone," she said, equal parts devastated and fuming.

And then, just as if they hadn't been in a shouting match seconds ago, her mother said, "Oh, Belle, I made up the other twin in your room for Louise. Please don't leave your things all over, since you'll be sharing the room."

Anna's stomach sank. Share a room with Louise? Could this get any worse?

"What do you mean? You have two other guest rooms..."

"Belle, please don't be rude. The other rooms are being redone and the workers are in the middle of the renovation. I couldn't have her stay with Clay, so this is the only alternative."

Anna looked at Louise again, who appeared to be just as upset. This was not a good idea.

Anna turned on her heel and headed toward the stairs. If it wasn't being berated by her parents, it was the constant specter of the big mistake named Louise. Anna vowed to savor her moments alone as the hits just kept coming.

❖

Louise dropped her bags and paused outside the door to her bedroom for the night, the room she was inconveniently sharing with "Annabelle." The Nelsons had finally wrapped up the dinner from hell. As much as she had been praying for that part of the night to end, she wasn't looking forward to the next chapter in this horror story. She still hadn't gotten a moment alone with Clay to process the last couple of hours, especially the abject humiliation she'd witnessed the Nelsons heap onto their daughter. Louise could not have properly prepared for that display. It wasn't just the Nelsons who bothered Louise, it was also watching Clay do close to nothing. What was that about? It had taken everything in her power not to tell the Nelsons off on Anna's behalf, not to mention her own—that reference to Louise's "humble roots"?

Were they even living in this century?

But Louise had taken a deep breath and kept her mouth shut, reminding herself that:

A. This was not her family,

B. She was in the middle of eating the meal they'd provided, and, perhaps most importantly,

C. She did not need to be drawing any unnecessary attention to her and Anna and whatever vibes might still be lingering between them.

When Anna finally left the dinner table, Louise thought she would be relieved to be temporarily free of the constant reminder of her infidelity. Instead, she'd felt oddly hollow. Still, at least Anna wasn't being persecuted anymore. Clay had warned her the Nelsons were "intense," but that had been borderline emotional abuse.

Louise took advantage of her brief respite outside the door to the bedroom. Collecting herself, she took a deep breath, grabbed her bags again, and opened the door. Anna was stretched out on one of the two twin beds, staring intently at her laptop with a pair of headphones on. She did not look up. Louise closed the door behind her quietly and waited for Anna to acknowledge her. A few seconds passed.

"Hey," she finally said, putting her luggage down on the unoccupied bed.

Anna still didn't look up. She did, however, respond. "Hey."

Louise waited another moment. When she realized nothing more was coming, she redirected her attention toward unpacking. She glanced around for a place to put some of her overnight things, but there was only a shared bedside table. Well, it would have to do. She dropped her charger, iPad, and sleep mask onto the table. Springs creaked as Anna shifted her position, and Louise was suddenly aware that the space between their beds was a bit narrower than she would have preferred. She moved around to the other side of the bed and pulled her bags down to the floor, stacking them neatly. Fresh out of things to do, Louise sat on the bed and let herself look over to where Anna was continuing to ignore her. Louise couldn't stand the feeling in the room. She felt too close to Anna or too weird about their dynamic.

Louise stared intently at Anna. Anna stared just as intently at her computer screen. Anna began to type something.

This was ridiculous. There was no way they weren't going to acknowledge what just happened, right?

"Anna..." Louise said.

Finally, Anna looked up, her face unreadable. She said nothing.

"I know this is awkward, us having to share a room..."

Still nothing from Anna. Louise continued.

"I just feel like it would help if we cleared the air a little." She leaned toward Anna a bit.

Again, no response.

"I mean, not just about the Bar, but also that dinner we just had to sit through."

Louise saw Anna's face change at the mention of the dinner. A flash of something, and then it was gone. She removed the headphones from her ears.

"I thought we established that you didn't want to talk about this during our bathroom interlude."

Louise bristled at the implication.

"I didn't want to discuss it there, with Clay and your family ten feet away."

Anna rolled her eyes. *Childish.*

"What do you need to talk about?" Anna asked.

The question felt like an accusation.

Thrown off, Louise responded awkwardly. "I guess, I just...I mean, I don't know how it usually is in your family, but that was just kind of like, well, I mean that dinner was pretty awful," she said, sounding neither diplomatic nor articulate.

"Yeah, you *wouldn't* know how it usually is," Anna shot back.

Louise was taken aback by the anger in Anna's voice. Her own hackles stood up.

"Wow, did I do something to you?"

Anna did not respond. She went to put her headphones back on, but hesitated when Louise stood up and moved to stand at the foot of Anna's bed, forcing them to face one another.

"Did you hear what I just asked you?" To her surprise, Louise could feel the fury starting to boil inside her. She crossed her arms across her chest in defiance. This was not the first time today she had been pulled so completely out of her character. There was one common denominator, Anna. Usually she'd coolly ignore anyone who acted passive-aggressively, but the long day of travel combined with the cross-examination at dinner and her conflicting feelings about Anna had worked her patience and she was on her last nerve.

Anna snapped her computer shut and pushed it off her lap and onto the bed, dropping her headphones on top.

"Okay, Louise, you want to talk, let's talk." Anna stood up from the bed. Now the look in her eye was clear. Anna was angry too. "Let's talk about how I just had to sit through one of the most humiliating and demoralizing conversations I have been in since, oh I don't know, the last time I was in this house."

Louise held her arms a bit looser.

"Or we can talk about how everything I've built, my job, my life is all falling apart, just like they predicted."

Louise was startled by how raw Anna sounded as she listed all the things she was going through.

Anna began to move closer to Louise.

"Or oh, I know, Louise, let's talk about how I now have to share a room for the next week with my brother's GIRLFRIEND who I literally just made out with five hours ago. That feels really good. I would love to talk about that. Where do you want to start?" Anna crossed her arms across her chest just like Louise, staring her down as she buzzed with electricity. Louise started at the mention of their kiss. It felt taboo having it said aloud.

Louise let her arms fall. As much as she didn't like being blamed like this, she could see that Anna was struggling and she felt herself soften in response. Louise moved back a few steps and leaned against a wall.

"I'm sorry, Anna, I really can't imagine being treated that way. Your parents were unforgivably cruel."

Louise's words didn't seem to have an effect on Anna.

"I really don't need your sympathy," she said, holding her stance.

Louise looked down, her rage fully replaced with regret. She didn't feel good about anything that had just happened. She knew if it was her, she would feel exposed.

"I wanted to say something…to stop them," Louise said. Her words felt hollow.

Anna sat exhaustedly back onto her bed. "But you didn't, did you?" she scoffed.

Louise searched for a way to explain. Saying she didn't feel comfortable commenting on other people's families felt cowardly. And she didn't want to acknowledge their connection by explaining she'd been trying not to draw attention to the two of them. Neither response seemed helpful in the moment anyway.

"No, you know what you did do? You gave an award-winning performance of perfect hetero bliss." Anna's words had extra venom.

Louise took another hit, sparking her new temper yet again. "Excuse me?"

"For someone who's 'not in love' with her boyfriend, you sure looked it. Or is that just what you say when you meet randos at bars. Let me guess, it 'doesn't count' when it's with a girl?"

The words stung. The idea that she would do that to someone, that she'd dismissed what she'd had with Gwen as frivolous was deeply painful. She was broken in places Anna couldn't even imagine. The hubris Anna had, imagining she knew anything about Louise and what counted in her life, made her want to crawl out of her skin. She was being painted as some sort of straight girl villain.

"You have no right to tell me how I feel!" Louise was angry, but underneath that anger she was holding back a deep sadness that had been growing more present every second of this never-ending day.

"I think I got to know you pretty well tonight," Anna shot back.

Louise tried as hard as she could to block out her thoughts of Gwen and her grief. "First of all, you have no right to throw in my face what I said to you in confidence. You and I were both there, we both thought we were never gonna see each other again. Second, I cannot believe you would accuse me of being some sort of a…you know what…I don't even know what to call it, but that was definitely some sort of bi-phobic smear. And third, I am in the same boat as you are here. What was I supposed to do? Tell your family that I made out with Clay's sister? Tell me, *Belle*, what should I have done?"

It was Anna's turn to deflate a bit. What was it with Anna? She had gotten under Louise's skin in every possible way.

"I don't know what you should've done, I really don't," Anna finally said. "But what I do know is that my brother is under the impression that you are in it for the long haul, and I don't see any reason why he shouldn't think that. Honestly, it makes me sick just thinking about how good you are at acting like it's mutual."

Louise closed her eyes in shame. Clay was a good person, and she did not want to hurt him. She knew on some level she already had.

Louise spoke quietly. "You're right, that was awful. I feel awful."

Anna seemed to calm down fully at Louise's defeated words.

"Listen, let's just leave this here. We're obviously not helping the situation by fighting. It's been a long day. We should just go to sleep and wake up when we're both further along in this psychological experiment. It would probably be best to just ignore each other for the next week."

Louise had started this conversation hoping that she could smooth over some of the awkwardness, or at the very least, make sure Anna was okay after that awful dinner. Clearly, her effort had the opposite effect. She was both seething and in despair, and she couldn't imagine spending another moment sparring. It was obvious that whatever she'd set out to do by starting this conversation, she had failed miserably.

"Fine."

"Fine."

Louise quickly walked away from Anna and picked up her night clothes, before escaping to the en suite bathroom. She took her time brushing her teeth and washing her face. What she really needed to do was to get control of her heartbeat, but she was having the hardest time calming down. Finally, she somehow succeeded in talking herself into a manageable state. When she came back into the bedroom, Anna was already in her bed with the lights off, her back to Louise. Louise got into her bed, slid her sleep mask on, and did the same. The air felt heavy. Sleep would not come for some time.

CHAPTER FOUR

Anna woke from a fitful sleep. At first, she couldn't place where she was. As her surroundings came into focus, she could see a person cuddled up in the bed next to her. She didn't register who the person was. Anna began to take in the sleeping face, letting a calm pass over her. Until the day before came rushing back in all its complexities. Anna's heart jolted. She was in her parents' house sleeping just a few feet away from Louise. Louise, who she had kissed impulsively right before finding out she was her brother's girlfriend. Anna took a stolen moment to consider the woman who had tormented her over the last twelve hours. It wasn't intentional, but it had been torment.

Louise was breathing faintly with her covers pulled close. As Anna let herself gaze more closely, she noticed a faint scowl decorating Louise's forehead. She looked deep in thought, dreaming with the same intensity she showed last night during their argument. Anna resisted the temptation to wake her, having already been the cause of that scowl the night before.

Even through her frustration, Anna couldn't help but notice how captivating Louise was. Seeing her now, so vulnerable and snuggled up, made Anna begin to let go of her anger. She could see the messy tendrils of hair falling haphazardly across Louise's face. She watched as Louise shifted, pushing the covers off of her body, drawing Anna's attention to her scantily clad body, her soft skin, the ever so visible silhouette of her breasts moving with each breath. The movement startled Anna and she reflexively closed her eyes to avoid being caught staring. The sounds of Louise shifting stopped. After a beat, Anna reopened her eyes to find Louise facing away from her.

This was better for everyone.

As the events of the night began to become clearer in Anna's memory, she found it was easier to recapture some of that earlier anger, especially when she wasn't actually looking at Louise's face. She decided that she needed to get out of that room, and she needed to get some space. Anna had promised Rachel that she would call them last night, but the dinner and then the argument with Louise had totally derailed those plans. Anna needed to talk to her friend desperately.

She snuck out of the bed and exited the room as quietly as possible. She usually wouldn't traipse around her house in boxer briefs and a T-shirt, but she didn't want to risk waking Louise by going through her bag.

It was still early enough that Anna had the house to herself, but even so, she walked downstairs and headed toward the back patio. Despite definitely not being dressed for the cold weather, she didn't want to be overheard calling Rachel in the main part of the house. Her mother tended to have extremely sharp hearing when it suited her, or rather when it didn't suit Anna. She grabbed her down jacket and stuffed her feet into a pair of unknown boots—which considering their size were definitely her father's or brother's—before heading out into the brisk morning air. She must've looked quite odd with her long, bare legs sticking out under her parka. She wasn't exactly comfortable temperature-wise, but she'd survive.

Anna 7:04 a.m.: *Hey you up?*

Rachel 7:04 a.m.: *No.*

Anna 7:05 a.m.: *Calling you now!*

Rachel 7:05 a.m.: *Ugh fine!*

Anna rolled her eyes and dialed Rachel's number.

"You must've been up, if here you are answering," Anna teased.

"Well, after you dropped that gossip bomb on me last night, I put my phone on loud thinking I'd get a one a.m. call, not a seven a.m. call." Rachel was clearly lying down in their bed, their voice sounding unused and irritable.

"Yeah, I know, I'm sorry. Things happened so fast and I was just too upset last night."

"I am only forgiving you because of your very particular circumstances. You will, however, have to make this up to me," Rachel replied.

Anna could tell Rachel was starting to wake up. Their voice was clearer, and she could hear the muffled sounds of them sitting up in bed.

"So spill!" Rachel demanded.

Anna sighed deeply.

"So I told you about the making out part and obviously dinner was a disaster, and then Louise and I got into a big fight in our room last night—"

Rachel cut her off. "Wow, wow, wow. Too much too fast! When you say 'our room,' how did you manage to make that happen?"

"I know you're joking, but trust me, that is not something I wanted."

"Okay, let's go back. I know you told me in broad strokes, but I need deets." Rachel sounded fully awake by this point.

"Okay, but I have to be quick. I'm freezing my ass off outside trying not to be overheard. Didn't have a chance to put pants on." Anna looked down regretfully at her goose-bumpy legs.

"Understood, now go!"

"So I went to a local place to get a drink before going to see my folks, you know, trying to cope."

"I hear ya."

"Exactly! I'm sitting at this bar and this creep starts trying to talk to me, getting pushy, and all of the sudden a woman just comes over and sort of helps me out."

"Like what, she gets him in a sleeper hold or what?"

"I mean, basically!" Anna laughed a bit. "A verbal sleeper hold at least. It was pretty amazing."

"Okay, I like this woman so far."

"Yeah, well, I did too. We started talking and it was nice." Anna smiled at the memory. Talking with Louise had been more than just nice, it had been intoxicating.

"She told me she was here to meet her boyfriend's family, which was, you know, obviously a huge red flag..."

"Hey, listen, this is a judgment-free zone. Go on."

"So I'm on my best behavior after that. Like I really tried to keep it on a friendly level. I know I can be slutty, but I'm really not in the habit of being "the other woman" when I can help it. But I don't know, we just clicked! And as we talked more, she eventually told me that she wasn't really as into her relationship as her boyfriend was." Anna paused a second, waiting for a comment. It didn't come.

"Listen, I know it's not an excuse for what happened next, but it just sort of became harder and harder to resist. Like I was thinking, is this my problem? I don't know the guy. Besides, all I was doing was talking. So I flirted. I flirted a lot. And then she flirted, and then when she was waiting for her boyfriend to pick her up outside, I just thought fuck it, I'm never going to see her again. So I kissed her."

"Let me get this straight. You decided it was a great idea to just jump some woman you just met—on the street, no less!—with her boyfriend rounding the corner?" Rachel's judgment-free zone had obviously collapsed.

"Well, not exactly. And actually, wait—now that I look back, she was the one who kissed me! I'd said good-bye and was walking down the alley next to the bar—very out of view, so don't get stressed out—and then she just came up and kissed me and then she was just like, 'Okay, bye, hope I never see you again' and walked away."

"That's really what she said?"

"No, but it was implied."

"Wow, and so the guy pulling up was your brother!"

"I didn't see him at the time, but yeah, turns out the boyfriend was Clay." It dawned on Anna how close they'd been to being discovered in that moment. Her guilt multiplied again. "Oh my God. I can't imagine what would've happened if he'd seen us. Fuck, am I a bad person? I mean even if it wasn't Clay, it's definitely shitty of me."

"Listen, there are no bad people, just bad actions. And honestly, I don't know, this all feels sort of in the grey. She kissed you, right?"

"I mean, I for sure kissed her back."

"Okay, go on with the story, but we're going to come back to this once I get the whole picture."

"Right. So obviously I go home and begin fortifying myself for the usual Nelsons smackdown. And as soon as I come downstairs to say hi to my brother, there she is. Honestly, Rach, they looked like a full-on Barbie and Ken set."

"Gross."

"Exactly. So we both avoid each other and barely pull off the fake just meeting scene. Thank God my fam is not reading the queer undertones that are just like all over the room."

"God, it is nice to be queer sometimes, isn't it. I mean, obviously not really for you, right now. You know what, never mind...go on."

"So yeah, she goes to the bathroom, I follow."

"Bold move."

"Rach, please, I was freaking out. That was the last thing on my mind."

"Mkay, sure. You're gonna tell me you didn't even *consider* a clandestine replay of the kiss? Which, by the way, how was the kiss?"

"I mean the kiss was good." Anna paused and felt her face warm. She could feel Rachel's desire for detail. "Okay, the kiss was amazing, like kind of insanely amazing," she admitted reluctantly.

"Well, that makes sense that you left that out of your first go-around. I'm going to go ahead and assume you WERE looking for a clandestine make-out sesh in the bathroom and keep the story moving. So, what happened next?"

Anna growled in frustration. Mostly because she knew a part of her didn't have totally innocent intentions when she'd followed Louise into the bathroom, at least on a subconscious level.

"Okay, so anyway, I follow her into the bathroom so we can get on the same page as far as how we want to play this. She's in the other corner of the room, getting as far away from me as humanly possible. Like I'm going to attack her or something! She barely acknowledges what happened and more or less shoves me into her closet as fast as possible."

"Hmm," Rachel said.

"What's that hmm?"

"Nothing…"

"No seriously, I know you've got some commentary. Out with it!"

"Well, it's just kind of odd to me that you're so angry with her, what was it, 'shoving you into HER closet'? I mean what choice did she have? Hey, Nelsons! Just FYI, I made out with your daughter while dating your son—cool if I crash here for the rest of the week?"

"Yeah, but to not even acknowledge me, in private? At the time, it just felt so…I don't know…like she was ashamed. Of me."

"I mean, it was one kiss, right? It wasn't like y'all had a relationship or even planned to ever see each other again."

Anna's righteous indignation began to falter. Rachel did have a point.

Rachel softened their tone. "Hey, listen, I don't mean to say that you aren't totally human for feeling like shit when someone tries to hide you. I mean you and I both know how painful that can be. I'm just saying, take a look at your reaction. You seem pretty invested in this person."

"I don't know about invested…I mean to your point, I guess she *is* basically a stranger. Listen, let me just finish the story and then you can psychoanalyze me."

"Fine, fine, I'll try and shut up."

"So we agreed to keep our situation under wraps and went back to dinner, at which point Louise and Clay did a crowd-stopping performance of the perfect son and future daughter-in-law."

"Vom!" Rachel interjected.

"Then as usual, they laid into me about all the ways I'm not living up to their standards, with the queerness and the not-real-job and yada, yada, yada. Honestly, it was a lot worse than usual. Maybe seeing Louise's perfection set them off—she's in med school for oncology. Anyway, I ended up leaving the table just so I didn't explode!"

"So, I take it you didn't tell them about the site closing down?"

"Wasn't exactly the right time."

"Listen, I know you think this is it for QueerConnect, but I really think if you can just keep it going a few more months, you'll be able to find another investor." Rachel's support felt like a breath of fresh air after the reception Anna had gotten at the table last night.

"I dunno, Rach, I think I've just gotta face that it's time to throw in the towel."

"Okay, again, putting another pin in this." Anna had started to lose track of all the pins.

"Fine, the last thing I need is to feel worse. Back to my French farce! This dinner was also where I learned I had to share a room with Louise. Which, again, not my dream situation."

"Sure...." Rachel said with sarcasm.

"Rach, I'm serious!"

"I know, I'm sorry. I'll stop teasing."

"So I'm still pretty salty from the whole blowup at dinner when Louise comes into the room a little while later. I'm trying my hardest to just sort of leave her alone, and then she does a one-eighty and starts trying to talk about the dinner and the bar, and I'm just getting more and more angry, and well, I guess I kind of told her off."

"Well, that's not surprising, you always run hot. I always say it's the Cecilia in you." Anna winced at the comparison. "What did you say and what do you need to apologize for?"

"Listen, I just said the truth!" Anna said defensively. "I don't need to apologize for anything!"

"Anna, how long have I known you?"

"A long time."

"Right. What did you say to Louise that you shouldn't have?"

Anna thought for a moment and let some of her anger dissipate. "I may have called her a fake...and possibly made a barb about her sexuality..."

"And there it is! So. How are you going to apologize?"

"Listen, I hear you. I shouldn't have said what I said, like I don't even know her, but can't I just let this lie?"

"You and I both know that won't last long. You are a dweller. If you don't nip this in the bud, you're gonna wind up torturing yourself. You don't judge people like that. Not for long, anyway. You need to make it right." Rachel's assessment was, as usual, spot-on.

"Fine, you're right! Jeez, why do I even call you!"

"Literally, this is exactly why you call me, bitch."

"Okay, okay. But still, she kind of fucked with me too. I mean she is the one who cheated on her boyfriend, my brother."

"Let me ask you something, Anna, and take a moment before you answer."

"Okay..."

"Do you seriously think she doesn't already feel bad about that? Do you really think it's something you have a right to punish her for?" Again, Rachel was making some solid points.

"Well, no but..."

"But what? Tell me what she's actually done to you other than save you from some jerk at a bar."

Anna wilted. "She...I don't know, I guess I just don't like that I feel shame around her..."

"You are not the decider of who is at fault. And besides, that isn't who you are. I suggest you take a look at where that's coming from and figure out why this girl has you all misaligned."

Anna sighed. "Here we go with the psychoanalyzing," she said good-naturedly.

"Fine, I'll stop, but mark my words, Annabelle! You have a week to survive here in La Casa de Nelson. If you don't get some peace of mind, you're gonna be exploding on everyone, in more ways than one."

Anna snorted. "Don't call me that, you remind me of my mother. Also, I don't even want to ask you what that means so I'm just going to assume you are referring to my short fuse and leave it at that."

"Denial is not a good look, my friend!" Rachel laughed.

"Fine! Fine! Enough! Thank you for talking to me. I know you're busy with family and these holiday calls are always so one-sided."

"Hey, listen, my family is supportive and kind and the holidays are a chance for me to refill my tank. It's the opposite for you. Let me be here for you. You always show up in my hard times."

"Thanks, Rach," Anna said. "It just seems like my hard times have been a bit more frequent lately."

"Our friendship is a marathon, not a sprint. And don't worry, I'll give you plenty of opportunities to make it up to me! Now go inside, put some pants on, and find a way to apologize to this mysterious future sister-in-law." Anna pictured Rachel's mischievous smile.

"Don't even joke!"

"Fine, go find a way to apologize to Louise. Love you, Anna!"

"Love you too, Rach."

Anna hung up and considered all that Rachel had said. She knew she had a temper, and that she had a tendency to say what she was feeling, regardless of who it might hurt. Part of it felt like a relic of growing up in a family like hers, around people who could be so vitriolic, but part of her knew it was also something within her. She was constantly trying to make space for herself, not just in her family but in her world. She didn't want to be like Clay, always looking for approval from others, but at what cost? Rachel was right. She needed to make amends.

❖

Louise was acutely conscious of the silence in the bedroom where she'd just awoken. It was a silence that was much appreciated. She'd had very little time to herself in the last day and a half; from her plane ride to that argument with Anna last night, she was on sensory overload. Louise reached for her phone. She saw a missed text from her mom.

Mom: *Hope it is going well! Love you <3.*

Louise smiled, thinking about her mom checking in on her, and then shot off a quick reply saying as little as possible. She didn't want to worry her mom with the ugly elitism she'd witnessed. Though they were close, she wasn't really eager to have new eyes on her situation with Anna. Mostly she was hoping for a text from Clay. She really wanted to speak to him. Why was it that visiting a boyfriend's family felt like she was in a fishbowl? Louise hadn't even registered that Anna wasn't in the room. When it occurred to her to look, she was relieved to have the room to herself. She sank back into the bed, allowing her body to relax.

Louise was tired. She was starting to think she had been tired for a long time. Adding on last night's argument, she had gotten herself stretched so thin that her exhaustion somehow morphed into sleeplessness, keeping her awake for what felt like the whole night. And then, as indicated by the minor headache she felt coming on, the sleep she did get was restless. Louise's thoughts were fixated on the "Anna situation," as she'd started to call it in her head. More than their alleyway transgression and even that horrible dinner, it was their fight last night that had her truly distraught. Anna had lashed out at her. Louise understood to some extent that talking about Anna's family was a sore subject, but she didn't think it warranted that level of animosity. Anna's words still tumbled around in her mind.

What was it she'd said, exactly? *"Let me guess, 'it doesn't count' when it's with a girl?"* That was it.

The dig might've been a throwaway line to Anna, but the words had added meaning for Louise. Louise was again brought pointedly back to thoughts of Gwen. Gwen, who she thought she would spend her life with.

Anna does not know me. Louise began to rev up her anger again.

Louise had a controlled and structured life. One that kept her from running her hands over the spots where her heart still hurt. Louise had learned there were some pains that didn't get better with time. She thought she had learned to live with her pain, but Anna's words had opened her up to feelings she didn't want to revisit, not here, and not now. Maybe not ever. But Louise had to admit those feelings were more than just her buried grief—she had identified with Anna, both at the bar and at dinner. She had felt a connection. She cared what Anna thought.

The good mood brought on by her mom's text had all but left Louise's body. She got out of bed, hoping a change in position might jolt her back. She stretched and began to look around the room. It was large, with enough space for a separate reading nook, and full of tastefully muted colors. Nothing like the slightly cramped but vibrant home she'd grown up in. It was hard to imagine this had ever been Anna's childhood bedroom. Louise decided the Nelsons must have changed it after she moved out. She did notice a few trophies on the bureau, highlighting past success in math team and chess club, and she couldn't help but smile. It was surprising thinking of cool Anna with her tattoos and hipster haircut being a little nerdy in high school. Louise chastised herself for her interest. Her feelings were oscillating by the moment.

Louise crossed the room toward the window that looked out over the Nelsons' backyard. The grounds were expansive and beautiful, even in the somewhat desolate winter season. She could not imagine growing up in a place that large. Outdoor space like this was everywhere in her Oregon hometown, but the difference was that Louise didn't personally own it. What an odd thing to have so much to share and choose to limit it to so few.

Louise noticed a figure pacing on the backyard's brick patio. Anna was instantly recognizable. Her mannerisms were on full display as she appeared to be on an enthusiastic and hand-gesturey phone call.

Was Anna wearing nothing but a parka and boots?

It was almost humorous, until Louise let herself take a closer look at Anna's silhouette. Louise couldn't help but note how spectacular Anna's legs were as she paced around the backyard. Anna was a bit too far away for Louise to see her face, but she'd had hours to study it yesterday. Anna was stunningly gorgeous.

It was...*miserable.*

Even if they'd never met, Louise knew if she was ever in a room with Anna, her eyes would be automatically drawn to her.

Why did she have to be Clay's sister!

Below her, Anna threw her head back in laughter, looking so young and full of life. Louise hadn't seen this version of Anna. Maybe a little at the bar, but nothing like the unbridled joy she was witnessing. She recalled the way Anna's eyes had sparkled with mischief after she'd made Anna laugh. The memory made Louise's pulse quicken. She closed her eyes to try to dampen the effects of what she clearly recognized as desire. It was a weak attempt.

Changing gears, she brought herself back to their fight the night before, to the words that were said. To Anna's narrowed and piercing amber eyes. Anna was confrontational and frustrating and very, very hot. God, what an annoying feeling! Louise was mostly angry at Anna, but even in midst of that anger, she was profoundly affected by her attraction to her. All of this contributed greatly to last night's insomnia. As she'd lain in bed hoping sleep would come, Louise became increasingly aware that the altercation with Anna had done more than energize her, it had turned her on. What a disaster. She decided she would just have to fight her feelings. She was not going to accept her desire, not while also feeling so run over by Anna's words and the grief it brought with them.

Louise saw Anna end her call and stop pacing. Anna looked up at the window. Had she spotted Louise staring? Panicking, Louise dropped to the floor. She hoped to God that somehow Anna hadn't seen her, especially not her incredibly sketchy scramble to hide.

Fuck. She crawled toward her bed, barely holding on to her dignity.

She considered pretending to be asleep in case Anna came back upstairs but decided against it on the off-chance Anna had witnessed the whole debacle. She didn't really want to be on her back foot in another sparring match. Louise did, however, go to the en suite bathroom and wrap herself in one of the Nelsons' seemingly complimentary guest robes, perhaps giving in to an unconscious desire to hide the body that had so recently responded to Anna in her pants-less parka getup.

❖

Louise scrambled back to sit on her bed and look through her phone. She frantically went through emails for fifteen minutes and was just about to accept that Anna was not coming back to the room anytime soon, when she heard a light tapping on the door. She had just enough time to arrange herself in the stiffest possible position on the bed when Anna came in with two mugs of coffee. Louise watched Anna stop in her tracks at the sight of Louise awake and alert.

"Good morning," Anna said in a much gentler tone than she'd used last night. "I thought you might want some coffee." Anna held up one of the mugs like an offering. She was no longer covered in the ridiculous parka. She was instead wearing boy shorts and a surprisingly skimpy shirt, a getup that unfortunately showed off every sexy inch of her body. Louise was fully drowning in her attraction.

She was also trying hard to read the situation. Was this a trap? Louise searched Anna's open expression for any sign of the injured and angry woman she remembered from the night before. It was a delicate balance, being so turned on she could barely think while feeling so little trust for the object of her lust.

"Thank you," Louise finally said, reaching for the delicious-smelling salvation in a cup.

"You're welcome."

Anna moved to sit on her own bed and faced Louise as she took her first sip. Louise's discomfort increased with her proximity.

"I…want to apologize for last night. Among other things." Anna shifted uncomfortably. "I was out of line to come at you like that and there is no excuse. Please forgive me."

Louise expected an explanation to come next, but none came. Anna stayed in her spot seemingly waiting for Louise to say something.

"To be honest, I'm not sure what you're apologizing for. You seemed pretty clear on what you thought of me."

It wasn't that Louise wanted to be petty; in her head, she wanted to take any opportunity to end this feud, but in her heart, she was still hurt. When Louise thought back to the Anna she met at the bar, she wanted to forgive. That Anna had been kind and open. As they talked, Louise could feel the pain Anna was feeling, and she was able to connect with it. Yes, her losing Gwen was not the same kind of pain as Anna's, but there was just something so vulnerable about Anna that made Louise's heart open with a quickness she had never experienced before. But the consequences of that openness had been made clear. Anna had the power to hurt her. Now, Louise was hardening herself, making sure she didn't leave herself exposed to another attack.

Anna didn't take the bait. She maintained her open and apologetic expression.

"That's fair. I guess I deserve that." She leaned forward a bit, making sure Louise was unable to look away. As if Louise had any choice in the matter. Since the moment they met, she had been powerless.

Anna took a moment to pull out her phone and click around. Louise could see that she had opened the notes app and was reading from it. She cleared her throat, seeming to prepare a statement. It was annoyingly endearing.

Anna continued. "I'm sorry for acting childish last night. I shouldn't have blamed you for anything that my parents put me through. I made how they made me feel last night about you and it wasn't. That wasn't fair. I'm sorry also for what I said about it not counting with a woman. I had no right to pretend to know you like that or to judge you for however you identify. And finally, I'm sorry for throwing what you said to me at the bar in your face. There was nothing wrong with what you said, and I invited you to be honest only to betray your trust. I have as much to feel guilty about here as you do, and it was hypocritical and unkind for me to push all the blame onto you." Anna looked up at Louise with big, sincere eyes.

Louise was shocked by the comprehensiveness of the apology. She gave herself a moment to let the words sink in. She had to admit, it was actually a pretty good apology.

"Did I miss anything?"

Louise knew there were a couple of other places that still hurt from Anna's words, but it was unfair to hold her responsible for things she couldn't know about.

"I think that's everything."

Louise couldn't help but let a small smile escape. Anna did as well. A calm passed between them.

"I should probably apologize as well," Louise added.

Anna leaned back casually, the tension seeming to leave her body.

"You really don't have anything to apologize for."

"I do though. I shouldn't have left you alone last night when I could tell that you were upset."

Anna let out a guffaw. "That's sweet, but it's not your job to anticipate when someone else is going to act like an asshole."

"You didn't act like an asshole," Louise protested. She realized that in a bizarre turn of events, somehow she was the one defending Anna's actions now. "Well, maybe a small asshole."

Anna laughed openly. It reminded Louise of her laughter on the patio outside, so free. Louise could feel the tug of attraction pulling her again.

God, not again.

Anna was bewitching, and not just because of her beauty. Anna was magnetic. There was an easy intimacy with Anna that Louise couldn't help but fall into. But that intimacy was also what she was most afraid of. Louise needed to put the brakes on this connection as soon as possible. She closed her eyes and forced self-control back into her body.

"I'm also sorry about earlier at the bar."

Anna's expression changed to confusion.

"What about at the bar?"

"I shouldn't have kissed you. If I hadn't, we wouldn't be in this awkward situation."

Anna didn't respond. She seemed taken aback. Louise rephrased.

"I mean, if I hadn't done that, we maybe could have been friends."

Anna looked hard at Louise. Then she cleared her throat, shifting back into a less casual sitting position.

"Yeah, maybe. I mean that's what we were doing before we kissed, right? Being friendly."

As much as Louise didn't want to slip back into an agreed upon denial, she felt compelled to. Her attraction to Anna was clearly an issue, and the more they settled into normal conversation, the more she forgot the seriousness of her transgression.

"Yes, I honestly think I might have gone temporarily insane. But I want to start over. I'd like to try and be friends, if that's okay. At least for the week?"

Anna's look held what was unspoken between them. But after a moment, she seemed to give in to Louise's plea.

"I can do that." Anna held out her hand as if for a handshake. Louise took her hand. The moment their skin touched, a jolt of energy passed between them. Their eyes met instinctively and she could see that Anna felt it too. But it didn't matter. This was the way things had to be until Louise could get herself back on the plane to Seattle. Just one week, that was all. She just had to not act on her attraction for one week, and then she would never see Anna again. And things could go back to the way they were supposed to be.

"Friends," Louise agreed, in a voice that wasn't hers.

Anna let go first. It took Louise a moment to pull her hand away and she felt like the awkwardness almost erased the established truce between them. Anna got up from the bed and walked to her suitcase to begin getting dressed. She threw on jeans and a sweatshirt, clearly reaching for the quickest things she could find. Meanwhile, Louise pretended to distract herself with her phone.

"Well, I'll leave you to enjoy your coffee. I'm heading downstairs to see if I can get something to eat before I'm put through another firing squad." Anna hesitated at the door as if to say something else, and then seemed to reconsider. "See you down there!" she finally said.

"Yeah, see you."

Anna closed the door and Louise fell back onto the bed with a sigh of relief. They had come to a final truce. They would be friends, and they weren't going to fight anymore. Still, Louise couldn't help but wonder why, if they had come to the decision to be friends, her heart was still beating so fast.

❖

Louise walked into the Nelsons' kitchen feeling strange. She still hadn't touched base with Clay and despite Dr. Nelson's insistence to "make yourself at home," she felt odd walking around unescorted in someone else's house. This was all exacerbated once again by the size and grandiosity of said house. "Kitchen" somehow felt inadequate to describe the space she was in. The room was, of course, full of all of the typical things that made something a kitchen: a fridge, a stove, a sink. Only all of the appliances must have been double their standard sizes and looked more like stainless steel computers than anything Louise had ever used to cook. And the room itself was sparklingly clean, not to mention enormous. Which meant it took Louise a few moments to notice she wasn't alone. Seated at the large kitchen table overlooking the grounds out back was Clay, casually sipping a cup of coffee while he awkwardly typed on a computer with his remaining free hand. Louise was charmed by his small idiosyncrasies as he scowled at the screen. Clay was easy to like, and honestly, seeing him at that moment, Louise was reminded why she'd fallen so effortlessly into a relationship with him.

No one else seemed to be around. Well, most importantly, Anna wasn't around. Louise did, however, continue to be extra conscious of where Anna was or wasn't. Something that she was very much choosing not to dwell on.

Clay looked up and his face brightened when he saw Louise standing at the island. He looked well rested and his eyes were full of kindness.

"Good morning, how did you sleep?" he asked, motioning her over for a kiss.

Louise gave him a light peck as he scooted across the window seat to open a space for her to sit.

"Honestly, not so well."

Clay looked at her with concern. "Really? Was the bed too stiff? I can't imagine it's easy sharing with Anna, the snorer." He laughed good naturedly.

Louise was pulled back into the room with Anna, thinking about her standing across from Louise in her short sleep shorts and her revealing T-shirt. Yes, sharing a room *was* hard, but not because of any snoring. Louise attempted to refocus herself on the more pressing things she wanted to discuss.

"Honestly, Clay, I'm surprised you slept well considering that awful dinner last night."

Louise could feel Clay almost shrink beside her as he processed her words.

"I know, that was bad." He didn't expand.

"Yeah, it was." She looked at him. "Is it always like that?"

Clay struggled to maintain eye contact. "I mean no, but it wasn't that surprising either. It's kind of only when Belle comes home."

"Why didn't you say something?"

"I mean, I don't know, it kind of all happened so fast."

Louise did not find this answer adequate. "Well, you just said it's not uncommon. It's not right the way they talked to her. You need to say something to them, defend her."

Clay shifted uncomfortably. "I know, I need to. It's just, I wish she wouldn't bait them with her sexuality stuff. She knows it'll get them all riled up."

"Bait them! What is she supposed to do, lie to them about her life and her job?" Louise was indignant.

"No, I'm not saying…lie. It's just uncomfortable for them is all. You can see they're kind of old school." Clay gestured vaguely at their surroundings.

"It sounds like you're the one who's uncomfortable."

Clay looked at her taken aback. They had never really fought much, so her tone must have been quite shocking for him.

"I'm not uncomfortable with her being gay or whatever, I just don't know why she always has to talk about it. My parents are set in their ways. They're never going to change their minds."

"Well, it doesn't help when no one ever tries."

Clay was silent for a beat.

"I was more preoccupied with introducing you and making sure you were comfortable. I wanted them to like you and for them to know how important you are to me." Clay looked at Louise sincerely, and Louise felt herself soften slightly.

"I understand that me meeting your parents was important to you, but there's no way anyone could've been comfortable during that meal. I definitely wasn't. I don't want to sit through another one like that, and if you don't say something next time, I will."

Clay seemed to gather himself.

"Okay, I promise, I'll do better. You are totally right."

Louise looked at Clay apprehensively. Was he just saying this to end their conflict?

Perhaps sensing her skepticism, Clay doubled down. "Really, I think you're right about Belle. It wasn't fair how they treated her, and I've looked away for too long. I promise I will do better."

Louise considered his words, still not fully grasping his relationship with Anna. "Why is it you two aren't close?" The question had added weight as Louise felt she was inviting attention to her interest in Anna. Clay didn't seem to notice.

"I don't know. I guess in a lot of ways, I'm proud of my sister, I think I just want to avoid conflict with my parents. I want to sit through a meal without feeling like there's a war happening around me. In the end, I guess staying away from her seemed like the easiest way not to get hit in the crossfire." Clay was thoughtful for a moment. "I'm seeing now that maybe I left her behind to deal with the fallout on her own."

"Okay, I think I'm starting to understand…" Louise responded, still struggling to let it go.

Clay seemed to notice her reticence. "Obviously, this hasn't been the best start to our week together. I'm sorry. Do you think we could start over, or at least recover a little?"

Louise looked at his apologetic expression and, with a jolt, noticed a striking similarity between Clay's and Anna's "I'm sorry" faces, their prominent eyebrows arching the same way above dark, repentant eyes. Louise was reminded of her own recent misdeeds, Anna's hot breath on her ear, Anna's hand grabbing her hip, the feeling of Anna's lips on her. Just as quickly, she felt the now-familiar rush of shame as she looked at Clay's kind face. Quickly, she pushed the memory back into the recesses of her mind and tried to refocus. She decided to let Clay off the hook.

"All right, all right," she said. "But first, you have to give me the rest of your coffee. I left mine upstairs." Louise grabbed Clay's mug from where he'd left it on the table and took a defiant sip. Clay's shoulders relaxed and he laughed sweetly.

"Deal," he said, visibly relieved. "How'd you get coffee already, anyhow?"

Louise's face grew warm again. She tried to shrug playfully. Clay laughed again.

"All right, keep your secrets," he said. "Anyway, I'm glad you came down. I wanted to know if you'd be interested in coming to cut down a Christmas tree?"

"Sure!" Louise agreed readily.

The day was beautiful, and she liked the idea of spending some...uncomplicated...time with Clay out in the fresh air. And it didn't hurt that she'd have a good reason to be away from Anna. Not that she was avoiding her exactly.

"Seems pretty late in the season to get a Christmas tree though."

"It's one of our traditions," Clay explained. "My parents used to put the tree up late on Christmas Eve so Belle and I would wake up to a bunch of presents underneath on Christmas morning. Over the years, though, we pushed it back a couple of days and it became me and Belle's job to cut the tree down and decorate. Belle already agreed we should go this afternoon."

Realization hit Louise like a ton of bricks.

"So, An...Belle's coming too?" she asked.

"Yeah, of course." Clay looked at her. "That's okay, right? I promise, it'll be fun. We used to get along really well together. Maybe all we need is a good restart with a hatchet at Spruce Tree Farm."

"Of course!" Louise attempted to sound lighthearted. "Can't wait," she finished weakly, and realized it was at least half true.

CHAPTER FIVE

Y ou two hang tight, I'm going to ask this attendant which way to go for the best trees."

Clay shut the car door and walked toward a small hut a ways off the gravel road, leaving Louise and Anna to stew in the soundless awkwardness. Louise had tried not to feel hurt when she watched Anna do her best to wriggle out of the group expedition. She knew she would've done the same if she'd had the foresight. Clay had practically begged Anna to come with an earnestness that really only he could pull off. Anna had caved, of course. Now Louise was in the front seat, looking out into the beautiful span of fir trees and doing everything in her power to avoid looking at Anna in her adorable Trenton snapback.

"Sorry you got roped into our sibling thing."

Louise turned to look at Anna's genuine expression of apology. It was a mirror image of Clay's. Louise wondered whose expression she found more charming.

"No, it's fine. Mostly I just didn't want to intrude."

"Trust me, it's not that serious of a tradition. I mean, I haven't even been home to do this in years." Anna looked sullenly out her window.

"But still, I could have found something to do. Especially with your parents in DC for the night."

"What a relief, right?" Anna turned back to Louise and gave a halfhearted smile. "I almost feel like they went to avoid me." Her eyes darkened.

Louise was struck by the sadness of that statement.

"Would they really do something like that?"

"Nah. They'd have to care to feel weird about last night. Plus, I'm pretty sure their trip has something to do with my father's political career."

Louise felt that protectiveness over Anna that had been present since the dinner. Why couldn't the Nelsons see how wonderful their daughter was?

"It's cool you and Clay have this tradition. I don't have any siblings, so this is sort of special for me to get to witness."

A dark look passed over Anna's face again. "I'm lucky to have Clay. I know we aren't close, but we used to be. I think it's just hard to be very close in a family like ours, always pitting us against each other."

Louise found herself wanting to ask more questions. Why were the Nelsons so cruel? How had she survived to turn out so different from them?

The door opened and they both jumped. Clay got into the car with a map and a giddy, childlike grin.

"Found the perfect spot." He looked between them and seemed to notice the awkwardness in the air. "Did I miss something?"

Louise replied quickly. "Nope, just ready for some nature!"

Anna said nothing and turned to gaze out the window. Clay couldn't help but show his excitement again.

"I know! So it's about a mile or two up this path by car and then a mile on foot."

"And then what? We carry it ourselves back to the car?" Anna turned back toward Clay with indignation.

Clay and Louise shared a look. Louise knew Clay and Anna were rich kids, but she hadn't really seen Anna show her primness till that moment.

Clay laughed good-naturedly. "Come on, Belle, you don't think the three of us can handle one tree?"

❖

Anna looked up at what must have been a fourteen-foot-tall mammoth of a tree. She held tightly onto her uncomfortably large ax and set her legs up in what she imagined was a "tree cutting stance," whatever that was.

She looked over her shoulder to see Louise and Clay watching her with what could only be described as the most artificially serious faces, clearly holding back laughter.

"I don't know why you both are making me do this!" she yelled back at them. "If you two are so 'outdoorsy' or whatever, why don't you show me how it's done?"

"No, no, no...this is the best part. You have to give it a whack," Clay said with a sinister smirk.

Clay hadn't been playful with Anna in years. It felt good to let her guard down a bit with a member of her family. Resigned, she turned back to the tree.

"Fine, but if you laugh, I'm walking back to the car and I'm taking the keys. You can drag this tree to the house all by yourselves!"

Anna squared up again and held the ax in an awkward pre-swinging position. She cocked back and released, closing her eyes right before she came in contact with the trunk. A sharp pain shot through her forearms, and she dropped the ax as she hopped around, shaking her hands in agony. The pain was short-lived, unlike the cackling she could hear behind her. As soon as the pain subsided, she went up to the tree to see how much she had cut. There was barely a ding. Clay came in close behind her looking on with more laughter.

"That's a good start, Belle. Just another five hundred whacks and we should be good to go."

Anna shoved him playfully and stomped performatively to the fringe where Louise stood.

"How about I sit this part out as usual," she said, crossing her arms playfully.

Louise was struggling to keep her laughter under control.

"Oh, so this is funny, is it?" Anna said mockingly. "Let's see how easy you find chopping down a tree."

Louise waved her hands as if calling a foul and tried again to stop laughing.

"That's okay, you clearly have a handle on this."

Clay picked up the ax and leaned jauntily on it next to the tree.

"She's right, Louise. If you're going to laugh, you've got to put your money where your mouth is."

Louise glared at Clay with mock contempt.

"Is that so? You're both going to set your guest up for humiliation and possible injury?"

Clay almost faltered, but Anna stepped in.

"Turnabout is fair play, my friend!" Anna walked over to take the ax from Clay and shoved it into Louise's hands. The slight force behind the ax handoff suddenly reminded Anna of the force she felt when Louise had pushed into her in the alley. The memory was paralyzing.

"Fine, I'll give it a try," Louise said, sounding exasperated.

Louise stood next to the tree and held the ax as if she had never seen one before. She seemed to almost take a practice swing, but then she gave Anna a mischievous look. Anna felt it all over her body. Louise's stance abruptly changed into something considerably more athletic. She set herself up and took an incredibly graceful and practiced swing. The ax sunk deeply into the trunk. She expertly pulled it out with an easy strength. She quickly set herself up again and with a few more swings, took the tree down in its entirety. As it fell, she held a smug pose and raised an eyebrow to Anna in challenge. Anna realized her jaw was on the floor. Clay laughed, if possible harder than before.

"Bet you didn't see that coming, did you?" Clay said with pride.

"Sure didn't. I'm glad we didn't put money on it." Anna laughed too.

Louise smiled and said with regret, "God, I really missed an opportunity, didn't I?"

Anna liked this side of Louise. She was competitive and confident. Anna wondered for a moment about what it might be like to be with someone like that all the time. Most of her relationships back in New York, if you could call them relationships, didn't even get far enough to see what it was like to just hang out, let alone get close. Anna wouldn't have minded being teased or getting to be playful with someone, particularly someone like Louise. Perhaps they could be friends after all.

The three of them took a water break and chatted about the times Clay and Anna had done this before. Their parents had stopped coming with them when they were teens and somehow Anna just could not get the hang of anything having to do with tools, against all lesbian stereotypes. Anna was laughing freely for the first time since being at her parents' house. It was nice seeing Clay laugh as well, especially outside of their house of horrors. Anna thought she would feel some of that discomfort from seeing Louise and Clay together joking around, but she found instead that it was more like hanging out with two good friends. She stole a glance at Louise's face and saw that her cheeks were flushed pink, perhaps left over from her heroic ax-swinging efforts. She looked so at ease. Anna wished for a moment that it could always be like this.

After a time, Clay got up from his stump and began to net the tree for easier carrying.

"I'm going to excuse myself a moment. Drank too much before we left," Louise said, and she walked out to find a private space in the woods.

Clay and Anna were left alone. The tension between them from the night before was mostly gone, but a quiet had fallen over them. Then Clay began to say something, but seemed to stop himself. Anna waited.

"Belle, I…I just want to say I'm sorry about last night."

Anna listened as he stumbled through his words.

"I hate that they treat you like that, and I should have said something. I love you and I'm not like them. I don't have any issues with who you are."

Anna was touched. She knew that it was cowardly that he never stuck up for her, but acknowledging this was a start. And she knew how hard it was to go against her parents, especially for Clay, who tended more towards avoidance than direct conflict. Looking at her brother's remorseful expression, she was hit again with a pang of guilt. Would he be apologizing if he knew what she and Louise had done, or what was in her heart every time Louise was nearby? And even more, should he?

"Honestly, I've never really told you this, but I think it's cool that you do your own thing. I wish I could be more like you." Clay was looking out toward the woods, almost like he was saying the words to himself, not to Anna.

"No, you don't," Anna replied.

Clay grew serious. "No, I really do." He took a deep breath and a haunted look came over him. "You don't know how hard it is some days to…I don't know…be this…" He trailed off.

"Be what?" Anna prompted him.

Clay seemed to lose some of his nerve. "I don't know, I don't know what I'm saying exactly. I just…I want you to know I am proud you're my sister and I want to do a better job of defending you."

Anna tried to hold back her curiosity about what it was that Clay wasn't saying, but she was genuinely floored by his words. Clay always seemed so comfortable as the golden boy that it never even occurred to her that it could be causing him pain. On paper, Clay seemed the polar opposite of Anna. Clean-cut, preppy, always doing and saying the right things, but maybe they weren't so different after all.

"Thanks, Clay," she said with emotion. "I'm proud of you too." Anna really was proud of him. He was so accomplished, and he was honestly a really sweet person. Not too many people with his status in life would be so kindhearted. She was beginning to wonder if the only thing standing between Anna and her brother was their parents. Maybe they could rebuild something together.

Clay looked at her with deep love.

"Honestly, it's Louise who has opened my eyes lately to the things I look away from. I think she really likes you."

The now familiar and creeping feeling of guilt continued to slither through Anna's body.

"Yeah, she's great," Anna said, trying to keep her voice as normal as possible. The crinkling of leaves brought them back to their task as Louise rejoined the group.

"So, who wants to bet me fifty bucks I can't drag this tree back to the car by myself?" Louise joked, breaking the ice.

"No one is gonna take that bet!" Clay responded, putting his arm on Louise's shoulder affectionately. Anna tried not to cringe.

❖

The trek back to the car was more difficult than any of them had anticipated. Finally, muscles protesting, they strapped the tree onto the roof and headed back to the Nelson home with a sense of accomplishment and contentment. Anna, again relegated to the back seat, was pleased to find that her position was actually a great vantage point for watching Louise interact with Clay. Gone was the "perfect couple" on display at last night's dinner table. Instead, the two seemed to have an easy rapport and spent the drive casually being comfortable together. It reminded Anna a bit of her relationship with Rachel, only with a lot less snark.

Watching Clay and Louise's interactions wasn't the only benefit of Anna's back seat position. It also provided a fantastic and somewhat undercover view of the left side of Louise's face. It was almost pathetic how quickly Anna gave up trying not to stare. Even with her resolve to try to rebuild things with her brother, she couldn't help noticing that every time Louise smiled or laughed, a dimple would appear on her cheek and Anna could feel time slow down.

When they got back to the house, Anna realized the journey had eaten up most of the day. She tried to slip away as quickly as possible. As well as they had all gotten along, she reminded herself that Louise and Clay were a couple and most likely wanted to be alone. And admittedly, part of her wanted to make sure she wasn't spending too long in Louise's presence. Resisting her attraction to Louise had become exhausting.

As she began to sneak up the stairs, Clay stopped her and asked if she wanted to hang with them that evening. Part of her wanted to. She surprisingly wanted to spend more time with Clay, but she resisted because there was also a part of her—a big part of her—that wanted to be around Louise as much as possible. That part of her she couldn't trust. She needed to try harder to see Louise as a friend only. Clay's vision for the night sounded cute: decorating the tree, ordering pizza, drinking eggnog or wine by the fire. When Anna tried for the second time that day to kindly decline, Clay again hit her with the sweetest plea. Once again, Anna couldn't help but agree. She assured him she'd be back downstairs shortly, but then took her time showering and putzing around the bedroom, answering emails and checking in with Rachel.

Rachel 3:05 p.m.: *I guess this is the one situation that can't be solved with a threesome!*

Anna was still trying to recover from the trauma of that text! She was relieved that she was able to be alone. She thought it was odd that Louise didn't come upstairs at any point. Maybe Louise knew that they both needed time apart to reset some of the intimacy they had built, or maybe she was just avoiding Anna.

Finally, feeling significantly refreshed, Anna rejoined Clay and Louise in the living room. Hanging out together during the evening was surprisingly fun. Anna was gratified to find the three of them were able to recapture the chemistry they'd had during the tree-cutting excursion. At one point, Anna thought she could almost see herself hanging with both of them in New York. Eased by the wine and the good vibes, Anna kept letting her guard down, laughing and joking with Clay and Louise. But then there would be a moment. A brief touch, a shared look, some other act of synchronicity between her and Louise, and her stomach would drop, jokes abandoned. The moment would stretch. The more wine they had, the more it kept happening. And the more Anna tried to keep her eyes trained on something—anything—other than

Louise, the more she felt pulled toward her. Anna had never been so aware of someone else. All her work to extinguish her attraction only served to increase it. Eventually though, it got late, and they decided it was nearing time to go to bed.

Anna was moving dishes into the kitchen when she heard Clay and Louise whispering.

"Are you sure you don't want to sleep in my room tonight? You might have to sneak out early, but we can set an alarm."

Anna caught her breath as she came to grips with what was happening. Of course they would want to hook up while her parents were away. As much as she hated sharing a room with Louise, it was much worse to imagine her having sex with her brother all night.

Get over it, they're a couple. Of course they have sex.

Somehow this had never occurred to Anna. Seeing them all day hanging out just like any friends was easy to digest, but this image was too much. She needed to get out of earshot and quick.

"I don't know Clay. I really don't want to get caught breaking your mother's rules."

Anna exhaled in relief. Maybe listening in wasn't such a bad idea.

"Plus you snore."

Anna heard Clay laugh. "Okay, fine! I've been enjoying having a giant king bed to myself anyways. Your loss!"

They stopped talking and soon Anna could hear the sound of lips touching in the other room. It bothered her, the kiss. Not all the joking and the friendliness between Clay and Louise, it was the kiss. The feeling of jealousy settling deep in her bones was what really told Anna this situation was not improving. Her mind understood that this was her brother's girlfriend, but her body did not.

Upstairs in their shared bedroom, the room seemed to shrink. Anna felt like Louise was everywhere. They were more comfortable and a little buzzed, which meant Louise's smile came easier, her movements were more languid, and the tension between them was becoming more palpable. Anna watched Louise change in the room, something she'd studiously avoided the night before. Was Louise aware of its effect on her? Was this tension not mutual? Louise turned away from Anna and pulled her shirt off in one smooth motion. Her back was smooth and braless, and when she bent to grab her tank top for bed, Anna could see the curve of her breast and she froze on the spot. Louise seemed not to notice. Once they had both used the bathroom and were in their respective beds, Anna turned off the light. Her body was thrumming with energy. She struggled to find a comfortable position on her pillow, under the covers. All she could do was try as hard as she could not to acknowledge the truth. Even with all her efforts, she still wanted Louise.

"Good night," Anna said, cursing the breathy lust she could hear in her own voice.

"Good night," Louise responded so softly she could barely hear.

Anna spent another night tracing Louise's shadow with her eyes, knowing sleep might never come.

❖

Louise slowly opened her eyes, trying in vain to hold on to the last moments of an extremely pleasant dream. She found herself unable to remember anything about it, but her body tingled with arousal. She sighed with pleasure before remembering where she was. Feeling guilty, she glanced over at the bed a couple of feet away where Anna's pert nose was peeking out from the covers. The bedding shifted, revealing Anna's delicate and peaceful face, long eyelashes moving ever so slightly. Louise allowed herself a moment to admire Anna's beauty before she found herself staring into piercing brown eyes. Louise stayed still, caught. Neither looked away. Louise felt her body continue to hum. Her phone dinged. The tension broke. An awareness set in, and Louise turned away, reaching for her phone. The message was from Clay.

Clay 11:02 a.m.: *I can't believe you're still asleep! Come down for...lunch?*

It was eleven a.m., a far cry from Louise's typical seven a.m. wake-up time. Disoriented, she sat up in the bed, stretching self-consciously. Anna was moving around as well. They were no longer connected. Louise got out of bed quickly and let herself into the bathroom. With her back against the door and with the privacy the room provided, she put her hand to her chest and tried to calm herself with slow breaths. How was she going to survive another minute, let alone another night with this woman? She grabbed her phone to text Clay back.

Louise 11:04 a.m.: *Be down in 5*

She went to the sink to wash her face. The mirror reflected a deep flush across her cheeks and chest, and she swore under her breath. Honestly, could she be any more transparent? Once she had righted herself and gone through her morning routine, she reentered the bedroom with a prepared "normal person" good morning she had rehearsed, only to find the room empty.

❖

Louise ended up taking longer than five minutes to get downstairs, now that she had the room to herself. She showered and dressed for the day, not wanting to look too casual after she'd already accidentally given the impression that she habitually slept in till noon. As she came down the stairs, Louise could already feel a different energy in the house. The Nelsons were home. If the house were a shirt, it was as if it had just been starched. She entered the kitchen and found Sebastian moving around very quickly with Dr. Nelson close on his heels dictating meal plans for the week. Dr. Nelson was not suggesting, she was telling.

"I want the roast beef marinated for seventy-two hours, and don't forget the onions will need to be caramelized...Oh, Louise, dear, you're awake?"

Louise did not miss the slight snark in Dr. Nelson's tone as she commented on her tardiness.

"Good morning," Louise responded. "Welcome back."

"Yes, well, very happy to be back. Luckily, we got in at six, so we didn't lose half our day!" Another barb. Louise got it; she should have been up earlier.

"Yes, sorry about sleeping in. I must be recovering a bit from finals." She flashed a sheepish smile.

"It is no problem, dear!" It clearly was. "Why don't you go over to the dining room? I think there's some leftover coffee cake."

Louise excused herself with relief and joined Anna, who was clearly also picking through the breakfast scraps. Scraps being an incredible homemade coffee cake that was beautifully laid out for them on a rose-patterned serving dish. She watched as Anna pulled a bite-sized crumble off the cake and popped it into her mouth before sucking the leftover sugar off of her thumb with relish. Catching Louise's stare, Anna licked the remaining sugar off her first finger. Before her weakened knees could fully betray her, Louise stumbled awkwardly into a chair and, trying to find something to occupy her, began serving herself breakfast. Clay and Mr. Nelson were a room over and Clay came into the dining room as soon as he saw her.

"Good morning, Lou," he said, bending down to kiss her softly on the cheek. Louise was relieved to have him there as a buffer. Clay spoke under his breath.

"Did she give you shit for sleeping in?"

"What do you think?" she replied.

Clay grimaced knowingly. "I'm glad you survived!"

He sat down next to her and began chatting with Anna. The easy chemistry between the three of them had all but dissipated and the tension of knowing the Nelsons were in earshot seemed to stunt Clay's and Anna's conversation. Once the meal had become sufficiently awkward, Dr. Nelson came in with an announcement.

"I know we've had a bit of a late start, but I need you all to be ready to go in about an hour."

Dr. Nelson began to clear the table. Being that she'd hired somebody to do that exact job, Louise had to assume the gesture was a clear direction to her and Anna that they needed to get moving. But get moving for what?

"If you don't mind me asking, what is going on in an hour?" She directed the question to Clay.

Clay got up from the table as if from a Pavlovian response to his mom's subtle communication.

"Didn't I tell you? Today is the Trenton Christmas Festival."

Louise looked at him blankly, racking her memory for any mention of such a thing.

"No, you didn't tell me. What is it exactly?"

"Oh sorry, I guess I was just so excited with all the travel stuff. Basically, it's a festival in the Trenton main square with Christmas lights and hot cider and a Santa. Exactly what you expect from a Hallmark Christmas movie."

"Sounds cute!"

Anna stayed put, sipping her coffee slowly.

"Are you coming as well?" Louise asked Anna, testing her ability to carry on a normal conversation with her.

"Couldn't miss it, even if I wanted to!" she said with a saccharine smile. The comment was clearly meant more for the Nelsons' benefit.

Dr. Nelson gave her a look. "Anna, please leave that attitude at home. It's hard enough dealing with the questions regarding your sudden reappearance in Trenton."

"Don't worry, Mom, I'll be on my best behavior."

Louise could feel tension growing in her shoulders again, hoping this wouldn't take another turn for the worse, but Anna's comment seemed to diffuse the situation a bit.

"And, Louise dear, Clay has some errands to run, so you and I should have some extra time at the festival to get to know one another and chat." Dr. Nelson gave her a conspiratorial wink—so different from her daughter's—which Louise attempted to respond to with openness. Dr. Nelson was giving her whiplash from all the different personalities she seemed to hold.

"Yeah, sorry, Lou. I should be able to meet up with y'all later on, but you might have to fend for yourself among Trenton's finest!" Clay put his hand on the small of her back affectionately.

"I'm sure I'll have a wonderful time," Louise said as she ransacked her mind for some possible excuse she could make to avoid this one-on-one with Dr. Nelson.

❖

Anna couldn't help but be charmed by the Trenton Christmas Festival. She usually self-identified as a Christmas grinch, but her heart was swelling two sizes just from the pine smell and the corny holly decorations. Anna loved New York, but sometimes her small-town upbringing would seep out, especially during the city's brutal summers when the smell of trash hung thickly in the air. But the feeling always faded as soon as she got used to the odor and remembered once again the incredible feeling of anonymity she felt from walking around the city. Having no one know Annabelle Nelson, Trenton weirdo.

The festival spanned a four-block area of the town center. In front of the centermost point next to the Trenton clock tower was a giant tree dressed in red and green ornaments (Trenton was not known for originality) and the typical random professional Santa sitting for the kids. The whole endeavor was being organized by church volunteer elves who seemed to be aggressively enforcing the queue on the ten or so families in line. There were booths selling homemade crafts and hot apple cider, as well as a little stage area off to the side, where a school band was solemnly playing very simple versions of Christmas carols. Each time they hit a right note (which seemed to be less often than not), the conductor's face would light up with surprise and he'd bounce forward a bit on his toes. Throughout the day, there would be different and yet similar performers and eventually a prize awarded to whoever had decorated the most Christmas-y booth. It was truly a Hallmark movie.

Anna had quickly separated from her family upon arriving downtown. It wasn't difficult now that her mother had latched onto her one-track goal of indoctrinating Louise into the family via interrogation. Anna only felt a little bad slipping out of their view. *I mean, this is why Louise is here, right? To get in with the fam.*

She stepped up for her hot apple cider.

The steaming cup was just the right amount of cinnamon and warmed Anna to the core. She was enjoying herself thoroughly, feeling almost unrecognizable among the Trenton residents. She was leisurely strolling around the square wondering what made a booth particularly Christmas-y when she spotted a group of women about her age coming right down her path.

The women looked familiar in a way that made Anna want to abruptly change directions, but she couldn't quite get away with that without drawing attention to herself. And anyway, they'd already seemed to spot her and were approaching her quickly. Anna braced herself for a flashback to the hell that was high school.

"Belle Nelson? Is that you?"

A Barbie doll that had come to life named Jessica Taylor gushed in a dramatic, high-pitched voice. Anna stared at her blankly.

"Oh. My God. How weird! You look...so different! I almost didn't recognize you."

Her comment was annoying, to say the least, but it was definitely less judgy than when they had all been in high school. Anna was mildly impressed to find that Jessica seemed to have learned some restraint.

"Hi, Jessica," she said, not trying very hard to mask her irritation.

The two women standing slightly behind Jessica were ever-present fixtures in her past life. One was Alison Hudson, Jessica's twin soul and best friend, a title which was shockingly displayed clearly on their matching gold "BFFL" necklaces. At least from first glance, they appeared to have changed close to zero in the years since high school. It was both a comfort and a disappointment. The third person, who was not wearing a matching necklace and seemed slightly out of place in this group, was Gina Perez. Even in high school, Gina had been different from the other two. She never quite clicked with Jessica and Alison, though all three had been close friends.

Actually, Gina and Anna had been "sort of" friends back then too. At least, that's what Anna thought. Gina and Anna had been in band together. She was clearly one of the "cool girls" and so their friendship wasn't quite open to the public, but they would hang after school and on the weekends, when Gina wasn't wherever with her clique. Anna hadn't thought about Gina in a long time. She had to admit, the two of them drifting apart had not been an accident.

When Anna left Trenton at eighteen, she never looked back. She couldn't remember if Gina texted or messaged her on Facebook, but knowing herself, she'd most likely ignored it. Gina was looking at her now with a raised eyebrow. Anna couldn't decide if it was indifference, contempt, or curiosity.

"So where have you been? You basically fell off the face of the earth," Gina said, her tone still unreadable.

Anna took in Gina's new look. She was definitely one of the country club bunch in her Ugg boots and lululemon ensemble. To Anna's dismay, she was still very beautiful. And that undercurrent of…something…was still beneath the surface. Anna had suspected that some of the reasons their "friendship" wasn't common knowledge had something to do with the knowing look Gina gave her at that moment.

"I live in New York. Don't get back too much." Anna shrugged, trying to project nonchalance.

"Oh, I love New York!" Jessica squealed. "I just love Times Square and all the people and Broadway! Do you live near there?"

Anna tried not to laugh at the very earnest and very ridiculous question.

"Not exactly."

She tried and failed not to be judgy.

"I live in Brooklyn. Not quite Times Square."

"Oh, that's too bad." Jessica seemed truly disappointed not to know someone who lived on the Jumbotron.

"I can't believe how many tattoos you have!" Alison chimed in, touching Anna's wrist. Her sleeve was poking through her winter coat, something that always drew attention in a town like Trenton. Anna was thrown off by how entitled Alison seemed to that level of intimacy. Again, people didn't touch other people without at least some kind of rapport in Anna's world.

"Yeah, I'm about to get another one right here," Anna said, drawing a large circle on her forehead.

Alison balked, clearly not catching Anna's joke.

"That's umm cool, Belle," Alison said, beginning to almost walk backward from the conversation.

Jessica seemed unperturbed by Anna's bold fashion choice.

"Are you going to Josh's family's Christmas party?" she asked.

"I think maybe, I haven't really checked in on that."

"Do you know if Clay will be there?" Alison asked, feigning nonchalance.

"Umm, I don't know. I guess?"

Jessica elbowed Alison who gave a small yelp in pain.

"Well, we won't keep you. Come on, girls, let's hit the spiked cider booth!" Jessica tossed her hair and flashed Anna a bright smile. "I'm sure we'll see you around this week." Jessica almost sounded earnest.

Just as Anna was about to let out a sigh of relief that the popular girls were leaving, she noticed Gina had stayed put.

"I'll catch up," Gina called after her friends.

Alison and Jessica seemed to do a double take but then kept walking away.

There was silence until they were both out of earshot.

"So," Gina said. "You're back."

So, I guess we're going to talk about it.

"Yeah...I'm here for the week. Maybe longer. We'll see!" Anna said with a shrug, thinking about the prospect of a long stay with her family. She was only planning on staying for the week and then making a new plan, but she had considered staying longer if absolutely necessary. But with the way the week was going so far, she was honestly thinking of cutting the week short and asking to crash on Rachel's couch indefinitely. No matter how bad her financial situation was, this wasn't worth it. It was so easy to forget what coming home was like. Why did she continue to try?

Gina seemed to consider what she was going to say next.

"You look good." Gina looked at Anna appraisingly, letting the comment stick in the air.

Undertones were what Anna remembered about their friendship, not overt compliments on physical appearance. Clearly, Gina wasn't wasting time this go-around.

"Uh, thanks. You too," Anna replied, meaning it.

"Yeah, well, one of the perks of being a personal trainer!"

Of course, Gina knew she was hot.

"I'm surprised to see you hanging with Romi and Michelle back there," Anna joked. "Well, not Romi and Michelle, more like those other girls who hated them..."

Gina laughed and as she did, she leaned in, allowing her arm to lightly graze Anna's.

I guess people don't really change.

"Yeah, well, once you left, I was alone. I had to find friends where I could get them. And there wasn't anyone else around to... broaden my horizons." Gina quirked her eyebrow, leaving no mistake about what she meant by her comment.

Anna was brought back to one of their sleepovers sophomore year, after they had both gotten ahold of some very low proof schnapps. Gina had interrupted one of Anna's long monologues about the hypocrisy of high school sports with a kiss. The taste of synthetic peach still reminded her of that night and how it set in motion a lot of angst and self-discovery. Anna and Gina never explicitly talked about that night, or any of the other nights. They usually happened after some form of "chemical excuse" was introduced and mostly went about as far as making out and some fumbling. At the time, Gina was extremely vexing to Anna. She couldn't figure out what their relationship was, if Gina was just experimenting or if there was something deeper between them. Now, it was less vexing. What young Anna really learned from the experience was that her wants and desires needed to be hidden. As a result, she'd spent most of her adult life trying to unlearn that exact lesson.

"I'm sure you could've found someone to be friends with. If not in Trenton, then a town over," Anna responded pointedly.

Gina seemed to ponder a moment but then she leaned in. Anna thought she was trying to kiss her—a bold move for the middle of Trenton's town square—but then Gina turned to her side to whisper in Anna's ear.

"Maybe I've been waiting for you to pick up where you left off." Her lips were so close that Anna could almost feel their vibrations as she spoke. Gina backed away trailing her hand along Anna's shoulder as she did. Gina then reached into her bag and pulled out a card. It was her business card for her personal training business. On it was her cell number.

Anna was stunned again by Gina's boldness.

"Give me a call, Anna, if you're interested in a training session. I have a lot of openings this week for the holiday."

Her tone was less flirty now that she was in earshot of Trenton residents.

"Let me go catch up with Jessica and Alison before they come looking for me. I'll see you soon, Anna," she said with a confidence that only someone who had been turned down as little as Gina could pull off.

"Yeah, see ya," Anna said with someone else's voice.

She watched as Gina sauntered away. There was something so frustrating about a girl like Gina. If Anna were in her right state of mind, she would have taken the opportunity to turn Gina down with a flourish, high fiving her teenage self as she rode off into the sunset on a motorcycle. But because she was feeling so down, and because she was coming off of a huge lusting-after-her-brother's-girlfriend debacle, she was almost considering giving Gina a call. Would it be so bad to have a little fling while she was home? Maybe it could take some of the pressure off the Louise situation.

As she walked along her recently interrupted path, the object of her turmoil came into view across the street. Louise was walking alone, making Anna wonder if she had found a creative way to ditch her mom or if her mom had sprung into socialite mode and left Louise to fend for herself. Either way, Louise was better off. Anna watched her as she took in the Christmas festival atmosphere.

Louise looked peaceful. She had an elegance to her and an openness. Anna was again floored by the pull she felt toward Louise. Even with the awkwardness peppering a significant chunk of their interactions, Anna couldn't help wanting to be near her. Louise reached over to receive a candy apple from one of the booths, and her smile spread, punctuated by that dimple. It was infectious. Mr. Jennings, the middle school art teacher, handed the fruit to her with the same exuberance, and Anna knew she was not the only one affected by Louise's charm and beauty. Anna held herself back from moving closer.

What would it be like to be able to go over to Louise now? To walk around with her, stealing small touches, brushing the tendril of hair that always seemed to fall in her face? What would it be like to be able to talk, to really talk, like they did at the bar? The connection she felt, the shared interests, the trust, that didn't happen every day. Seeing her now, when no one was looking, Anna could see the lingering sadness that seemed to hover over Louise. Was that part of what Anna found so attractive? Anna knew what it felt like to feel alone in a crowd. It was what brought them both to the bar that day, a loneliness. Anna could see that loneliness now. If Louise hadn't been her brother's girlfriend, maybe she could have gone over to her, asked her about that sadness. Or better yet, maybe they would have run into each other here coincidently after their shared kiss at the bar. She might have persuaded Louise to steal away with her. There was of course the problem with the unnamed boyfriend. Maybe that would have been enough to keep them apart, if they had run into each other like Anna was imagining. Deep down, Anna knew it wouldn't have been enough for her to stay away. Maybe this was a flaw in Anna. It was troubling how comfortable Anna was with being a dirty little secret. She considered her high school track record with Gina and decided she needed to get some self-respect. But the reality was, she couldn't act on her feelings. She had to keep things at friend level. She couldn't betray her brother, especially not after his heartfelt apology and their new effort toward a better relationship.

Just then, Anna noticed her mother coming up behind Louise, clearly looking to rejoin her. Anna acted without thinking. She crossed the street and approached Louise quickly. Catching Louise's eye, Anna grabbed her hand and pulled her lightly through a crowd of people, speed-walking as quickly as she could.

"Whoa, what are you doing!" Louise asked, surprised. Clearly, she had not spotted Anna's mom.

"Giving you a break from Dr. Nelson's examination," Anna said over her shoulder.

Once they were sufficiently far from the prying eyes of her mother, Anna let go of Louise's hand, trying not to care about the tingling she felt just from that momentary touch.

"There, now you can decide if you want to spend the rest of the day with my mom or if you want to do what you want."

Anna had become exceedingly conscious that she'd acted without thinking, and that the exact thing she was avoiding was happening presently. But now that it was upon her, she realized she hadn't been avoiding it at all.

CHAPTER SIX

As they walked, Louise was acutely aware of how close Anna was walking next to her. She could see every one of the freckles in Anna's eyes.

She realized she had been distracted when she heard Anna ask for the second time, "Louise, did you hear me?"

Louise came back into the present conversation.

"Right, uh...Yeah, thank you for...I guess rescuing me."

Louise was relieved to not have to endure another hour of Dr. Nelson listing accolades and name-dropping. Anna was looking at her in that unwavering way that made Louise feel on edge.

"Okay, well, I guess I'll leave you to it," Anna said, looking ready to turn and leave.

"Wait!" Louise was surprised to hear the word come out as a plea. She tried again. "I mean, maybe we could walk around together?"

The question hung in the air as Anna seemed to contemplate the situation before her.

"I don't know anybody, and it would be nice to have some company, that isn't your mom obviously." Louise tried her hardest to project the most platonic friendly vibe she possibly could. Louise could tell that Anna was hesitating.

"Okay," Anna said carefully.

Louise was surprised by Anna's response, but she tried not to show it. She wanted to be Anna's friend, and honestly, Anna was the only person Louise liked in Trenton, apart from Clay.

They awkwardly debated where to start but eventually picked a direction, laughing as they noticed their difficulty with such a simple task.

As they walked through the booths, Anna explained who everyone was and some of the main staples of the festival. It was clear to Louise that Anna loved all the super corny booths and DIY stations, stopping each time to compliment the booth owner on their creativity. Louise could tell from the interactions she observed that the people of Trenton were surprised to see Anna, and almost all of them mentioned how different she looked. Louise also noticed the way Anna spoke to them with kindness and curiosity. Something Louise wasn't expecting after hearing how hard of a time Anna seemed to have when she used to live there. People really responded to Anna with interest and affection. Whatever negative feelings the Nelsons must have instilled in Anna, she had survived with her heart intact.

"It's funny seeing you interact with everyone. I would have thought you hated Trenton, just based on the way you talked about it at the bar." Louise knew it was bold to reference that time, but she was getting more comfortable with Anna, and she wanted to know more about her.

"Yeah, it's interesting. I thought I hated Trenton too, but"— Anna gestured to the scene around them—"look around! It's hard to hate a cheesy festival like this!" Anna's smile was infectious. It turned out, she could be kind of a softy.

"I can't disagree with you there. We have something like this in my hometown. I was devasted to miss it this year."

"How funny, I hope our festival doesn't disappoint?" Anna asked the question with a slight competitiveness that Louise was starting to notice was a trait of hers.

"Trenton could never disappoint, at least not in holiday spirit. I mean look at all those children in reindeer antlers and masks, could anything be more picturesque? I guess I just meant because you love New York so much, it seems like it would be hard to reconcile these two places."

Anna seemed to think on this for a while.

"Well, I guess I'm starting to think differently about a lot of things. Like maybe I'm not just one thing, if that makes sense."

Louise didn't quite follow, but she was curious. She knew getting closer to Anna was dangerous, but it wasn't like friends don't talk about these sort of things.

"Think differently how?"

Anna seemed to hesitate. The conversation was clearly getting personal. Louise couldn't tell if Anna was uncomfortable or just not sure what she felt.

"I guess I've just been thinking a lot about why I left Trenton and what I'm doing back here. Like did I leave because of this town, or my parents, or because I wanted a new adventure? A lot of it feels like it's about my parents and I don't like that. I don't want to do things because of them, I want to do things because of me. Being here, I can see that there are things I love about Trenton. Should I throw all of that away just because of them? And then it's like with my company shutting down. I had other places I could have gone for the holidays. I have friends, why did I come here, where I knew I would be berated? Am I still just looking for their approval? Like Clay?"

Louise didn't know how to respond.

"Sorry, I know that was heavy."

"No, it's fine. I like heavy." Louise realized this was true as she considered Anna's words.

Anna looked at her with what looked like relief. Louise knew how hard it was to be vulnerable. Louise had been so careful with who she showed her soul to that even hearing Anna made her realize how lonely it was, keeping it all inside.

"Maybe it's okay to like both places, and maybe it's okay to want their approval. I mean, it's only human to want your parents' approval. I do think that wanting it shouldn't hurt. They shouldn't hurt you like they do."

Anna glanced at her. "Honestly, I think it hurts too much right now."

Anna's words were poignant and made Louise sad for her. She wished she could do something to take away that pain, but she knew this was something Anna was going through on her own. It also comforted Louise to know that Anna seemed to be leaning toward protecting herself. Louise felt deeply that Anna was worth protecting.

They continued to walk through the festival and allowed the lightness and playfulness to slowly reenter their interactions. It was amazing how easy it was to move through emotions together. The awkwardness between them was gone.

Louise found that she was having a much better time than she'd anticipated. Once it was a respectable time—afternoon—they went over to the craft beer stand. The line was short—maybe it wasn't the *most* respectable time—and they reached the counter quickly.

"Belle?" A tall and conventionally good-looking man behind the booth formed a visor with his hand as he pretended to inspect Anna.

"Hi, Josh," Anna said with a smile.

"Come here, girl. I haven't seen you in ages!"

Josh came out from behind the booth and embraced Anna in a giant bear hug. From her vantage point, Louise was able to take in the man in his entirety. He had a scruffy beard and a trucker hat placed lightly on his head with a casualness that only a certain kind of man could do. He was tall with a soft middle that actually looked pretty good on him. His baseball-style shirt read "Harris Farm Brewery" as did all the swag around his booth.

Josh let go of his bone-crushing hug and held Anna by the shoulders.

"You look amazing, Belle! Who would have thought that lanky little kid who used to hang around me and Clay would turn into such a looker?"

His flirtatious words were clearly harmless and Louise had heard stories about Josh from Clay, but Louise felt prickly about this burly man being so intimate with Anna.

"Thanks! You look good as well, very much playing the part of brewery lumberjack." Anna elbowed him lightly in the gut.

"Yeah, well you know, my job is drinking beer," he said good-naturally. "Where's Clay?" Josh was looking around and finally noticing Anna wasn't there with her brother. His eyes landed on Louise. "Oh, who is this?"

"This is Louise Tanner," Anna said. "Clay's girlfriend."

She seemed to stumble slightly on the word girlfriend, reminding Louise that she was in fact Anna's brother's girlfriend and not Anna's girlfriend.

"Really nice to meet you, Josh. Clay has told me a lot about you."

"Likewise, Louise! I've been looking forward to meeting you all week. I was hoping it wouldn't be at the wedding," he said playfully as he gave her a warm handshake.

The word "wedding" rang in her ears. Had Clay been talking to Josh about them getting married? The thought chilled Louise to her bone.

"I don't know about wedding talk so soon..." The words sounded hollow, and Louise noticed that the exuberance and comfort that she had been radiating since hanging with Anna had dimmed.

"Didn't mean to put you on the spot there, Louise. I just know my boy likes you is all."

Josh had a way about him that put Louise at ease. Even with the grenade he'd just thrown into the conversation, she could tell he was just being friendly.

"It's fine," she said, hoping they could move on quickly. Josh looked between them and started to pick up on the awkwardness.

"So, what can I get you both? Obviously, I have to hook you up. What'll it be?"

"Thanks, Josh," Anna said, clearly relieved to have the subject changed. "How about that blood orange lager? I tried it the other night and was totally blown away."

Josh lit up at the compliment.

"Yeah, I tinkered with that one a lot. Can you taste that blood orange?"

Anna took a sip of her nice frothy beer right off the tap.

"Definitely, it's my new favorite flavor, perfectly bitter."

Louise noticed a bit of froth had caught on Anna's upper lip. Anna licked it off, drawing Louise's eyes from her lips to the slow cascade of her tongue. There was still a little froth left.

"I'm going to finish showing Louise around, but we'll catch up later."

"That's a promise, Belle," Josh said, pointing a finger gun as he moved back behind the booth.

"Nice meeting you, Josh," Louise said.

"You too, Louise. I'm sure I'll be seeing you later this weekend."

They continued on their path with Louise completely distracted by the line of froth still sitting on Anna's lips. Once they were out of sight of any onlookers, Louise held Anna's arm, bringing her to a stop. Anna furrowed her brow in confusion. Louise moved into Anna's space, holding her chin with one hand and bringing her other thumb to Anna's lips. She slowly moved her finger over Anna's skin. The move was a necessity in Louise's eyes. She couldn't let Anna walk around face full of froth. But as she became more aware of her hands on Anna's face, her lips, she could feel that pull in her stomach, that feeling of want. They held each other's eyes, aware of the energy that continued to thrum through them both. Louise stilled with her fingers still touching Anna's lips. She pulled her hand away, slowly regaining her composure.

"Sorry, I should have asked. You just had something on your face."

Louise's voice was breathy and slow. Anna cleared her throat and backed away, touching the place Louise had just touched.

"Thanks."

They fell back in step, Louise hyper-aware of Anna's proximity. They walked farther apart but even the forced distance felt odd, like they had something to hide. Admittedly, Louise did have something to hide.

Eventually, they made it over to one of the boundaries of the festival. Off in the corner there was an entrance to what looked like a corn maze. At the front stood a snowman who looked like he had had just about enough of yelling at kids through two eyeholes all day.

"What do you think? Want to see if we can make it through the Trenton Christmas maze?" Anna asked in that "platonic friends" tone they'd become so good at.

"If you think we brought enough provisions?" Louise made the quip implying a yes, but then it dawned on her, there were no other people around. They would be alone. Was this the best idea considering all she could think about was Anna's lips and what they felt like under her fingers, under her own lips?

❖

Louise took in the surprising intricacies of the Trenton town maze. Not only was it tall and adequately confusing, but it was also covered in Christmas lights and bows, making it the perfect Instagram background for anyone who didn't feel like what they were doing was a secret.

Anna set the pace, which was slow. It seemed that there was no one yet in the maze. Most likely it would become more popular as the sun set so that the lights could be more noticeable.

A silence hung between them. Louise searched for things to say, but she came up with nothing. It was one thing to be alone in their shared bedroom in her boyfriend's family house, it was another to be alone in this maze, away from prying eyes. Their stroll together was starting to mess with Louise's head. It was like she had stepped into a new timeline in a multiverse. They continued to walk, pausing when they came to a fork.

"Which way do you want to go?" Anna indicated to the right and the left.

Louise looked as far as she could down each pathway and still hesitated.

"It's okay if you pick the wrong way. It'll either dead end and we can come back, or it'll lead to something that leads to something that leads to a way out."

"I guess I'm not really the best at making uninformed decisions," Louise said with a smile.

"Yeah, I can tell!"

Louise gave Anna a playful nudge and Anna pretended to be hurt.

"Okay, let's go right."

Anna looked at her skeptically. "Are you sure? I mean this is pretty high stakes. Right is your final answer?"

Louise hesitated again.

"Oh my God, you're definitely about to stress out again, aren't you?" Anna laughed, continuing to tease Louise. "I'm going to decide for both of us. We're going left."

"Left!" Louise exclaimed. "So, you're just trying to do the opposite of what I want?"

"Based on my observations of your decision-making process, I don't think you know what you want." The tone was teasing, but the words were not.

"Fine, you go left, I'll go right, and I'll see you on the other side, how about that?"

Anna turned serious for a moment.

"Would you rather I leave you alone?"

Louise became aware that their conversation had changed. Anna thought she wanted to ditch her or something.

"No, I was just kidding."

"Are you sure? I mean, I know this is awkward and seriously, there is no pressure to spend time with me, especially after… everything."

"No, Anna, I…I'm having a good time." Louise left it at that. Clearly, there was still so much unsaid. Somehow they had spent the entire afternoon together and all Louise wanted was for it never to end. Louise wasn't so sure that was how friendship should feel. Louise turned down the left passageway and then looked back, holding her hand out.

"Come on, let's go your way."

Anna approached slowly and Louise took Anna's hand in hers. The gesture could have been meant to be friendly, but when Anna let go, Louise was confronted with the oddness of it. She tried not to think about her impulse to be tactile with Anna. She didn't hold hands with friends, not even in passing. She wouldn't even really think to do it with a girlfriend or boyfriend. She was crossing lines with Anna, but if she didn't look too closely at it, it could have been innocent. The silence between them came back. They continued to walk.

"Why do some people call you Belle and others call you Anna?"

"Or if you're my mother, Annabelle," Anna added.

"Yeah, it's been kind of confusing. Do you have a preference?"

Anna seemed to consider for a moment. "Well, I guess I prefer Anna. I definitely don't like Annabelle, it's so old and weird and… Southern."

Louise laughed. "It isn't very fitting, is it?"

"Yeah, I mean, pick a name, right!" Anna laughed too. "But honestly, I don't mind Belle. At least I don't mind when *some* people call me Belle, like Clay or someone who just doesn't know me by any other name. When I left Trenton at eighteen, I just wanted a new start. So, I had a handy second nickname to switch to."

"I guess that is convenient," Louise replied. "What made you leave so decidedly, I imagine right after high school?"

Anna shrugged. "I guess it was just the way I felt here at the time. Have you ever felt like you were trapped? Not in a place or anything like that, but in yourself? Like that everyone had already decided who you were and as long as they could see you or be near you, you could never change or grow or anything."

Louise felt as if she were experiencing that sensation of being trapped right along with Anna.

"I think I do know that feeling."

Louise couldn't help but think about her life with Gwen and how many of her decisions felt like they were made for her. How when Gwen died, it seemed like everyone around her, her friends, Gwen's family, even her mom looked at her as someone wounded. Once she was able to get past the worst of her depression and she was able to leave that environment, she finally began to learn new things and grow. Sometimes she wondered if she and Gwen would have even lasted. Maybe not, but living without her, without her best friend? That was what trapped her most of all. She didn't feel comfortable sharing that with Anna, but Anna didn't push.

"Do you feel free now?" Louise asked.

Anna seemed very contemplative. Their gaits were matched, and Louise could feel that their hands kept accidentally grazing.

"Sometimes."

For the first time in a long time, Louise wished for that feeling for herself.

"I feel it with you," Anna added, catching Louise off guard.

Louise didn't know what to say. This was a territory she had been working hard to steer clear of. Instead of speaking, she found herself involuntarily reaching to hold Anna's hand. They walked in silence just holding hands. Louise was completely shocked by her own actions. Finally, Anna spoke softly, almost as a statement of fact. "We're holding hands."

The silence continued.

"Is this okay?" Anna asked in that same soft tone.

"Probably not." Louise's voice was not her own. She could feel the seconds tick by, her feeling of "wrongness" growing. They came to another fork. This one had three different options. Louise went ahead and chose the middle one, bringing Anna along without so much as a pause. The feeling was heady.

Louise was struggling to concentrate on anything but the feeling of holding Anna's hand. She was trying as hard as she could to persuade herself to let it go, but instead, she felt herself being pulled in the entirely opposite direction.

"What are we doing, Louise?" Anna asked more forcefully.

They passed another corner of the maze and came to a dead end.

Anna stopped walking. Louise couldn't take it anymore. Anna was much too close. Louise found herself moving closer.

"Stop talking," Louise said, the only thing she could think of to say.

Louise couldn't stop, she pushed up against Anna, inching her backward toward the stalks. They moved easily aside, forming an Anna-shaped divot in the maze wall. Louise grabbed Anna's hips and pulled her in closer. She could see Anna's heartbeat on the pulse point of her neck. As if in a trance, she placed her lips to Anna's neck in what started as a delicate kiss, her breath coming fast. There was no space between Louise's desire and her decision to act on it; everything felt at once out of her control and completely within her grasp. Anna's moan of pleasure hit Louise hard and she opened her mouth running her tongue and then her teeth over the skin in front of her. The taste and smell of Anna was intoxicating. Louise was on sensory overload, but she wanted more. She tried to show Anna with her hands, her mouth, her tongue, but she was still frustrated. Louise spoke between bites.

"I can't help wanting you." The words came out as a plea.

She was asking for something, she didn't know what—help resisting Anna, or maybe to have her like this, more than this. Louise felt Anna let out a groan of exasperation. It was the sound of that same wanting. Had Anna been fighting this desire just as much?

Anna's hands traveled down Louise's back. They were strong and forceful, just the way Louise had imagined. Anna tugged her closer, the contact desperate and fervent.

Louise could feel Anna's hands find her ass, pulling their bodies together with little care for how quickly this was going. It left Louise gasping; she felt her wetness just from the friction of the last few desperate moments. Louise moved her kisses down Anna's neck to her collarbone as she moved her hand up to Anna's breast, exploring openly.

"Fuck, Louise!" Anna moaned, appearing to struggle to stay standing. Louise pulled Anna's shirt open to reveal bare breasts, not caring when a button broke off, her lips on every inch she could see. She moved back up Anna's neck and her breath was erratic, her body nearly shaking with want. Louise found the front of Anna's jeans and pulled at the button, undoing it easily, then moved to the zipper.

"Louise, wait."

The words crashed into Louise and she froze. Her teeth were now firmly around Anna's earlobe. She noticed where her hands were, what she had been about to do. She had to stop. She abruptly pulled away and stepped back. Anna looked completely dismantled. With growing horror, Louise slowly became more and more aware of how profoundly fucked up what she just did was. Shame washed over her.

"Oh my God. I can't believe I just did that." Louise took a few more steps back. She ran her hands through her hair frantically. "Fuck, Anna, what is wrong with me!"

Anna seemed to be unable to speak. The way her hair was all frazzled and her shirt was misaligned sent a jolt of energy through Louise's system, forcing her to close her eyes, anything to stop herself from acting on the feelings she was having.

"Louise, I don't know what—"

"There you both are!" A voice called from the other end of their current path.

Louise's heart stopped. Anna turned away for a moment and pretended to pick something off the ground, giving her time to button her shirt, at least as much as she could. It was Clay and Josh who both appeared completely unaware of what they had walked in on. Did they see anything? Louise couldn't imagine what they thought—she must have looked guilty at least.

"I looked everywhere for you both, and then Josh said he saw y'all go into the maze."

Clay came over and kissed Louise on the lips. The sensation was like razor blades. Louise was at a loss for what to do or say. All she could do was wonder if Clay could tell her lips were swollen. Or think about the salt from Anna's neck that she could still taste on her tongue.

"I'm on break, so I was hoping I could come hang with you all," Josh said with his usual charm, moving in next to Anna.

Louise continued to blunder. It was Anna who ultimately saved them.

"Yeah, we got a little turned around." Anna's voice sounded odd, almost haunted, but Clay and Josh didn't seem to notice.

"I can see that," Clay said looking around the dead-end alcove that Louise had just pushed Anna up against.

When silence hung in the air, Anna spoke up again. "Actually, can we try and get out of here? I'm starting to feel claustrophobic." Her voice was stronger now.

"Same," Josh said, throwing his arm over Anna and beginning to walk with her back down the path they had come down. Clay looked at Louise thoughtfully.

"Are you okay, Louise?" The words were kind but worried. Louise had had enough time to get herself together to reply.

"Yes, I'm just...." Her mouth moved next, but nothing came out. His caring eyes made her feel like scum. "It's just been a long day."

He held her close, only magnifying her awful feelings. She loved that Clay wasn't the kind of person to push. He knew she was a more internal person and he was respectful of her boundaries in that way. Louise was acutely aware of how much she had violated in their relationship. They walked behind Anna and Josh. Louise was trying to slow Clay down to get some space between Anna and Josh, but they kept inching closer. They were coming to new parts of the maze—maybe they were closer to being out? God, did Louise want to be out. She could overhear a bit of Josh's conversation with Anna.

"So, I was thinking, since you're back this week, maybe you want to hang out just you and me." The irony was not lost on Louise. The complete misalignment of everyone in this group made her feel that claustrophobia Anna expressed a moment ago. She could hear Anna hesitate.

"Josh that's…really nice of you. Um, but…I'm actually…not dating right now." Louise thought she was going to say she was gay. *But maybe Anna isn't gay, I mean she actually said queer, didn't she?*

Louise could not believe she had already been distracted from her self-flagellation to wondering who Anna dated. She had to get out of there and quick, but before she knew it, they reached the end of the maze. Finally out in the open air, she felt she could breathe again.

The boys were formulating a plan on what to do next, forcing Louise to accidentally catch Anna's eyes again. Anna looked upset. Louise was as well, but this was different. Anna looked almost angry.

"Hey, Belle, your button broke," Clay said, pointing at Anna's open shirt.

Louise's stomach dropped. Fuck, she had done that. Anna looked shocked as well. She straightened her shirt and tried to make it look presentable. Her haphazard actions didn't go unnoticed by Clay.

"Uh, thanks…Clay…I actually have to get going."

"What! But we just got here," Josh said pleadingly.

"Yeah, I'm sorry. I have some work to get done at home and, um…I promised I'd call Rachel."

Rachel? Who was Rachel?

Louise tried so hard to focus on the moment, focus on her boyfriend, focus on hiding what she had just done, but she was still unable to let Anna go from her mind.

"Yeah, um, so, see you all around I guess." Anna gave a short awkward wave as she turned to go.

"Oh, Belle, some of the old gang from town is going to be at the bar tonight. You have to come!"

Anna didn't pause from her exit, but she shot back an appeasing, "We'll see," as she continued down the main road and in the direction of the Nelsons' house.

When she was out of earshot, Josh turned toward Louise and Clay.

"That was weird, right? She was acting weird?"

Clay agreed and looked toward Louise.

"Did something happen between you two?" he asked innocently.

Yes, something had happened, but it couldn't have been what he picked up on.

"I don't know, it was a bit awkward today maybe," she said halfheartedly. Josh and Clay seemed to find this reply acceptable.

"Well, since my goal of asking Belle out fell pretty flat and you two probably want to be alone, I'll go ahead and get back to my booth," Josh said. Louise almost didn't want him to go. She was afraid of what her face would show once she was alone with Clay.

Josh said good-bye to them both and Clay turned to her again.

"What really happened?" he asked pointedly.

Louise began to walk down the street in the opposite direction of the festival, the car, and their house. Clay followed, confused.

"Louise, what is going on? What's wrong?"

Louise's halfhearted attempt to fast walk her way out of this was obviously not going to work.

"Honestly, I don't know, Clay. This has just been a lot. Meeting your family, the couple-y stuff. And today, where were you?" Yes, this explanation had huge omissions, but it wasn't untrue.

He looked at her as if he didn't know this person looking back at him. Her tone was too tense, too argumentative. They weren't like this with each other.

"I just had an errand to run. I really didn't think it would be so bad hanging with my family for a morning. Where's my mother? I thought you were going to spend time with her?"

Why was Clay suddenly so concerned about who she hung out with? Was he picking up on something?

"I did, but it was a lot, Clay. Anna sort of rescued me and then I don't know, we just kind of got in a bit of an argument."

This was a lie. But it was the only thing Louise could say that would make sense considering the energy when Clay came up. I mean, it was kind of a fight, toward the end, after they almost had sex right in the open maze.

"What kind of argument?" Clay asked carefully.

"Honestly, I don't want to talk about it. It'll be fine, we just feel different about some things is all." This might be true, but there were also obviously a lot of things they really connected on. A shiver ran through her body. Louise tried so hard to dampen it as much as possible.

"Okay, okay, I just, we were all getting along so well. I really liked having Belle…you know…back sort of."

Louise could see in Clay a person who needed family. He was healing his relationship with Anna. Another reason she could not be a part of this mess anymore. Clay was too good of a person to have this sort of betrayal happen to him. And it wasn't just the betrayal from her, but the betrayal from a sister who so far had not instigated anything that had happened between them. It was all Louise and this desire she could not get control over.

"I'm sorry, Clay, yes, it's gonna be fine. I'm gonna talk to her later and make sure we're all okay. I promise, it was nothing." She tried to smile in a way that communicated the sentiment. That whatever had happened between them could be fixed with a conversation. Louise knew that wasn't true, but she needed to find a way to make it true.

❖

Louise and Clay drove back to the house in total silence. Louise could not figure out what to say or how to handle the situation she had caused for herself. When they pulled into the Nelsons' driveway, Clay turned off the car but didn't get out. He stared straight ahead and let out an exhausted sigh.

"I don't want to fight," he started. "I know things are weird between us right now and when I think about it, I'm probably to blame. I've been so stressed with school and now my parents…"

He gripped the steering wheel harder when he mentioned his parents.

"Can we just hit the reset button? But for real this time?"

Louise could not stand the idea that Clay was blaming himself. It felt ridiculous after everything she had done. She wanted to tell him the truth, but sitting in the car next to him, she just didn't know where to begin. It was all so recent and raw, and she needed to process what was going on with her before inviting someone else into her chaos. Still, she had to say something.

"It's not just you, Clay," Louise said slowly.

He looked at her now, clearly hoping for more.

"I'm going through something right now. I'm not ready to talk about it, but it's made it hard to…to be here this weekend."

Clay nodded in acceptance. Louise put her hand on Clay's cheek and looked into his eyes, the eyes of someone she deeply cared about.

"I promise, I will talk to you when I'm ready."

Clay gave her a small smile.

"Okay, I'll be waiting."

Louise could not live like this. Her deceptions, her betrayals, they were stacking up. She left the car with Clay but hesitated before they reached the front door. Just the idea of entering the Nelsons' house again, a house with Anna inside it, turned her stomach.

"I'm going to go for a walk, okay?" she announced, already turning down the long oval driveway toward the desolate rural street.

"Do you want me to come?" he asked, a little too eagerly. Maybe he also didn't want to go back inside just yet. But Louise needed time alone.

"No, thank you. I just need a moment to recharge."

Clay walked over and gave her a gentle kiss on the forehead.

"Be careful. The street looks empty, but when cars come, they come fast."

"I will," Louise said, waving as she headed toward somewhere unknown.

❖

Getting some space was helpful. From the Nelsons, from Clay, but especially from Anna. Louise had spent the better part of forty-five minutes reviewing everything that had happened since she first stepped foot in Trenton. In a way, she could almost rationalize that first episode in the alley. A momentary lapse in judgment, an indiscretion. She knew what she'd done was wrong and that she'd violated her commitment both to Clay and to herself; this was not in dispute. She also knew that, had that been all it was, she could have kept it to herself. She would have waited until after the trip to break it off with Clay. She would have told him about the kiss with a stranger, how that was the moment she knew that what she felt for him was not romantic. While she still wanted Clay in her life, she knew deep down it could only be as friends, good friends. Lying didn't come easy to Louise, but she could have done it at least for that long.

This was, of course, no longer a possibility. And not just because she'd since added another notch to her belt of indiscretions. The alley kiss was so much more than a simple lapse in judgment. Images flashed through Louise's mind—Anna up against the maze wall, her breath coming fast, the sounds she made when Louise bit her neck hard. Louise shut her eyes and stopped walking. She couldn't stop the feeling of arousal coursing through her, so powerful it was almost scary. She opened her eyes and tried to think about why this person was so beguiling to her.

"Fuck!" she yelled to nobody.

It felt good.

"Fuck fuck fuck fuck!"

At first, she thought Anna reminded her of Gwen, and that maybe this was all just an echo of her grief. But even with Gwen, the gravitational pull had never seemed so debilitating. Gwen grew up with her, they learned of their attraction together. Yes, they had been overwhelmed with feelings, but it never felt like something she needed to resist. She had never felt lust like this. Gwen made her feel complete. Anna was pulling her apart.

Louise was dwelling on this when her phone went off. It was her mother, apparently trying out a video call. Part of her wanted to decline the call, but she realized in desperation that she really needed to talk to someone she loved, and who loved her unconditionally, because she was struggling to love herself at the moment.

Louise swiped to answer and her mom's plump, jovial face appeared on the screen. Well, more like plump, jovial under-face, as her mom struggled to figure out how best to angle the phone. The view switched suddenly to display a pair of practical winter boots that Louise knew well, stomping up a stone path. Her mother swore good-naturedly under her breath and Louise almost smiled at all the jumbling before remembering the reason she'd answered the call.

"One sec, honey, I'm trying to get this stupid phone to work right, but I think my gloves are messing it all up. Let me get inside here and I can get them off."

A couple of minutes later, her mother was inside the house, gloves off, and finally able to get the camera to show a serviceable view of most of her face. Situated, she finally took a look at Louise.

"Honey, what's wrong?"

The question was so disarming. Louise hadn't even spoken and her mom already knew something was off.

"It's nothing, Mom. Can we talk about it in a second? How are you?" Louise didn't want to worry her mom by going straight into a crisis.

"Everything is fine here. I was just checking in on you to see how everything's going, meeting the parents and all. But you're upset, what happened?"

Her mother was studying Louise's face intently and Louise knew there was no chance she'd be able to skirt around the disaster that had become her life.

"Mom," Louise said pleadingly, then she felt the tears begin to fall. Seeing her mom's loving face was too much. All the strict controls she had built to manage her emotions promptly fell apart.

"I've done something, just so bad, I don't know what to do." Louise brought a hand to her face to wipe the streaming tears. She felt so small, like a child. Louise couldn't find a way out of these feelings, and all she could think was that she was a bad person. It was the only explanation for her behavior.

"Honey, there is nothing you could have done that I would judge. I love you no matter what. So, tell me, what happened."

Louise tried to speak, but found that she could not, instead crying harder now. She needed to let it out, the shame, the guilt, but also the pain she carried with her. The pain that only her mother really understood.

She took a deep breath and got back some semblance of control.

"Mom, I really messed up."

Louise wanted to get the worst out first. Her mother waited patiently, continuing to look at her with love.

"I cheated on Clay."

The words came out harsh and blunt. She looked into her mom's pixelated eyes, looking for the judgment she felt she deserved. She didn't find it.

"I feel so bad I...I don't know where to begin."

"Just start from wherever you feel most comfortable, love."

Louise sniffled. "I was just feeling so trapped. I didn't want to go on this meet the parents trip. Clay is great, I mean you know I care about him, but things are just going so fast. I don't know."

Louise took a moment to sort her thoughts.

"I flew in early and ended up at this dive bar in town waiting for Clay to pick me up, and I met this woman."

Louise paused, seeing the knowing look on her mom's face. Louise wanted to ask what her mom was thinking, but then decided to get her story out as quickly as possible.

"Mom, I don't know what it was about her, but we just... clicked. And one thing led to another and...I kissed her. I kissed her and I didn't even think about the consequences. I didn't think about Clay or where I was or anything, I just kissed her." Her mother's look was kind, a smile teasing at the corner of her mouth. Louise couldn't hold back her question any longer.

"What are you thinking?"

"I'm just absorbing everything. Honey, go on..." Louise could see her mother attempting to school her face.

She calmed herself a bit more, deciding how to say the next part. The words finally came, the one thing she didn't want to talk about.

"She reminded me of her." Louise's words were soft. She knew her mom knew who "her" referred to. She understood Louise's reluctance to say Gwen's name. "Not in every way, not even in most ways. God I don't even know, maybe it's just her. She's the first person to see me, to really see me in so long."

"Oh, Lou."

Her mom's tone was sympathetic. She could hear the grief in her mother's voice. She had lost a daughter in Gwen as well.

"I've worried about something like this happening."

"What do you mean?" Louise asked, not sure she wanted to know the answer.

"I just know that you carry so much of what happened with Gwen around with you. You deny so much of yourself. For a long time now, I've watched you perform this character, this controlled person. It's almost like when Gwen died, you let the parts of you that loved her die with her. Honey, you are too young to be without those feelings and I'm sorry to say this, but when you ignore those parts of yourself, they find a way to come out."

Her mother gave her a knowing look. Hearing her mom talk so freely about Gwen felt like a knife in her chest. Her mom never brought her up casually like this. She usually let Louise lead that conversation, knowing how much it still hurt.

"I don't know what to say to that. I live the way I live because I have ambitions. Because I've already spent too much time hurting. I don't want my life to be one big roller coaster. I don't want any more pain."

Louise's rant was loud and sort of incongruous to her mom's comments. Her mom nodded in acceptance.

"I know, honey."

Her mother sighed, seeming to let go of the point she had been trying to make.

"Is this the whole story? A kiss?"

She seemed to be almost minimizing the indiscretion. "Listen, I'm not saying what you did was right, but in my day I'm not even sure a kiss would be categorized as 'cheating.' Is this all that has you so upset?"

Louise was silent for a moment.

"There's more," she said faintly. "The woman I kissed, Anna, I found out later she's Clay's sister."

The widening of her mother's eyes was unmissable.

"Oh sweetie, that's... Well, shit!" The expletive wasn't uncommon for her mother, but it was definitely not comforting to Louise in this moment.

"And there's more," Louise said.

Her mother leaned back in her chair.

"You know what, honey, I might need to go pour myself a little something real quick here for this next part."

Her mother's face dropped out of view and was replaced with the blank white of the ceiling.

Louise waited patiently, gathering her thoughts as her mom retrieved a glass of wine and settled back into her chair in the living room. She picked her phone back up and nodded.

"Okay, Lou, continue."

"So once we both realized our connection to Clay, which might I add, all took place in front of the entire Nelson family, we agreed to just pretend it didn't happen." Her mother raised an eyebrow and took a delicate sip of her wine. Louise could almost hear the "sure" in her mother's expression.

"So, as you can imagine, this went about as well as could be expected. Not to mention we're sharing a room!"

"Oh, dear…"

"So, we did okay for a while. But, Mom, I just…I…"

Louise tried to compose herself to say the next part.

"I've never been so drawn to someone before, so attracted. It feels almost like I don't have control over myself. I like her so much. I've never felt anything like this before."

Louise looked at her mom's patient face and said the next part oozing with guilt.

"Not even with Gwen…"

The words stuck in her throat. Most people wouldn't be this honest with their mothers, but Louise's relationship with hers was different. Her mother was a single mom raising a child who had lost someone so close to her at a young age. She had listened to Louise as she cried herself to sleep, she had watched her struggle to get out of bed in the morning. There weren't secrets between them. Not when bigger things had happened.

"Is there more?" her mother asked carefully.

"Yes," she replied. "More…happened between us."

She considered a moment.

"Enough happened for me to know I need to tell Clay. I need to get out of here, I need to get as far away from Anna as I possibly can." Louise spoke quickly, already formulating a plan to get a flight out of Virginia as soon as humanly possible.

"Louise, take a deep breath."

Louise stopped her racing thoughts and listened to her mom. She let in her mom's soothing presence and let out all the anxiety that was building within her. She felt her heart rate slowly begin dropping back to normal.

"Let's talk this out a little more before you make any decisions."

"Okay."

"So, you met this woman, Anna, who you feel a connection to. And Clay, how do you feel about him?"

Louise considered how best to put her feelings for Clay.

"I care deeply for Clay, but I think I've realized I'm not attracted to him. Not like that."

"Okay, so that's something," her mother said. "Knowing that, what do you think you want to do about him?"

"I'm going to tell him, today. All of it. I'll tell him that it's not working between us, I'll apologize for leading him on by coming to Trenton, and I am going to tell him I kissed someone else."

"Are you going to tell him who?"

"I don't know, should I? They have a strained relationship, and they were finally starting to rebuild. They are both so good together and I just feel like their connection is so fragile. And I just…it was me, Mom. I instigated both times."

Her mom looked at her skeptically.

"And what, was Anna handcuffed or something? Was she not a willing participant at all?"

"Well, I mean, yes…" Louise shook her head at the thought. "But I just don't know how fair it is to drag her into this."

"Okay, honey, this is all very much up to you. But as for this Anna woman, what are you going to do about her?"

"What do you mean? I'm going to leave this stupid town and that'll be that."

"Just like that?"

"Well, what do you expect me to do? She's Clay's sister, not to mention I know nothing about her. She may be seeing someone as well; I really don't know anything about her life."

Louise thought back to Anna's mention of somebody named Rachel. Her mother looked at Louise as if she had just caught her with her hand in the cookie jar.

"I meant more, what are you going to do about these feelings that have come up? About the connection with Gwen?"

Louise thought about this. She was so focused on getting space from Anna that she hadn't even considered what Anna might be going through. How the push and pull may have been affecting her. Did she owe Anna some sort of explanation? Did she owe her a conversation at least?

"I might need to talk to her…or apologize…or something."

Louise's mom waited patiently for a moment. "Louise, can I tell you what I see?"

Louise was already regretting her nod of yes.

"You are a beautiful, intelligent, kind, wonderful woman. Yes, you may have made some mistakes here, but the biggest one is not being honest with yourself. Nobody is perfect, nobody does the most logical or the most ethical thing every time. And usually when we try so hard to be perfect, that's when something lands in your path to remind you that you can't control or predict everything that comes into your life. This woman is someone you want, and you haven't wanted anything outside of your career in such a long time. I've learned the hard way that opportunities like this, opportunities to have a strong connection with somebody, they can be few and far between. It would be a shame to miss your chance."

Her mom took a large sip of her wine before continuing.

"Now I'm of course not saying you should go do whatever and hurt everyone in your wake. I'm just saying you don't always have to run from your feelings. Be honest. And give yourself a break."

The words hit Louise hard. She couldn't easily forgive herself, but the muscles in her neck loosened. Maybe she could find her way out of this, maybe she could be honest. That was a start.

"Okay, Mom, I'll try."

She heard strength in her voice that had been missing at the start of the call.

"Thank you for talking with me, for the advice. I'm going to talk to Clay, then maybe I'll talk to Anna." The plan felt solid, authentic.

"Okay, honey, just know I love you and I will always love you. There's nothing you could do that would ever change that.

I am so proud of you!" Her mother's pink cheeks rose in a warm smile for her.

Louise felt the love her mom always shared with her, and she smiled back, hoping her mom felt just as well loved.

"Bye, Mom, love you."

"Love you too, baby."

The call ended and Louise allowed herself to breathe easier for the first time in a long time. She had a plan. She was going to tell Clay the truth and then she was going to let him decide what to do about the rest of the trip. If the conversation stayed civil, she would talk to Anna as well and apologize for her behavior, and maybe, if Anna seemed open, she could be honest about what was happening between them. Even if she was leaving, she felt she owed Anna—and maybe herself—some sort of closure.

Louise set out back to the house already feeling some of the relief she'd so desperately craved just a short time ago.

CHAPTER SEVEN

Louise approached the Nelson house a new woman. She was no longer falling victim to circumstances, she was retaking control of her life, starting now. Louise opened the door and entered the foyer quietly. She needed to find Clay without being spotted by any other Nelson, especially Anna. As she softly searched the rooms she was familiar with, she heard a raised voice coming from the other side of the house. So far, she had not explored that area as Clay had warned her in no uncertain terms that it was where Mr. Nelson spent most of his time. She had to admit, he was a man of few words, but she had sensed enough to know she wouldn't want to be in his cross hairs. She was about to turn away, toward the stairway, when she made out Clay's voice mixed in with what had to be Mr. Nelson's.

Against her better judgment, Louise followed the voices down a hallway and then crept over to the slightly ajar door leading to what had to be Mr. Nelson's office. The overdone masculine decor—wooden walls and mallard duck figurines—was visible through the crack of the door, as was Clay, whose stance was almost visibly set in fight-or-flight mode. The room reeked of cigar smoke.

"I don't give a damn what you feel, no son of mine is using his education and achievements to be a goddamn teacher."

"Professor, Dad—"

"I don't care what you call it!"

Louise could hear a shuffling and what sounded like Mr. Nelson putting out a cigar. And the clinking of a tumbler.

"Son, I don't know how many times we have to go through this. You continue to waste your life navel-gazing in academia, indoctrinating yourself with liberal bullshit. You need to start proving yourself as a man. Do you understand me?"

"Yes, sir." Louise heard the emptiness in Clay's voice.

"Now, let's talk about this girl you've brought home. You better have a plan there."

Louise knew she shouldn't be listening, but from the way Mr. Nelson was talking to Clay, she was almost concerned for him.

"Louise is great," Clay stated trepidatiously.

Mr. Nelson gave a mumbled response that didn't seem to say much for his opinion of her.

"I don't care what kind of girl she is, I just want to know if my son knows what is expected of him. Do you understand what I'm saying, Clay?"

Louise sure didn't understand.

"Yes, sir."

"Women don't wait around forever. You need to secure this relationship."

"We haven't been together very long…I don't want to put too much pressure on her."

"Son, this is exactly what I am talking about. It is weak to wait for life to happen to you. If you want her, if you want a marriage and a family, you have to take it. Are those things that you want, Clay? Because if not tell me now, I don't need to waste my time on a pansy only to be caught up in some scandal again."

Louise saw Clay's cheeks redden.

"Yes, sir, I want those things."

"Good." Louise heard another clanking and slurping of the glass. She didn't know Mr. Nelson well enough to know if he was drunk, but she continued to be shocked by the level of hatred she was feeling toward these people.

"Did you take care of the errand your mother asked you to do?"

"Yes, sir," Clay said glumly.

"Well, then, aren't you grateful? Your mother didn't have to do that for you, did she?"

"I'm very grateful, sir."

"All right, son, that'll be all. The next time we speak like this, I want there to be no more talk of staying in England or any more indecisiveness. Understood?"

"Understood, sir," Clay said. Louise quietly scrambled out of the way, slipping behind the hall wall. Clay came around the corner and nearly walked right into her without realizing it. He jumped at the sight of her.

"Shit, sorry, Lou."

Louise could see that his face was pale and his eyes were watery.

"Clay, come with me."

She took his hand and led him through the house and outside to the backyard where she knew they couldn't be overheard. They walked for a while hand in hand until they had enough distance from the house and enough open space for Clay to let out what he was so obviously holding in. Clay brought his hands to his face as he began to cry. Louise pulled him into her arms and rubbed his back. She had never seen him like this. He was always so level-headed and optimistic. As she rubbed his back, he tried to stop his tears and straighten himself up. He pulled away from Louise and began pacing back and forth a couple of yards away.

"Clay, I'm here, you can talk about whatever it is."

Clay shook his head and took a deep breath. "It's nothing, just stress." His voice sounded empty, monotonous. Louise considered keeping what she heard to herself, but then remembered her overall goal, honesty.

"I heard your conversation with your father," she said, trying to strike a tone that conveyed both support for Clay but also condemnation for his father's words and aggressive masculinity.

Clay looked at her sharply, eyes wide with—what—fear? Louise felt that maybe her attempted tone hadn't gone over that well after all. But almost immediately, the look faded and Clay let out his breath in what sounded like relief.

"What was that about, Clay? Why does he talk to you like that?"

Clay seemed confused by her question. "Talk to me like what?"

Louise realized she needed to tread carefully around how she characterized Clay's family. What she wanted to do was say what she really thought—*your parents are full psychopaths and honestly shouldn't have been allowed to be parents*—but she realized that might be too much.

"He was really coming down on you in there," she said instead.

"He was just trying to toughen me up is all."

"Clay, do you really need 'toughening up'? I mean, what does that even mean?"

Clay's eyes searched Louise's face. She tried to show how safe he was with her. There was nothing about him that she could judge him for.

"I'm just not...I struggle with..." He couldn't get his words out. Finally, he landed on something understandable.

"My dad loves me. He just wants me to be a better man. I'm trying, but I think I just fall short sometimes."

The tears began to fall again. Louise could see how hard he was trying to hold them back.

"Fuck! Look, I can't even talk without crying like a bitch!"

Clay brought his hands to his head hard and started grabbing his hair in pent-up anger.

Louise was shocked at Clay's obvious distress. She'd never seen him like this.

"Hey, Clay," she tried to say soothingly, channeling her mother's calming aura. "Take a deep breath, it's okay."

Clay finally seemed to calm a bit, muscles visibly relaxing, but his tears kept falling.

"I'm sorry you have to see this. I'm sure it's not attractive."
Louise softly took his hands in hers.

"You could not be further from the truth. It's not unattractive
to cry and I don't want you to apologize for sharing what you're
going through with me. I just wish you wouldn't be so hard on
yourself."

Clay moved his hands on top of hers and rubbed them softly.
Then he leaned in to kiss her. Louise let him. The kiss started
soft, but suddenly became more demanding. Clay was never
demanding. He pulled her closer and tried to push his tongue into
her mouth. She stopped him by pushing him away gently. There
was no resistance, but he looked at her bewildered.

"Clay, I…I need to talk to you."

Clay looked upset again, deflated.

"Is this the part where you tell me this whole thing scared you
away?" His usually happy face was so sad and hurt.

"No, it's not…listen, I've been needing to talk to you for a
while now."

Desperately, Clay cut in.

"Let me stop you there. I know this trip hasn't been easy. I
know the whole thing has been full of miscommunications and
feeling distant and I totally understand you wanting to step back…
but please…I am begging you." Clay literally kneeled in front of
her and held her hands, pleading.

"Please, don't break up with me. I can't face them, I can't
get through this, I…." The tears were gone but his expression was
panicked.

"I'll do anything. If you want, I can promise you that the
moment we leave this house, we can discuss every single thing
that is not working between us and if it really isn't something I can
fix, we can fix, we can break up. But please, Louise. As my friend,
please just stay with me through the next couple of days."

Louise was thrown for a loop. She could have guessed a lot of
responses, but she couldn't have anticipated this. His desperation

was palpable, surprisingly focused more it seemed on his family than on the possible end to their relationship. Even more striking was his plea to be a friend to him, a request that resonated with her deeply. Louise truly cared about Clay, and watching his pain like this was destroying her. The whole reason she wanted to tell him was to be honest with him, to show him respect, to give him the opportunity to be mad at her, which she felt she fully deserved. But looking down at his anxious eyes, she saw that that wasn't what he wanted. He didn't want her to be honest. He wanted her to play the part. He wanted her to help him escape the pressure his parents were putting on him. When Louise thought about it, she realized she could do this for him, maybe even that she owed him this in some way. Even if it meant she had to hold her secrets a little longer, she could do this for her friend. Her friend who was hurting.

Louise pushed his hair aside and pulled on his hands, gesturing for him to get up. He awkwardly climbed to his feet and she smiled at him.

"Okay, Clay, I'll put this conversation on hold. But when we leave…"

"I know. I'll accept whatever you decide." Louise searched for sadness in his voice but heard only relief. She tried to refrain from wishing terrible things on his parents.

Clay went in to hug her, and she accepted, feeling relieved that the embrace felt almost platonic. That strange energy was gone from him, almost as if it was never really there.

"You know, Clay, that stuff your dad was talking about. About you not being a man, and being a teacher and all that, it isn't true. You are amazing, just as you are."

Clay looked at her and seemed about to say something, but then turned away and looked up toward the house.

"I appreciate you saying that, but I think I just need some time. Really, I'd love to try and leave some of this heavy stuff behind and get out of here. What do you think about going over to the Bar now? I know Josh'll be there already and I could really use a break from the Nelson house of horrors." He flashed her a watery grin, but Louise could still see the pain behind it.

Louise looked back to the house, finding the window to the room she shared with Anna. She imagined Anna flung across one of the beds in the room and debated for a moment whether or not her plan could still be carried out partially. In a way, she'd told Clay; at least, she'd told him she wasn't happy. Although she'd agreed to play the part for the rest of her stay, at least some of the pressure had been released through both of their partial honesty. What about Anna? Should she be honest with her? Louise wasn't sure. It seemed like her whole plan had been turned around.

"Okay, sure, let's head to the bar. A change of scenery would be nice."

Clay smiled in appreciation.

"Great! Are you sure you don't need to grab anything?"

Louise looked up at the house again. The bedroom window remained empty.

"No, let's just go."

❖

Pissed, that's how Anna was feeling. She paced her room feeling like a caged animal. First, Louise dumped all her fears and vulnerabilities onto a total stranger. Then she kissed that stranger, putting into motion the most awkward and frustrating week of Anna's life. Then, she somehow swept it all under the rug, put everything in its right place, and all at Anna's expense. And then finally, when Anna had at last landed on some sense of equilibrium, Louise pounced on her in the corn maze. Anna felt a shiver run through her as she remembered Louise's hands on her fly, her mouth on her neck. If Anna hadn't had a moment of clarity brought on by what she could only imagine was an act of God, she knew she would have let Louise do anything she wanted to her. It was a scary thought, how difficult it was to stop herself when Louise's hands were on her. But then, there she was, smack in the middle of a nightmare. Louise and her boyfriend, Anna's brother, and Josh, who somehow missed the memo that she was the town dyke. The whole thing was hypocritical, bizarre, and honestly made Anna feel like shit. She didn't want to hurt her brother. She had taken painstaking efforts to prevent this from happening, to protect her tentative relationship with Clay. She couldn't believe how easy it was for her to give in to her desires. It was honestly pathetic. She also didn't like that the whole situation had her so turned around that she'd hesitated to come out to Josh. Anna stopped pacing and looked at her phone. Seven missed calls from Rachel and six unread texts.

Rachel 5:12 p.m.: *Yo call me back ASAP*

Rachel 5:17 p.m.: *Okay it's been 5 mins, what are you doing?*

Rachel 5:18 p.m.: *Or should I say who...*

Rachel 5:20 p.m.: *Nm I know who ;)*

Rachel 5:21 p.m.: *Okay now I know you won't text me back. Just please! I'm for cereal here! You're gonna want to hear this from me!*

Rachel 5:33 p.m.: *Okay whatever you can run but you can't hide Annabelle Nelson!*

Part of Anna wanted to call Rachel back to know what was so important, but it came at a risk. If she called Rachel, she would be forced to reexamine her own role in her thing with Louise. She wasn't ready to do that. She liked being mad. If Anna continued to be mad and continued to put all the blame on Louise for what happened, she wouldn't have to deal with the want that still pulsed through her body and the unrelenting shame that went with it. She was still thrumming with energy and her heart had never fully calmed down. When she flashed back even for a moment to the feeling of teeth on her neck, she was reminded of how wet she was still. Not to mention the anticipation. Even now, with every moment that passed she was more at risk of Louise coming into the bedroom. In her mind she knew that if or when she did, she would let Louise know exactly what she thought of her. How she thought Louise was selfish and a mind fuck. How she didn't want anything to do with her. But deep down, somewhere her anger wouldn't allow her to feel, she wasn't sure at all that was how the confrontation would go. Maybe Louise wouldn't make it past the door. Maybe Anna would fuck her right there.

"Damn it!" Anna exclaimed, pulling at her hair. "I can't be doing this."

Anna sat on the bed and took some deep breaths.

You do not have to act on this. She does not get to have all the control.

Anna let herself lie back. The more she ruminated, the more resolute she became. Why was she feeling so much guilt? She didn't do anything wrong. Anna wasn't the one in a relationship. She wasn't the one breaking a promise. Yes, she had reacted to Louise—honestly, who wouldn't—but Louise was the one who kept pushing it.

Still, the fact that it was Clay on the other end felt awful. And the closer she became to Clay, the more guilty she felt.

I'm such an asshole.

Once she let herself feel the guilt that was building, her anger began to dissipate. Because the truth was, the anger Anna felt wasn't real. It was a tool, one she had used many times to protect herself. Louise wasn't some magical seductress. The whole situation with Louise had made Anna feel small and overlooked, the way she seemed to always feel in her family. Louise had been kind to her. She had listened and supported her. Even with her parents, Louise was the only one who asked her questions or seemed to notice her at all. But being a secret was a trigger for Anna after so many years hiding who she was. Anna wasn't always the most rational person, but she usually came around to the truth in the end and unfortunately, she had come around to it.

God, just the thought of another night sleeping in the same room was enough to make Anna want to get a hotel. Maybe she should text Gina. Kill two birds with one stone. She could exorcise some of this pent-up sexual energy, then enjoy a safe place to sleep that wouldn't end up with Louise between her legs. Anna covered her eyes and groaned. Every time she thought about Louise, the feeling came back, the pulsing between her legs.

She noticed that she'd ended up on Louise's bed, not her own. She could smell the scent of Louise's hair on her pillow, remembered how it had smelled next to her face. Just the thought of her here made Anna more wet.

Anna ran her hand down her stomach and into the front of her pants. She worked the button loose. Not long ago, Louise's hands had been there, about to discover just how turned on Anna was. The thought made her moan. It was insane, she wasn't even touching herself yet, but she could already feel the beginnings of her orgasm. It had been building and now it would take so little. She thought for a moment of what would happen if Louise came back through that door, if she found Anna like this. What if she watched? Anna pushed her fingers through the folds of her cunt and begin to rub her clit. She couldn't remember ever being this wet.

It was unusual for her to be this turned on without someone touching her for a while. But then again, hadn't she just had three days of foreplay? She tried not to think anymore, she just needed release. Her thoughts returned to Louise, watching from the door. Saying "Harder." That got Anna close. She began to lift her back from the bed and push two fingers in deeper as she pressed her palm against her clit. She imagined it was Louise against her, inside her, saying in her ear, "I can't help wanting you." Just like she did in the maze. Anna fell over the edge of her orgasm, quaking and totally incapable of hiding the sound. If anyone had walked by her door right then, they would have heard Anna's intense release. She could feel herself tightening around her own fingers, fingers she'd imagined were Louise's and she let herself fall apart on her bed, covered in the smell of her perfume. Anna opened her eyes, blood returning to her head, and realized what she had just done. She got off the bed quickly and tried to straighten the sheets. God, what would she have done if Louise had walked in? At her level of turned on, she clearly couldn't make rational decisions.

At least this would make it easier for her to deal with Louise. Maybe all she needed was to ease some of the pressure that was on her. Some of the need that was building. The more she thought about it, the more she convinced herself that she was now truly free from her desire. She just needed to get it out of her system. She saw another text on her phone form an unknown number.

Unknown Caller 7:03 p.m.: *Hey it's Josh, I got your number from Clay. You have to come tonight!*

Unknown Caller 7:03 p.m.: *No pressure but also George is on the bar and he said to get your ass here.*

Unknown Caller 7:05 p.m.: *Same with Gina Perez. I didn't know y'all were friends?*

Unknown Caller 7:06 p.m.: *Please?*

Anna looked at the texts with frustration. Yes, she needed to let Josh know he was barking up the wrong tree, but she was also feeling an unfamiliar feeling in Trenton—FOMO. And yes, she was a little curious about the Gina situation, but she was also really looking forward to hanging with George again. As the two major (out) members of the Trenton lavender club, she was kind of hoping to cultivate that connection a bit more. And most importantly, who the fuck was Louise to scare her off? This was her town, this was her family, unfortunately, and these were her friends—well, acquaintances anyway. But regardless, she wasn't going to let someone else's issues, someone else's fucked up relationship, mess with her life. She updated her contact.

Anna 7:35 p.m.: *Fine! Give me 10 :)*

Josh 7:37 p.m.: *<3*

Anna rolled her eyes. Poor Josh. She began to change her clothes. Once she was adequately assembled in the sexiest look she had—for no particular reason—she looked at herself in the mirror and allowed herself one more pep talk.

"I will not talk to Louise. I will not hang with Louise. I will not do anything with Louise," she promised herself. Feeling as prepared as she'd ever be, she grabbed her stuff and headed for the front door. Even after "taking care of the problem" as she thought of it, Anna could still feel how turned on she still was.

High school nostalgia should help with that.

❖

The Bar was packed. In a totally cliché moment, "Wagon Wheel" was playing from the faux jukebox in the corner, and the smell of fried food and hops gave Anna a strange feeling of affection for Trenton. The faces she saw when she came in the door were familiar, but older—a bit of the youthful fullness had left their cheeks. It was odd seeing how small-town living could age people. Looking around, Anna decided that it wasn't so much their faces as it was their clothing choices, or maybe just their general vibes. Everyone seemed to be coupled up or regretfully moving toward the door, heading home early to let off the sitter.

Anna pushed her way through the crowd until she found a spot with a bit more elbow room tucked in a corner of the bar. From there, she had a good vantage point on who was coming in and—more importantly—who to avoid. It was also close enough to the bar that she might be able to catch George for a chat if he got a moment. Apparently, he had clocked her as soon as she came in and was on the same page. Anna watched him casually ignore several disgruntled Trentonites waiting for a drink so he could say hi to her.

"Well, look what the cat dragged in!"

"Yeah, yeah, I got your message through the grapevine."

"Damn right! Who else is going to save me from the Heathers?" he quipped, gesturing toward a section of the bar where Jessica, Alison, and Gina stood looking bored.

"I figured it was always this busy, since you run the only decent bar in town."

"You'd think, but no. That crowd usually gets their vodka waters at Westbrook Country Club a town over. I guess Josh was persuasive today."

"Yeah, why was he so persistent? I was kind of thrown off by him finding my number and texting me," Anna asked as he passed her the beer she liked from the other night. "Thanks."

"Yeah, well that has a very simple answer," he said with a knowing look. "But as far as getting the 'cool kids' to show up, I'm not really sure. He stocks his beer here, so I guess he must like the bar?" George hesitated a moment. "He comes around a lot with Clay." George began distractedly clearing out a beer tap. He seemed not to notice the steady buildup of thirsty patrons crowding the bar and eyeing him with increased irritation.

"Umm...George, if you don't start slinging drinks soon, I think there might be a mutiny."

George rolled his eyes dramatically but left her there to sip her beverage and acclimate to her surroundings. She hadn't yet seen Louise or Clay, but she was sure they were somewhere in the crowd. She needed to get eyes on them, to continue her avoidance. It probably wouldn't be easy to keep that up all night, but she had to try. She was still angry, or at least she wasn't done pretending to be. Anything to dampen her desire to be closer to Louise.

Anna looked back toward where Jessica, Alison, and Gina were standing. So far, she was pretty certain that Gina had not spotted her yet. She couldn't decide what she wanted there. It was flattering to have Gina's attention, but her own receptiveness to that attention felt almost like a reversion to an earlier version of herself. One who knew herself less and accepted whatever someone like Gina deigned to give to her. But then again, maybe Anna hadn't changed as much as she thought—after all, stolen moments with the popular girl wasn't too far from her current situation. Anna could feel the shame of her high school self course through her body. As a queer person, that pain was not easily forgotten. Anna scanned the room again and let out a resigned sigh.

"Oh no, are you already having a bad time?" George reappeared at her side, apparently having adequately placated the thirsty crowd, at least for now. "I thought I could at least get you to the forty-five minute mark before you were sulking out of here."

Anna pushed her hair back from her face and tried to rearrange her features to look more open. She didn't want George to think she was always surly. Anna had seen him two times in three days and both times were atypical, to say the least.

"No, I'm fine, it's just been a long couple of days is all."

"I can only imagine, life with the Nelsons!" The second bartender, Tony, came back on from his break, giving George a chance to pay more attention to Anna.

"I meant to ask, did you ever get that girl's number you were chatting up the other day? I was pulling for you there."

Anna looked at him with mock disdain. "I don't know if you've forgotten, but that girl very explicitly stated she had a boyfriend."

George gestured for her to go on. "And?"

"And what?"

"Well, I just think from the small details I got from your conversation that it didn't seem all that serious."

Anna rolled her eyes. The last thing she needed was more thoughts of Louise.

"I mean, the guy I'm kind of seeing is in a relationship."

Anna was shocked to hear him say that so casually.

"And that doesn't bother you?"

"I mean, it does bother me, but it's just not that easy being queer in Trenton. Honestly, I might never meet anyone great if I took a hard line on things like that," George replied sheepishly.

"Yeah, I don't know if I agree, George. I mean no judgment, but I'm not sure it's good for the soul to be hidden like that. Especially on top of everything that comes with being queer."

George looked down and then seemed like he was almost going to say something. Anna softened as she picked up on the fact that this was bothering George.

"Hey, George, is everything okay?" George met her eyes and Anna melted a little more—there was a definite sadness there.

"No, I mean you're right. The closeted thing has really been messing with my head." He stood up straighter, and it was as if whatever dark thought he'd just had left his body. "Enough on that tragedy, back to 'has a boyfriend' girl," he said with air quotes. "So, what you're trying to tell me is that I was totally off base? Me, George, someone who's survived this town only by being an expert at picking up on these kinds of signals? You're telling me that was a totally platonic, perfectly run-of-the-mill, four-hour conversation with a stranger?"

"Okay, first of all! It wasn't four hours," Anna protested, trying to figure out whether she was going to tell him everything, or just let him figure it out when he saw Louise that night with Clay.

A moment of perfect timing presented itself. The crowd parted just enough for Anna to see Louise seated in a booth across the room. She was laughing freely, Clay next to her with his arm comfortably over the seat behind her. The scene was casual but intimate. Josh was sitting across from them gesturing animatedly. Anna was again transfixed by Louise. She was wearing the same sweater and jeans Anna had had her hands all over just hours before. Anna tried to suppress her attraction and focused instead on the kick to her gut. She pulled her eyes away and back to George.

"Why don't you ask *her* if it was platonic? She's right over there."

George put down the glass he was cleaning and took in the scene. His smile fell away.

"How does she know Clay?"

Anna was a bit disoriented by how slowly George was putting the pieces together.

"She knows him because he is the boyfriend you just moments ago told me was irrelevant."

George looked away quickly and began wiping his hands on his apron. His action seemed a bit frantic in Anna's opinion.

"George, are you okay?" Anna asked him again.

She decided his flippancy about being the other man was much more of an act than she'd realized. Or maybe he'd finally picked up on how serious her situation was.

"Yeah, no, I'm fine, I'm just surprised is all."

"So now you see why the party line is that nothing happened between us. Actually, it would be better if you could just forget that I was even here that night."

"Got it," George said stoically. "I'm sorry, Anna. I could tell you liked her."

Anna considered denying it, but when she looked into George's eyes, she could tell that he was going through something in his love life as well. If anyone here would understand, it was him.

"Thanks, George, I did." Anna looked back across the room, and this time Louise wasn't throwing her head back in laughter, she was looking at Anna.

❖

"Shit, shit, shit," Anna said to herself as she averted her eyes from the person she was most trying to avoid. She dropped down onto an empty barstool. Louise had left the booth and was walking right toward Anna's corner of the bar.

"Uh-oh," George said, preparing himself for a quick exit.

"Wait, wait, don't leave me!" Anna gave George a pleading look.

"Sorry, girly, I'm gonna let you handle this one."

George moved to the other end of the bar and began doing his job with a gusto Anna had yet to see in him.

"Fuck," she whispered under her breath.

Anna could feel the air around her change. It was as if time stopped. She sat motionless on her stool, refusing to change her position or show any invitation for socializing. She sensed rather than saw Louise come up to the bar, stopping just inches away from her. To an onlooker it could have seemed like Louise was just there to grab a drink, but her proximity let Anna know that whatever was between them was not something Louise was trying to avoid anymore. Anna's body was stiff with tension.

"Hey." Louise's voice was like a caress.

Anna closed her eyes as she pushed her desire as far away as she could. She took a sip of her beer, refusing to turn toward the siren. The silence permeated, communicating more contempt than Anna could have expressed with words.

"Are you just not talking to me now?" Louise asked, an irritated inflection in her voice.

Anna continued to look anywhere but at Louise.

"Fine. I'll just wait here to get my drink."

Louise turned fully toward the bar but didn't change their proximity. She was close enough for Anna to smell her rose-scented shampoo. Anna tried not to acknowledge the way her body was reacting to Louise. Since the moment she'd seen her across the room, Anna had been clouded with thoughts and desires that were in complete contrast from her recent decision not to engage. She needed to focus right now on self-preservation. She needed to ignore the slenderness of Louise's olive-toned arm on the deep brown of the bar top. Or that hypnotic scent, soft, clean, feminine. She remembered how that scent permeated Louise's sheets as she came imagining Louise's fingers insider her. Having her so close now with that memory at the top of her mind was already wearing at Anna, tempting her to drop her convictions. George remained at the other end of the bar, but the other bartender, Tony, took Louise's order.

"Anna, I think we should talk," Louise said solemnly.

Anna couldn't stand it any longer. She could feel her frustration, confusion, and, yes, her lust, all mixing together into some kind of toxic mess bubbling inside her. If she couldn't act on her desire, the next best thing was to fight.

"Honestly, Louise, I'm really not interested in any more conversations with you."

Louise didn't falter.

"I understand you're upset with me, and I just feel like if we could just talk, I could explain—"

Anna interrupted before she had to sit through yet another of Louise's half-baked rationalizations.

"I think you should stop trying to explain things to me and instead, start explaining things to Clay."

Anna got up from her stool. She couldn't help that her body landed flush against Louise as she moved past her. The feeling was intoxicating, and every particle of her body was telling her not to leave the warmth of Louise's skin. Somehow, she forced through it.

"Excuse me," she said as she walked firmly away from Louise, toward the other side of the room.

Louise didn't follow. It was admittedly what Anna wanted, but she was disappointed nonetheless. Before she could beeline for George again, she found herself all but surrounded by the Country Club crew. Jessica, Alison, and Gina were looking at her like bored children who'd happened on a new toy.

"Hey, Annabelle, come settle something we were just arguing about," Jessica said, more as a command than a question. Anna decided a new conversation, however banal or annoying, could only help get her mind off Louise. She gave the group a perfunctory smile.

"Okay, what's the argument?"

Jessica looked at Gina with a slightly conspiratorial gleam in her eye.

"So, Gina here was just saying there aren't any attractive men in Trenton. Alison and I don't agree."

Anna looked at Gina who was giving Anna a sultry stare. Anna wasn't sure what Jessica and Alison knew about Gina's sexuality, but from the way the conversation was going, it seemed like not much. Alison chimed in.

"Since you're visiting from New York, maybe you could weigh in."

Anna didn't see how her state of residence had much bearing on the question at hand.

"On whether the men here are attractive?" she asked.

She was already irritated by how her experience here was somehow already flunking the Bechdel test.

"I honestly don't have an opinion."

"Oh, come on," Alison said with clear frustration. "What about Josh? He's always had a crush on you. What's the deal there?"

Anna knew these women were really just bored and looking to gossip about anything. She figured she might as well give them something to gossip about.

"I'm not sure Josh and I would make a good match," she said, hoping they would pick it up quickly. Alison looked at her puzzled.

"What, he's too country for your 'alt life' in New York?" she asked, actually gesturing air quotes at her. Anna was struggling to grasp how they didn't know already. But then again, maybe they did, and they were just baiting her.

"No, more like...he's a little too 'straight' for me." She gave the quotes right back.

"So, you're a lesbian? I told you, Gina."

Jessica gave Gina a not-very-subtle nudge. Gina shrugged and looked away.

How ridiculous. Gina was the one telling them Anna was straight.

"Yup, have been all my life."

"Well, that explains why you never went for Josh," Alison pointed out unnecessarily.

"Sure didn't help."

"So," Jessica said, clearly getting to what she really wanted to ask. "Did you ever hook up with any girls in our class?"

Anna tried hard not to look at Gina. She considered her options. She wasn't going to out Gina, but she also wasn't going to pretend.

Anna sipped her drink and shrugged mysteriously. This, of course, only made Jessica more curious.

"Oh my God, who! You have to spill," Jessica gushed.

Anna could see the wheels in Jessica's mind turn. Anna searched desperately for a change of subject. Thankfully, she noticed Josh walking by on his way back from the bathroom.

"Hey, Josh!" she yelled, getting his attention.

He turned to her with a 100-watt smile and headed their way. Jessica adjusted her hair and seemed to morph into a completely different woman.

"Hey, Joshy," she said in a voice about an octave higher than it was just a moment ago.

"Hey, Jess. Hi, Alison, Gina. What's up, y'all?"

Alison looked from Josh to Anna as if just noticing the opportunity to create some drama.

"Not too much," she replied with a smile. "We were just talking to Annabelle here about what she thought about the guys in Trenton."

He blushed very slightly at the comment. Anna wasn't looking forward to this conversation.

"Oh yeah? What did you say, Belle?" His casualness didn't hide his curiosity one bit.

"Well, I…." Anna felt a hand land on the small of her back and a memory of Louise's smile flashed involuntarily through Anna's mind. This time, it was Gina's hand. Anna didn't move away.

"Anna was just telling us that she isn't all that interested in men, and I have to say I can't help but agree."

Anna looked at Gina, totally shocked by the turn of events. Was she coming out?

Josh seemed lost. It was at that incredibly inopportune moment that Clay decided to join the group, with Louise in tow showing the exact expression of unhappiness that Anna was feeling. This was truly building into a crescendo of awkwardness.

"Hey, everyone," Clay interjected.

Always courteous, he introduced Louise in that same sort of forceful way he had used when talking to her parents. The group members said hello and Louise graciously engaged in some polite small talk, demonstrating how annoyingly pleasant she could be even when she clearly wished she was anywhere else. Everyone was interested in and kind to Louise, except Alison, who had clearly had her eye on Clay for a while.

The small talk petered off and Clay looked around the group.

"So, what were you all talking about?" he asked. Anna vowed to kick him later.

Gina didn't take her hand from Anna's back. "I was just telling Josh here that not everyone in this town is all that into the opposite sex."

Clay coughed weirdly and looked supremely regretful that he'd somehow brought the subject up. Josh continued to look confused. Jessica and Alison were looking at Gina slack-jawed. Anna was struggling to know how to react. All at once, she became aware of Louise's panicked eyes on her and put together how Louise might have interpreted the situation. It could have seemed like Anna outed Louise to the group. She acted quickly to assuage Louise's fear.

"Josh, I'm gay." Josh looked at her.

"Oh wow, seriously?"

"Yeah, I probably should've told you earlier." He took a moment to consider her words and then he gave a shrug.

"Well, that's a relief on my ego. I guess I can't blame you too much for not wanting to go out with me."

Anna smiled thinking about how rare it was for a straight guy to move on so quickly. Or was it rare? She considered that perhaps she didn't hang with too many straight guys. Josh then elbowed Clay.

"Could have warned me, bro," he said with mock irritation.

Clay shrugged but he still looked a little uncomfortable. Anna glanced at Louise again and saw the panicked look had left her face and she was back to playing Clay's perfect girlfriend.

Jessica was not going to let this Gina thing go.

"I'm sorry, what were you saying, Gina, about 'plural' people 'not being that into men'?" Anna considered options for helping Gina out but then caught herself. They weren't in high school anymore—Gina was an adult, she could make up her own mind about what she wanted to share and not share about her sex life.

Gina shrugged and took a sip of her cocktail.

"I was just saying that Anna isn't the only one in this town who has…broader tastes." The words left Gina's mouth with a flirty intonation as her eyes blatantly scaled up and down Anna's body. No one in the circle missed her meaning.

"Yeah, right!" Alison exclaimed dismissively. "Are you trying to suddenly act like some bisexual? Pshh."

She rolled her eyes toward Jessica and Alison, obviously awaiting backup indignation. Jessica looked at her with scrutiny.

"Gina, are you serious right now?"

Gina's hand continued to rub Anna's back suggestively. Anna tried to look anywhere else just so her face wouldn't give away her lack of surprise by this revelation.

"I'm not 'suddenly' bisexual," Gina said, holding her head up high. "It just never came up."

Jessica seemed to take in the words carefully, then she noticed Anna's avoidant stance and looked between the two of them.

"No!" she said as a moment of realization hit her. "You two?"

She pointed accusingly at Gina and Anna. Anna tried desperately to hide her blush. Gina seemed to have a similar reaction. Anna had never even spoken to Gina directly about what happened between them. Hearing it now in front of everyone felt like she was being caught by her parents or something. Anna caught Louise's eye. She did not look the least bit comfortable with Gina's announcement.

"Let's just say, Anna and I have a history." The statement hit the group like a ton of bricks.

"What!" Alison exclaimed in total disbelief. Everyone looked toward Anna for confirmation. Anna was still so shocked by the turn of events that she didn't know what to say. But then she noticed the fear in Gina's eyes. She knew what it felt like to have someone deny the things they did in the shadows.

"It's true," she said decisively. Her eyes again traveled to Louise who had been staring holes into the side of her head.

Jessica broke the awkward silence with a lighthearted laugh.

"Gina, girl, you are such a little skeeze. How could you keep a secret like that for so long?" The question was clearly rhetorical because she took her and wrapped her in a giant hug.

As much as Anna struggled to understand these women, she could still see that there was love there. Gina held on tight to Jessica and Anna felt the absence of Gina's hand on her back with some relief. It clearly wasn't as easy as it might have seemed to say all that, and even more so to an audience. With Gina gone from between her and Louise, Anna could feel the tension between them building. Louise was giving off a very weird energy.

"I think that's enough reminiscing for me," Anna said, backing up toward the direction of the bathroom. "I'm going to do a lap and say hi to some people."

Her comments were largely ignored by everyone as they were clearly having a moment, or at least witnessing one. Louise, however, held Anna's eyes. Anna headed toward the restrooms, feeling again that nothing in Trenton was quite what it seemed.

Chapter Eight

Anna saw that the group was still chatting. Apparently, the conversation continued just fine without her. Irritatingly, the only person who seemed to have even noticed her absence was Louise. Anna caught Louise watching from across the room as she tried to sneak unnoticed toward her original corner of the bar and away from the group. Guiltily, she looked away, but not before seeing that facade of happiness from earlier lift from Louise's face for a moment—Anna could see she was struggling. This bothered her. Still, she kept moving, reminding herself that whatever Louise was feeling was not her fault. By some miracle, Anna found her original stool by the bar was still empty. She settled back onto it with an almost affectionate familiarity and looked around for George. He was helping a group of women she thought she recognized from the class above as they tried to decide on their next shot.

"We just want something fun!" a woman explained with a slight slur.

The cluster of expectant faces around her nodded in agreement.

"Hmm." George looked thoughtful and then smiled.

"I can do a blow job, how about that?"

Anna snorted. The women looked at him with confusion. George held up his finger and started mixing the ridiculous concoction of amaretto, Irish cream, and whipped cream.

The shot was truly disgusting.

"But here's the deal…" George said. "You can't use your hands. You have to take it straight from the table with your mouth."

Finally catching on, the women started laughing and sealed their assent with an eager, "Wooo!"

As they lined up, ready to deep throat a shot glass, George slid over toward Anna.

"It's got like zero percent alcohol," he said with a sigh.

George clearly read his crowd well on that one and his salesmanship had not faltered. Still, Anna saw that his smile wasn't quite reaching his eyes.

"I see you made it into the 'in crowd,'" he continued.

"Yeah, that was an experience…"

"Awkward?"

"You have no idea." Anna glanced back toward the group. Gina seemed to have recovered well from her revelation since she was now laughing easily with Jessica and Josh. She noticed Anna looking and gave her a small smile, pushing her hair behind her ear. Anna turned back toward the bar to find George staring at her, and very accusatorially in Anna's opinion.

"What?" she asked defensively.

"So, you're not even going to admit there's something going on with you and Gina?"

"Oh my God, are you like a psychic or something? How do you even know about that?"

"Honey, please. One, she has been shooting you flirty looks like that all night. Two, when I told her I hung out with you the other night, she was over at the bar with Josh earlier asking me intense questions about 'how long you're going to be here' and 'if you're seeing anybody.' And if that wasn't enough—and just to be clear, it is—I'm pretty sure I saw her at a Tegan and Sara concert in 2009." George looked at Anna knowingly. "Now it's your turn to speak. "

Anna put her head down on the bar and let out a frustrated moan.

"This is not what I wanted to be dealing with right now." She looked back up at George with a pitiful face.

George didn't bother to hide his impatience as he raised a brow at her.

"We kind of had a thing in high school, way before either of us had exactly reached, shall we say, peak self-awareness. Honestly, I could never figure out at the time if she even thought our hookups were a big deal or just a way to pass the time."

Anna picked distractedly at a hangnail.

"And now?"

"And now…" Anna trailed off as she saw George's eyes widen and flick pointedly between her and something behind her, clearly trying to communicate something to her.

Before she could figure out what, she felt a hand on her shoulder.

"Hey, Anna."

Anna turned to find Gina had joined them.

"Oh! Ha, hi, Gina," she managed to squeak out.

Gina took a seat next to her.

"Was it me you were just talking about?" she asked, looking from Anna to George.

It seemed that she had overheard after all.

"Whelp, I think I am needed on the other end of the bar! Let me get you a refill, Gina, and then I'll get back to it." George moved miraculously quickly, leaving Anna alone to explain.

"Yeah, sorry, I was just…sorry."

Gina moved a hand onto Anna's leg and gave an indulgent smile.

"You don't need to apologize. I mean, you didn't say anything that I didn't just admit to."

Anna found herself startled again by Gina's sudden openness regarding their history.

"Yeah, well, if I recall, you weren't always so open, and I've spent quite a few years respecting that." She immediately regretted the sharp tone in her voice. Gina looked down at her fingers as they brushed over Anna's thigh.

"I guess I deserved that," she responded sadly. "Actually, I've wanted to talk to you for a while about what happened."

Anna watched Gina shift from confident and flirty to hesitant and nervous.

"Listen…" Anna said. "You don't need to explain anything to me. That was amazing back there, you opening up like that in front of…like everyone."

Anna was pleased to find she was genuinely proud of Gina.

"I can't imagine how hard that must have been."

Gina looked up from her hands and Anna could see that she was holding back a great deal of what she was feeling.

"Thank you." Her voice was soft. "It means a lot, coming from you. I always thought you were so brave." She gave Anna a small smile. "You being here has stirred up a lot of those old feelings and I just felt like fuck it, I'm twenty-eight years old, I don't know what I've been so scared of."

Anna considered Gina's words. "Well, if it's any comfort, I've found that usually fears about coming out aren't founded in nothing. Especially just thinking back to what it was like here when we were younger."

It looked as if Gina was about to respond, but she paused and took another sip of her drink instead.

"Anna, I'm sorry about the way I treated you."

Anna let the words sit in the air, words she had wished for longer than she would admit. Gina was very much her first everything, and the casual way she'd played with and then discarded Anna had hurt deeply back then. Sixteen-year-old Anna was telling her not to let Gina off that easily, but the adult Anna was stronger and knew more about the world. She saw now that what happened between them maybe wasn't as inconsequential for Gina as she'd let herself believe. It could be good to let go of some of that old hurt.

"Thank you for saying that."

The feeling was complex. Anna was thinking about herself, about what was happening with Louise, about what George had said, and she just decided that it was all too much. She was going to stop trying to figure everything out and just be present. Here she was, sharing a drink with a beautiful woman, who was not hiding her desire for Anna, and who she had known almost all her life. Anna let the heaviness of the moment go and chose to change the subject.

"So, tell me about yourself now! What have you been up to?"

Gina's laugh of relief washed over them both like a tonic. And with a coy smile, she began to fill Anna in on all the ins and outs of the last few years.

❖

What is wrong with me? Louise splashed water on her face, feeling more and more like she was going crazy.

This whole night had been a total disaster. Already, she was regretting the deal she'd made with Clay. She could feel her performance eroding little by little. She was not used to lying like this, and it was becoming increasingly clear to her that Clay was not having a similar experience. In fact, she found his ability to compartmentalize everything that had happened that afternoon— the fight with his dad, the near breakup with her—disorienting. She'd thought she understood Clay, truly knew him, but now she found herself wondering what he could be hiding from her.

His behavior had been downright odd. When they first arrived at the bar, Clay had left her in a booth with Josh while he went to get drinks for the three of them. But once he finally got back to the table, he'd somehow forgotten his own drink and his energy seemed off somehow. He kept looking around or losing the trail of their conversation. Even Josh said something about his behavior at one point. And then, just when Clay finally started calming down a bit and Louise started to relax, she spotted Anna. She was posted up at the bar, wearing her typical black sultry look and looking just as sullen as the first time Louise had seen her. Louise was hit again with a strong desire. What did it say about her that moodiness turned her on?

Right on schedule, Anna caught her eye and Louise was certain all the things she wanted to do to Anna were completely transparent. Anna turned away. Rebuffed again. Louise couldn't resist the deflection.

"I'll get the next round," she said, already moving toward the bar.

When she got there, it was just as she suspected. Anna wanted nothing to do with her. But if Anna wanted to be angry, two could play that game. Well, kind of. Louise wasn't necessarily angry at Anna, but she found herself infuriated by all the circumstances swirling around the situation and how it all seemed outside of her control. She was angry at the Nelsons and the way they treated Clay and Anna. She was angry that she was stuck in this godforsaken town for another few days. But most of all, she was angry at herself and the way she just couldn't seem to get a grip on her feelings. Who was she kidding? She was also angry at Anna, who so clearly blamed her for everything and who seemed very much in denial about the mutualness of their attraction. Louise wanted to apologize to Anna, she wanted to explain, but she wasn't going to beg.

Anna hadn't even given her the chance. Almost immediately, she'd shut down the conversation by standing up to leave with a resolve that was both surprising and devastating. The space was crowded, and Anna's body pressed against Louise's just for a moment as she pushed past her to leave. As resolved as Louise was to hate Anna, she was dismantled by the flash of desire that coursed through her at the intimate touch. The moment was brief, but she was once more totally powerless. But there was more to it than that. She'd finally been getting somewhere with her friendship with Anna. Louise had enjoyed every minute of her time with Anna at the festival. And the animosity now hurt even more knowing what was lost between them. She understood Anna was quick to anger, just considering her reactions over the last few days, but it felt like they'd really been making some progress.

With Anna gone, Louise took a moment to gather herself before returning to her booth with Clay. He again seemed preoccupied and kept glancing toward the bar and drumming his fingers with excess energy. Their conversation with Josh felt stilted and sparse, but Louise didn't have the bandwidth to care. She was spending nearly all of her effort on trying to quiet her racing thoughts and stopping herself from looking for Anna. She barely noticed when Josh left for the bathroom. But she did see when he waved them over to join him with a group of women near the middle of the bar—a group of women that included Anna. Louise was reluctant, but Clay didn't seem to hear her protests. He took her hand in his and she grudgingly allowed herself to be dragged over to the group.

As they approached, Louise realized that the beautiful and fit woman standing inches from Anna was the same one she'd seen at the festival. Her stomach dropped. She could see that the woman's hand was on the small of Anna's back, a gesture that looked familiar and sensual. Louise couldn't move. She stopped walking and let go of Clay's hand, letting him join the group while she tried not to scream.

This feeling was totally unfamiliar. Even when she was with Gwen, she had never felt this slithering in her stomach, this heat in her neck, this anxious rumination in her brain asking, *Who the fuck is this woman touching Anna?*

Realizing that her open-mouthed gawking wasn't quite how she wanted to present in front of these people, Louise smoothed her face into what she hoped was a smile and joined Clay. With some effort, she was able to maintain the mask as she met everyone— including "Gina," her five-foot-ten basic nightmare. Anna, for her part, did not acknowledge Louise at all. This avoidance made it all the more difficult for Louise.

Did Anna want Gina's hand on her back? Maybe it was just a friendly caress. Was there even such a thing as a friendly caress?

Louise's mind continued to race. The conversation didn't help. The focus on "coming out" made Louise feel like she was naked and everyone was talking about her. It wasn't that she didn't want people to know her sexual orientation—it was no secret that she was bisexual—but talking about it felt irrationally close to talking about Anna. And then she learned some new information, that Anna and this girl had a romantic history.

As the moments ticked by, Louise's slimy, slippery feeling began to escalate. She was jealous. She was jealous and she had absolutely zero right to be. When the conversation came to an emotional ending, Louise watched Anna escape to the restroom. Louise felt relieved that she no longer had to stand next to her and Gina as they got all nostalgic and flirty. But just like every other time that Anna left her space, she also felt empty. With Anna gone from the group conversation, whatever was being said just seemed to matter less and less. Louise nodded at the appropriate times and shared an anecdote or two, but her mind—and against her better judgment, her eyes—had followed Anna back out of the bathroom and over to the earlier barstool. She fantasized freely about what it would be like to be able to do exactly what she wanted right now. To sit down next to Anna and laugh like she had just a few days ago. But instead, she fled yet again to what had somehow morphed into her go-to processing spot: the bathroom.

Now, standing in front of another bathroom mirror, Louise was coming to terms with how little she really knew about Anna. Maybe her entire conceptualization of what was going on between them was just wildly off base. At the very least, each new piece of information she learned illuminated how absurd it was that she was so willing to lose herself in this unknown person. Louise thought back to just a few hours ago, when her hands had been all over Anna's body and she'd whispered into her ear the things she wanted to do to her. Little did she know that she might not even have been the only person TODAY to make that sort of offer to Anna. Louise knew deep down that her thoughts were poisonous, but this was what it felt like to be feeling things she hadn't felt since Gwen, for someone she had only known a few days. Had she always been such an insecure person or was it just her environment?

Another woman walked into the restroom, mercifully breaking Louise's train of thought and current stasis. But when Louise exited the bathroom and glanced toward Anna's corner, her nightmare continued. Not only could she not have what she wanted, clearly someone else could. Anna was smiling and turned toward Louise's new archnemesis, Gina. Gina was touching Anna's leg possessively. The sight of it made Louise see red, and not just because of Gina's touch. Anna looked content, interested, curious. Louise had been on the other end of that look before. Now, watching the scene from the outside, she felt small.

Louise moved without thinking. As she approached the two canoodlers, Gina noticed her first. She looked up at Louise with oblivious openness, casually leaving her hand on Anna's thigh. When Anna saw where she was looking her reaction was different. She abruptly pulled back and swiveled her legs slightly away from Gina's hand, causing Gina to pull away herself with a somewhat bewildered look. Louise added a tick to her W column.

"Hi, Anna, Gina. Bar's pretty packed! Looked like you all had a bit more room down here for ordering drinks." Her voice was artificial and totally unlike her. Gina looked dubiously down the length of the bar at several open spots farther on but didn't say anything about it.

"Yeah, I don't come here too often, but it's pretty hype tonight," Gina said instead, offering some normalcy.

If Louise wasn't so unfairly biased against Gina, she would have thought it a kindness.

"What about you, Anna, having a good night?" The question was asinine, but Louise was no longer speaking with any plan or forethought.

"Yeah, I guess," Anna replied.

No help there.

"It's just…" Louise said. "We were here the other night, Anna and me, and it was basically only the two of us and some drunk asshole the whole time. Right, Anna?"

Anna glanced at her with confusion and some irritation but didn't reply.

Gina looked between them.

"Oh, you two must be hanging out a lot, since you're dating Clay! It must be fun having a sibling so close in age," Gina said, turning toward Anna with interest.

Louise's heat rose again. She hated the reminder that she was literally here as Clay's girlfriend, not to mention watching this woman move in on Anna with no hesitation. And why shouldn't she? Louise had no claim on Anna and Gina clearly couldn't know what Louise was going through. Unfortunately, the knowledge wasn't enough to reel Louise back in.

"Well, actually, this was before I knew Anna and Clay were related," Louise blurted out, shocking even herself. She had no idea that she would give up the story she and Anna had agreed on. No longer avoiding Louise's eyes, Anna was staring at her incredulously.

Gina's eyes went wide. "I don't understand, you knew each other before?"

Before Louise could say anything else, Anna cut her off.

"We ran into each other here when we both first came to town, a few days ago, and I didn't know she was Clay's girlfriend." Something about the way she said "Clay's girlfriend" felt like a dig.

Anna looked uncomfortable and an awkward silence followed. The interruption gave Louise a chance to shut her mouth. She knew she was playing with fire and although she wanted Anna to acknowledge her, she wasn't truly trying to expose them to Gina.

But Gina had clearly picked up on something. Her hand returned decisively, if awkwardly, to Anna's leg and her eyes remained on Louise.

"What a funny situation..." She turned back toward Anna, lifting an eyebrow flirtatiously.

"I wish I'd been the one that caught you alone at the bar. Maybe we could've made better use of your time here."

The comment was pointed and dripping with innuendo. Louise was not a violent person, but this woman was testing her. She was at a loss for how to work through the chaos inside her. She couldn't bring herself to leave Gina alone with Anna, and she definitely didn't want to continue enduring their flirtation. Desperately, she tried to change the subject.

"So, Gina, you went to high school with Clay and Anna?"

Gina looked at Louise with skepticism. "Yeah, Clay was in my grade and Anna was a year below."

"And so you two hooked up?" The harsh words fell out of her mouth and both Gina and Anna reacted.

"Louise, what are you doing?" Anna said firmly.

"What? I'm just wondering how it all went down is all. I mean, I imagine it was a secret, right? Since tonight is the first time you've told your friends."

"What the fuck?" Anna said a bit louder now. She directed her next comments only to Gina. "Gina, you don't have to answer that."

"No, I can answer." Gina sat up straighter and looked directly at Louise. "I was an idiot when I was in high school. Anna was… is…smart and funny and sexy and everything I could have asked for in a friend, and I treated her like shit."

Louise was taken aback by the strength in her words.

"So. Any other questions, or do you want me to start asking why you seem so interested in Anna?"

It was like hearing a record scratch. Anna's face went white. Louise realized with humiliation that she was completely on display. She launched a futile attempt at damage control.

"I don't know what you're talking about. I just don't like anyone treating Clay's sister like that…" It sounded feeble even to herself.

"Sure, whatever you gotta tell yourself." Gina got up from her chair and turned toward Anna. "I'm going to go check on Jessica and Alison. When you're finished with whatever this is, come find me. I would love to pick up where we left off."

She gave Anna a slow kiss on the cheek. Louise felt the familiar heat boil inside her, every nanosecond like a hot poker. Gina turned toward Louise.

"It was nice talking to you. I hope you figure whatever this is...out." She gestured around the area between them.

And then she was gone, leaving Louise flooded with embarrassment as she stood in front of a very angry Anna.

Anna spoke in a frantic whisper. "What the actual fuck, Louise!"

Louise let the words hit her as the last five minutes came into perspective. The jealous feeling had waned, leaving her with only the incredibly awful feeling of embarrassment that was behind it all.

"Anna, I don't know what I was thinking."

"That's obvious."

Anna was very close to her, still full of that same exasperation from before.

"Do you know how hard it is for someone like her to come out like that? She doesn't need shit about it. And what is this bullshit about protecting me? The only person I need protecting from is you."

The accusation stung.

"I'm sorry, Anna."

Louise's words were faint. She wished she could just rewind the past fifteen minutes and find the self-control not to come over and make a fool out of herself.

"I'm having a hard time," she said, "seeing you with someone else."

Anna seemed to take in the words and a calmness passed between them. Some of the anger was gone from her eyes. Louise couldn't imagine feeling more pathetic than she did right then.

"I know the feeling," Anna responded. The comment wasn't pointed; it sounded almost consolatory. Anna started to leave but Louise grabbed her arm. They were close.

Louise whispered so only Anna could hear.

"Please don't go home with her."

The words were a plea. Anna held her gaze. It felt like she was on a tightrope. She was left with no response as Anna left her at the bar. The emptiness was back again. Louise tried to get her composure back. Once she was finally feeling semi-normal, George came over and asked if she wanted anything, she shook her head, but he lingered. He was looking at her with a wariness she had not seen the other night.

He finally spoke. "Be careful there. You have a lot of people's hearts in your hands right now."

He didn't wait for a response, he just left her there feeling if possible worse than she had a moment ago.

❖

Anna slipped out the back door and into a small lot with a couple of private staff parking spaces and some dumpsters. She didn't know what to do with herself. She could still feel her emotions simmering, but hearing Louise admit, with such vulnerability, that she was having a hard time seeing her with someone else had left her so...confused. This entire weekend consisted of Anna watching Louise with someone else—Anna's fucking brother! The angry simmer started boiling. And then, to top it all off, what an insanely selfish request.

"Don't go home with her."

The words still rang in her ears. Anna began to pace.

I can go home with anyone I want. I can fuck whoever I want. Why should I care what she thinks?

But the problem was that she did care. She cared very much what Louise thought. She cared very much what Louise wanted. Her pacing ended with a rather dramatic dumpster kick that left her hopping on one foot, left toe throbbing.

"Hey, watch it, that's my garbage!" George had slunk outside and was watching, leaning up against the wall with a casual grace. Anna was appreciative of how comfortable she was with George after such a short time. His tone was kind and playful, but she noted a glum demeanor underneath.

"Hey, sorry," she replied.

She stopped her pacing and took in her new, old friend.

"You okay?" Anna asked.

He straightened himself up a bit, like he had earlier.

"Yeah, I'm fine. It's just been a long night." He was clearly deflecting. "For you as well I can see. Are you leaving?"

Anna wanted to press him more on what was bothering him, but she couldn't be sure he'd be comfortable with further questioning.

"I think it might be a bit crowded in there for me."

"I know what you mean," George said in response.

Anna again noticed sadness in his voice. "Are you sure you're okay, George?"

George was quiet for a moment and looked at Anna with a kind of intensity.

"You know, it hasn't been easy these last few years here in Trenton. It's been lonely, you know?"

Anna came over and leaned on the wall next to him, listening carefully.

"I just feel like I'm the only one who is ever honest." He hesitated and then seemed to backpedal. "Never mind, I'm probably not making any sense."

"I don't have to understand all the specifics to listen," Anna responded delicately, feeling like George could easily scare.

George looked away from Anna and let out a sigh. It sounded like something he had been holding in all night.

"Whatever happens with that girl in there, don't feel like you don't deserve what you want. Sometimes being here makes you feel like it's their world and we're just living in it."

Anna was struggling to read through George's cryptic messaging. Was he talking about her or himself?

"You know, George, you deserve what you want too."

George let a smile spread across his face and brought Anna in for a hug. When he pulled away, he looked more like himself again.

"Well, now that I've fully 'sad boyed' my heart out, I should probably get back in there. I'm sure the Heathers are overwhelming Tony at the bar."

Anna still wasn't convinced, but his face at least had a bit more color in it. With his hand on the door, he looked back toward Anna.

"Thanks, Anna." He threw her a wink and swung the door open, nearly colliding into the exact person Anna was hiding from.

The numerous apologies of two overly polite people took over until George stepped back and courteously held the door for Louise.

"After you," he said with an absurd chivalrous gesture. He flashed Anna a look that very much asked, *you good out here?* Anna gave him a subtle nod, accepting her fate.

❖

The back door slammed shut after George and a deafening silence fell. A gust of wind ruffled Louise's loose curls—it must have lasted only a moment, but it seemed like hours to Anna. She felt as though she could see each strand of Louise's hair twist and unfurl in slow motion. The sound of the crowded bar melted into the background, replaced by the exhale of Louise's breath.

Louise looked at Anna for a moment and then pulled her coat tightly around herself and began walking off toward the alley, leaving Anna stunned in her wake.

"Where are you going?" Anna asked, hearing the words tumble out of her mouth before she could control herself.

Louise didn't answer. Anna followed. When she turned the corner into the alley, the place where it had all begun, Louise slowed to a halt and turned around. Anna gave herself adequate space to take in Louise and her confusing behavior. Louise's arms were folded in front of her, not in defiance, but almost as if she was holding herself together.

"Anna, we need to talk."

The words sparked anger in Anna again. She looked at Louise with total frustration.

"These things I'm feeling," she said, "they aren't going away. I know you feel it too."

The comment enraged Anna. "Don't presume to know how I feel!" Anna growled, squaring off against Louise.

"Fine, I'll speak for myself." Louise was starting to raise her voice as well.

"I can't think when you're in the room. I…" Her words dropped off and her expression was just as frustrated as Anna felt. Her cheeks were flushed pink.

Anna didn't want to let Louise run this conversation like she had every other time. So Anna hit first.

"First, you cheat on my brother. Something I never would have been a part of, had I known who you were—"

Louise cut her off. "But you would have helped me cheat on someone you didn't know? You're so noble."

"I made a mistake. And the moment I knew who you were, I let it go. I put the whole thing behind me. But you won't. You just keep needling and needling."

Anna moved closer to Louise unconsciously.

Anna continued. "You play with me, one minute hot, cold the next. I can't get a handle on what you want and then you've already changed your mind! You're giving me whiplash."

Anna could see the anger building in Louise as well, but she went on. "Then at the festival. I was kind to you, I was trying to be friendly and respectful, and you continued pursuing me."

"Okay, let's get one thing straight," Louise said. "There were two people in that corn maze. And I wasn't 'pursuing you.' I like you, and I think deep down, you know you like me too. I don't know why you're turning this around and acting like I've seduced you against your will. Was it against your will when you had your hand on my ass? Was it against your will when you begged me not to stop?"

Anna was again stunned, her breath was coming quickly and her anger and her desire were again, competing for control.

Louise didn't stop.

"I'm trying to be honest about what I'm feeling. I'm trying to get a handle on what is going on between us, but if you're just going to live in this denial-land you've created, then fuck it!"

Louise turned and started down the alley again to leave, but Anna reacted quickly. She moved behind Louise, grabbing her by the hips and stopping her exit. Anna found herself flush against Louise's back. Louise gasped as if startled, but then quickly gave in to Anna's touch. She moved Anna's hands from her hips and guided them over her body indulgently.

Anna couldn't hold herself back any longer. It was too much to stop, to pretend she didn't want this. She softened her hands as she moved them over Louise's hips and stomach. She couldn't see Louise's face, but she could hear her breath coming ragged with another soft moan of pleasure. Anna pushed Louise's hair to the side and brought her face to her neck. She could smell the flowery scent from the sheets earlier, the scent again turning her on more. Her lips touched below Louise's ear softly.

Louise stilled. "Anna...please..." Her words were ragged and desperate.

Anna pressed her lips harder then pulled her mouth away.

"Please what?" Anna moved her hands down Louise's legs as Louise pressed herself into Anna's body.

"You want to know what I'm feeling, what I feel when I'm with you?" Anna continued to kiss and lick her neck, moving her hand inside Louise's coat to caress her soft breasts. She could feel Louise's hard nipples through her shirt.

"Turn around," she whispered forcefully.

Louise didn't hesitate, she began to turn but was quickly pulled into Anna's space. She brought a hand to the side of Anna's face and their mouths collided with urgency, tasting each other deeply. Louise's soft moans became louder, a soundtrack to Anna's own thirst for more. Anna began to move Louise toward the wall, the same wall that Anna had been pressed against, back when things were less complicated. Anna didn't care anymore what the complications were. She didn't care that they were a couple dozen yards from the bar. Nothing mattered except the woman she was pressed up against, who was grabbing her ass, whose shirt she was opening, button by button.

They continued to kiss passionately as Louise's shirt fell completely open, exposing her full breasts and pink nipples, hard with desire. Anna's mind was so muddled, and she was so wet that she didn't even hesitate when she pulled her lips away to say, "I want you, now."

Louise leaned back against the brick and looked into Anna's eyes. She moved her hands to the button of her jeans, undoing her pants, her eyes still trained on Anna's. Her breathing was labored. Anna was so turned on she couldn't even think of the risks of fucking in public so close to everyone. When Louise had undone her pants fully, she pushed her hand under the elastic of her underwear and began to touch herself. Anna could tell the moment Louise's fingers touched her pussy because her eyes began to close. Anna was completely enthralled. The act was so surprising, so unexpected. But quickly she realized that she wasn't getting what she wanted. She wasn't the one fucking Louise. Anna placed her hand on Louise's moving wrist and stalled her movements. Louise opened her eyes again, clearly struggling to hold back her own pleasure. Anna slowly removed Louise's hand. Her fingers were glistening with her wetness. Anna brought Louise's fingers to her lips and took them slowly into her mouth. Anna could taste and smell Louise and the experience only made her more ravenous. When she pulled Louise's fingers from her mouth, Louise's eyes opened, taking in the scene.

"You taste amazing," Anna said. Louise seemed to be at a loss for words.

Anna couldn't wait any longer. "I want to fuck you." She kissed Louise deeply and slowly moved her hand to where Louise's just was.

"Someone could see…" Louise said, right before she moaned Anna's name, feeling Anna's mouth on her breasts.

Anna pushed past Louise's underwear band but paused using all the restraint she had.

"I have to fuck you, now. I can't wait." Anna meant it a question, but it came as a demand.

Louise nodded and guided Anna's fingers lower. Anna slipped her fingers between the folds of Louise's cunt. They both moaned in pleasure.

"You're so wet," Anna said, her words shaking. She could barely speak, but she wanted Louise to know just how amazing she felt. Louise was breathing erratically, truly unable to respond. Her arms were wrapped around Anna, one hand running through the back of her hair, the other scratching down her back. Anna slowly rubbed Louise's clit and she heard a frustrated groan come from Louise.

"Do you like how I feel?"

Louise moaned louder, and her hips thrust against Anna, making clear she wanted more. Anna was kissing and licking Louise's neck between her spouts of teasing words. She found the back of Louise's head with her other hand, fingers entwined in her hair, as she said in Louise's ear, "You've been teasing me since the moment I met you. How does it feel?"

Anna slowed her hand further, waiting for Louise to respond. When it was clear Anna was waiting, Louise groaned in frustration. "Fuck, Anna, please."

Anna was, if possible, more turned on just hearing the desperation in Louise's voice.

"Please what?" she asked, knowing exactly what Louise needed.

"Please, Anna…. Harder."

Anna couldn't bear to tease Louise any longer. She was about to come just from the feeling of Louise on her hand. Anna moved her fingers lower and slowly slid two of them inside. Louise stopped moving for a moment, Anna could feel her adjusting to Anna being inside her. The feeling was incredible, Anna almost didn't want to move she felt so connected. Louise looked at Anna, her eyes blazing. She pulled Anna toward her again and kissed her desperately. Louise started moving her hips, seeking the pleasure that Anna's hand promised. Anna began to fuck her slowly and then, just as Louise was starting to get frustrated again, she fucked her harder, pulling each whimper from Louise. Anna's pussy was pulsing with her, as they both got closer and closer to release. Anna pushed deeply and Louise let out the most staggering sound as her body squeezed Anna's fingers. She came hard, and Anna was transfixed. She wanted the moment to last forever, but Louise finally collapsed onto Anna's shoulder. Anna was reluctant to pull her hand out. With Anna's fingers still inside, Louise leaned back and looked up at Anna, clearly speechless. Finally, Anna reluctantly pulled her fingers from between Louise's legs and began to disentangle herself from their embrace. Anna was still so turned on and astonished by what she was feeling, but Louise seemed to be coming to her senses. She began to softly push Anna away.

"I need a second," she whispered, moving away and back toward the parking lot as she fumbled to rebutton her pants and shirt. It only then really registered to Anna that what they had done would have been totally visible to someone who accidentally stumbled into the alley, that someone could have come out back and heard their very audible moans. Anna was coming down now. The gravity of what they did was slowly creeping back in. Louise looked at her with an expression Anna couldn't decipher.

"I should go back inside," she said, clearly not wanting to mention what had just happened.

Anna was stung by the feeling of rejection she felt.

"Are you going to pretend this didn't happen?" Her voice was shaking.

Louise looked at her sadly. Anna was struggling to understand what was happening. Louise walked back over to Anna and kissed her gently on the lips. The kiss was soft and finite. She ran her hand over Anna's cheek.

"How could I possibly pretend this didn't happen?"

She smiled wistfully and turned back toward the door to the bar. Louise didn't look back. She left Anna confused and incredibly turned on, looking toward the empty space where Louise just was. Anna took a moment to get herself together. She couldn't think straight. She knew she couldn't go back inside. She couldn't face Clay or George. Not to mention Gina, who was sure to be looking for her as the night began to wind down. Worst of all, she couldn't face Louise. Not in front of people, not after what they had both done. Instead, Anna turned down the alley, away from Louise, and started the cold walk home.

CHAPTER NINE

A calm settled over Louise, a calm she had not felt in a long time. Even reentering the crowded and noisy bar didn't break her newfound reverie. She found herself at Anna's abandoned barstool. She tried feebly to still her beating heart.

"Another drink?" George asked with no hint of the edge from earlier.

"Just a water, please."

George came back with a tall glass of ice water with a small tiki umbrella in it.

"Thank you," Louise said, finally registering the extra look he was giving her. He'd clearly been scrutinizing her.

"What?" Louise asked.

George shook his head and held his hands up in surrender. "Nothing!"

"Seriously, why are you looking at me like that?"

He began to clean a glass distractingly.

"It's just...you look a little...flushed." George paused his cleaning to emphasize the last word.

Louise could feel her face flush deeper with embarrassment. She quickly looked away, took a sip of her water, and gave him a noncommittal "hmmm." He seemed to take pity on her, allowing the deflection and moving instead to tend the other end of the bar.

Shit.

Already, her post-sex euphoria was starting to fade as she caught herself furtively checking the bar for Clay. Her boyfriend.

Shit, shit, shit!

Her eyes landed on the back of his head—thankfully, way across the room—and she quickly looked away, having determined that five minutes after fucking his sister was a bit too soon to face him and all of his friends. Well, more accurately—after being fucked by his sister—in an alley no less, and with a very dangerous chance of being seen. Just thinking about it brought that fluttering feeling back.

The whole incident had been so unexpected. She'd followed Anna outside with the sole intention of being honest with her. She wanted to explain her conversation with Clay, hoping it would release some of the tension between them. But it seemed her body had different ideas for ways to release the tension. Anna had been so forceful, commanding, it was unexpected. It was so much hotter than Louise could have imagined. Louise knew she was attracted to Anna fairly instantly, but she had no way of knowing what it would be like to be with her. Her body was still thrumming from the most incredible sex she had ever had.

Louise closed her eyes for a moment, overwhelmed again with the aftershock. Once the feeling passed, she refocused on the less-than-ideal situation. She knew she needed to talk to Clay, even if just to say she wanted to go home. She wanted to go home not just because being there felt like standing naked in a crowd of people, but also because Anna didn't come back into the bar behind her. She could only guess the Nelsons' home would be where she was most likely to be. With her now-clearer head, Louise realized that leaving Anna in the alley like that might have seemed like she was embarrassed or ashamed of what had happened, but that wasn't it. She'd simply been overwhelmed; it was too intense. She'd needed a moment to get back in her own body and her own head. It was what she had been trying to avoid, this feeling of connecting too hard. She couldn't risk losing herself again in somebody who might not always be there.

Having sex with Anna, even in a stolen moment, had affected Louise more than anyone she'd been with since Gwen. The memory of her first love and all she had given up started to hurt and, jumbled up with the searing attraction Louise felt for Anna in her post-sex haze, well, it was just all too much. She wanted to talk to Anna about Gwen, explain why it seemed like she was so hot and cold, why her faltering feelings for Clay were not enough for her to leave him so easily. As Louise continued mulling over the past few days, she realized she'd made a sequence of errors. Understanding what was going on inside herself wasn't enough. Even being honest with others about what she was going through wasn't enough. She had to decide what she wanted and go after it with intention. Simply telling Anna she had feelings for her, and that those feelings scared her because of her grief for Gwen and telling her that she was breaking up with Clay didn't answer the question. What did Louise actually want?

It was at this moment of epiphany that Gina sat on the stool beside her. Gina, the cause of all of Louise's wildly irrational behavior over the last few hours. Well, not *all* of her irrational behavior.

Louise turned toward Gina to find her calmly sipping her drink and peering at Louise quite obviously. She was seated backward on the stool, facing out toward the booths.

"You okay?" she asked over her shoulder.

The question sounded sincere, to Louise's surprise. She knew she hadn't been fair or kind to Gina.

"Yeah, thank you," Louise said, trying to thaw the ice between them. "I'm sorry I was…so rude earlier."

Gina raised an eyebrow as she listened, looking around at the energized group of bar patrons.

"You were, weren't you." Gina let the comment linger and then nudged Louise playfully with an elbow.

"I'm just messing with you. Apology accepted." Gina looked back over with a smile and caught Louise's eye. Louise knew Gina had picked up on something, but it wasn't clear how much.

"So, I take it Anna left? I haven't seen her for a while." Gina looked disappointed as she asked.

"I'm not sure..." This was awkward.

"Well, since we cleared the air a bit, what's the deal with you and Anna?"

Louise searched her mind for a response that didn't make her want to dig her head in the sand and hide.

Gina, perhaps picking up on her anxiety, went on. "Let me also say, I know it may seem like I have an agenda right now, but I don't."

Louise flashed Gina a skeptical look.

"No, seriously! I'm obviously attracted to her, I mean who wouldn't be."

The comment was a little too pointed.

"Let me put it this way, it takes one to know one."

"Know one what?" Louise asked.

"Someone who has the hots for Anna."

Louise blushed relentlessly.

"Don't worry, I'm not going to blow up your spot. I mean, I don't think it's super great that you're literally dating her brother, but I think at this point in my life, I don't have a lot of space for judgment."

Hearing it spelled out like this was making Louise's ears ring. She knew she had to say something. She couldn't just sit there looking dumb or denying it anymore. She'd already made a fool of herself in front of this woman in more ways than one.

"Yeah, I'm, umm...dealing with some feelings...for Anna."

Gina nodded knowingly.

"And what about her feelings for you?"

"I'm not sure," Louise admitted. Even with their alleyway sex, Louise was confused by the push and pull over the past few days. And with Gina now added to the mix, Louise couldn't be sure she wasn't just the latest member of some previously unknown Anna Fan Club.

"Come on, even I can see this thing is not one-sided. I'm actually surprised Clay hasn't noticed."

The thought should have bothered Louise more, but it didn't. She was too taken aback, too relieved, by Gina's insinuation that Louise really might be special to Anna. Her heart did a backflip.

"So, I guess I might have to move on to greener pastures, won't I?"

The question was flippant and kind, but underneath Louise could still hear that tone of sadness. It brought her back to the moment.

"I'm sorry I...didn't mean to mess that up for you," she said truthfully.

Gina shrugged. "Listen, I'd rather know now than later that I'm runner-up. And no offense, but I don't really want to be there when this whole thing blows up."

The thought of the many bad outcomes that were possible in the next few days began to make Louise nervous again.

"Besides, I'm newly out and I feel...powerful. I'm grateful to Anna for being who she was when we were kids, and now, for reminding me that it can feel good to be brave."

Gina swiveled her stool toward Louise and seemed to brush off her Anna nostalgia.

"So. What about you?"

"What about me?"

"Well, what are you going to do?"

Louise was struggling to get a handle on Gina. Just a short while ago, she was her competitor, her enemy. But now, here she was asking the one question that Louise just happened to be grappling with.

"Listen, I'm not trying to pry, I'm just trying to pay it forward. For a kindred spirit," she said playfully, clinking her drink with Louise's stationary water on the table.

Louise searched Gina a final time for any evidence of a vat of pig's blood.

"I honestly don't know. I'm in this thing with Clay, but I did try to talk to him. Kind of. I promised him we could stay together through the end of the week. He's got a lot of pressure on him from the Nelsons."

"Ah, the Nelsons!" Gina quirked her eyebrow conspiratorially. "Dr. Nelson works out at my gym. Totally rude to all the employees, acts like she owns the place."

"That sounds like her. If you saw how upset Clay was, you'd understand. I can't break up with him right now." The words sounded hollow. "And then there's Anna…"

Gina sighed dreamily. "Yes, then there's Anna."

Before she could catch herself, Louise began to spill.

"I mean, even if there is something between us, what's the point? We live on opposite ends of the country. We have completely different lifestyles. I'm in med school and have like no time outside of studying. Not to mention the obvious problem that I'm dating her brother. Even if I did break up with him, how would that ever be okay?" Louise groaned in frustration.

"But how do you feel about her?"

"I feel…everything. She's beautiful, she's kind, she has this amazing, contagious laugh. When she's hurting, I just want to take all her pain away. When she listens, it feels like what I'm saying is the most important thing in the world. She's all I think about, I want her so bad it hurts. And this is all just moot anyway because this will pass, these feelings will pass. They have to." Louise swirled her glass on the bar and stared accusatorially at the remaining melting ice cubes.

Gina considered her words. "Maybe you're right."

"Which part?"

Gina laughed. "All of it! But can I just say one thing, just while I'm riding my high from coming out tonight?"

"Sure," Louise replied unhappily. "I could obviously use any advice I can get at this point."

Gina arched her eyebrows again, feigning offense.

Louise smiled grudgingly. "Let me rephrase. I would love your advice."

"Well, I guess I'd say that if Anna looked at me the way she looks at you, I wouldn't hesitate. I'd risk it all."

Louise took in Gina's words.

"And on that note, I'm going to head out of here. As much as I love playing matchmaker for the girl I've been crushing on since high school, I may have reached my limit for good karma." Gina dropped a few bills on the bar.

"Thanks, for talking to me," Louise said sincerely.

Gina threw her a wink. "See you around, I hope." And then she walked to the exit, turning multiple heads on the way.

Louise was left with an overwhelming sense of hope. She still wasn't sure exactly what she wanted, but she knew she wasn't going to find it here. Louise left some money on the bar as well, waving good-bye to George. He still had his hands full, but he gave her a brief salute. Then she located Clay who was definitely a few decibels louder than before and was regaling a group of less inebriated folks, including Josh.

Louise touched Clay's arm hoping to get his attention. He turned and a huge smile burst from his face. "Louuuu.... I was looking for you! Come hang with us!" His breath reeked of beer and his movements were big and sloppy.

"Clay, I'm really tired. I'm going to head out, okay?"

"Nooo, come on, a little longer." His words were slurred, but he didn't have a glass in his hand.

Josh chimed in. "We cut him off a little bit ago. If you want to go, I can make sure he gets home okay."

Louise felt bad about leaving him, but Josh seemed pretty comfortable and she didn't want her distracted mind to be a wet blanket on the fun he was having.

"Okay, Clay, did you hear that? I'm going home, but you're going to get a ride with Josh."

Clay seemed to only hear the part where he didn't have to go home with her and went back to telling stories from childhood.

Clay was usually a pretty moderate guy, so it was odd seeing him so drunk. But then again it had been an emotional day, maybe he needed to blow off some steam.

Louise checked one more time with Josh and he passionately reassured her.

"He can even stay in my guest room so he doesn't wake up his folks."

Louise thanked Josh and headed out, ordering a ride share as she walked. Standing with the alley in her sight line, she was again startled thinking just how close they had been to being caught. She couldn't help but wonder, would she get another chance?

❖

As the car pulled up to the Nelson estate, Louise was beginning to lose her nerve. She awkwardly stumbled out of the car—just the thought of Anna waiting in their shared room threw her off balance—and she quickly glanced around to confirm nobody had seen. A snort poorly disguised as a cough sounded from the car behind her.

Just the ride share driver then.

But Louise had bigger things to worry about as she shut the car door (perhaps a bit harder than was strictly necessary). Would Anna be waiting? The reality was that Louise had left her in that alley with no clear plan or understanding of what would happen next. She wouldn't blame Anna if she'd decided just to hop on the next plane back to her cool life in New York City, to leave all this messiness behind. Even if Anna felt there was something between them and she didn't want to flee, it was more likely that this fragile relationship—was it a relationship?—was about to implode.

Louise stopped and looked up at the guest room window. The light wasn't on. Somehow it hadn't occurred to Louise until that moment that Anna might actually be asleep.

Really, who could fall asleep under these circumstances?

But if she was asleep, what should Louise do? Should she wake her up to discuss what happened or should she go with satisfying her base desire and crawl into Anna's bed, hoping to pick up where they left off? The thought of having sex with Anna again sent a shiver down Louise's spine in a mixture of arousal and fear. She knew it was possible that Anna might not want a repeat of the alley, and imagining that rejection felt nearly intolerable.

A gust of icy winter wind shocked her into moving again toward the house. Unless she wanted to freeze to death in the Nelsons' driveway, she couldn't avoid the inevitable any longer, whatever the outcome.

Louise used the guest key to let herself in through the front door. The house was quiet and dark. She made her way up the stairs slowly, allowing her eyes to adjust to the darkness. Right outside their shared bedroom, she paused with a hand on the doorknob. She took a deep breath and let herself in.

In the same way that she always knew when Anna was in a room, she could feel almost with just her hand on the door that the bedroom was empty. Moonlight filtering through the window gave an eerie blue sheen to the room, but at least it provided enough light to confirm Louise's intuition. Looking around, she could see that the beds and everything else in the room remained untouched. No discarded wallet, nothing. It wasn't clear that Anna had come home at all, either to pack up and leave or to wait for Louise to return. Louise felt some of the fear in her body morph into relief, coupled with a surprising ache of disappointment. She was alone.

She sat on the bed and tried to relax her racing heart for a moment. Once she was pretty sure that no angsty roommate was about to barge in on her, she went to the bathroom to wash her face. She switched the light on and noticed something new—a pile of clothes next to the shower. Having been intimately acquainted with Anna's Breeders T-shirt, she realized Anna must have come home. Louise's heart skipped a beat. With this new information, it was easy to deduce that Anna was most likely in the house, and quite possibly naked. That last thought was just where Louise's mind was.

Shaking her head, Louise brought herself back to the task at hand—finding Anna. Maybe she'd decided to try to sleep in another room, or on a couch somewhere since the Nelsons' home renovations had taken over the other guest rooms. It was time to do some exploring. Louise left the bathroom and passed through the bedroom into the second-floor hallway, making sure to move carefully in the still-unfamiliar space. At the far end of the hallway, she could make out a narrow strip of light seeping out from the bottom of a door. From the brief tour of the Nelsons' home that Clay provided the first night, Louise knew the door didn't lead to Clay's or his parents' bedrooms. Well, she was pretty sure it didn't. She decided that if she came upon a Nelson that wasn't Anna, she could just say she got lost.

Louise softly rapped her knuckles on the door and paused nervously, fist still hovering midair, ears hyperalert to any sounds that might come from the next room.

No reply.

She waited a few beats longer, wondering if perhaps she'd knocked too quietly, before rashly deciding to just get on with it. She opened the door and was pleasantly surprised with the look of the room. It was gorgeous. Floor to ceiling shelves full of books covered three of the walls, serving as a luxurious backdrop to an antique-looking fainting couch, several plush chairs, and an assortment of eclectic side tables and lamps. The furniture rested on top of an intricate Persian rug that gave what could have been a too-expansive room a warm and inviting quality. The wall directly across from Louise boasted three towering windows, currently offering a picturesque view of the starry winter sky twinkling over the Nelson estate's sizable grounds.

And there, draped across a built-in window seat, propped up against several pillows, was the object of her search, Anna, with a paperback in hand, staring at whatever sound had pulled her from her reverie. Louise saw that the outfit change she'd predicted earlier had in fact materialized. Anna was now clad in a pair of black boyshorts and what looked to be a very old T-shirt. Worn thin from years of use and washing, the flimsy cotton draped alluringly over Anna's body, highlighting her preference for going bra-less. She was wearing a pair of dark glasses that made her look studious and, if possible, even more sexy than her usual too cool look. But it wasn't just how sexy she looked, it was her vulnerability. It was as if Louise had discovered her in the first place that had seemed like a home to Louise. She was stunned by the sight of her. All the feelings came crashing back—the anxieties, the fear, the anticipation.

Anna put her book down but stayed in her relaxed position. She clearly wasn't pressed to speak first.

"You weren't in our...the room."

Louise's voice sounded shaky and self-conscious. Anna said nothing. Louise struggled to read Anna's mood. Was this another fight they were about to have, or was something else going on? She realized she was still standing awkwardly in the doorway and stepped into the room instead.

"Is it okay that I'm here?" she asked.

She heard the heavy door shut gently behind her.

"Yeah, it's fine." Anna's words came quickly.

Louise walked over to the fainting couch and sat down carefully, vowing to avoid doing anything that could mess up the rich brocade. She was facing Anna but was far enough away to show that she wasn't trying to pounce on her, however much she might want to.

"I have a couple things I wanted to say earlier, that I never got a chance to..." Louise was brought back to the reason why she wasn't able to get her point across. "Can I tell you now?"

Anna nodded.

"There's a lot you don't know about me, a lot of things that I've been through."

What was it she wanted Anna to know? Why had it seemed so important for Anna to understand what was going through her head?

"When we met at the bar, I felt a connection. A connection I haven't felt in a long time. Maybe it was the fact that I would never see you again, or maybe it was just…just you, but I allowed myself to feel something. I've spent a long time trying to avoid feeling things like this."

Louise took a deep breath to try to calm her racing heart. She had spent so long hiding this part of herself.

"When we fought the other night about my sexual orientation, it wasn't just that you offended me. It brought up stuff, stuff I don't like to think about, stuff you couldn't have known." Louise paused preparing herself to talk about Gwen.

"I'm here, I'm listening," Anna stated with a genuine openness in her voice.

Louise found the courage in her words. "I loved someone very deeply once. Her name was Gwen." Gwen's name felt rusty and unused on her lips. "She was my first love and I thought I was going to spend the rest of my life with her."

Louise could hear her voice shake, she could feel the tears starting to gather on her lashes, but she was struggling to let in how she was feeling.

"And I got hurt, I got hurt so badly that I couldn't…" Louise's word's fell off. How do you begin to explain this kind of pain? "I think when it happened, I took all of my feelings and all of my desires and I put them in a little jar and buried it as deep as I could. I promised myself I would never lose myself in someone again. And I haven't, not until you. I've dated other people, people who didn't feel like her, people who didn't have the power to hurt me." It was here that she finally starting to realize how unfair this was to people who liked her, people like Clay. "Clay's a wonderful friend. He's a wonderful person, but I know he can't hurt me. Not like that."

Louise wiped tears from her checks and looked at Anna, searching for understanding in her eyes.

"What happened with Gwen?" Anna asked.

Louise flinched. She could feel the sharpness of the question. It wasn't intended, but even so, her grief was still raw.

"She died. She was nineteen years old and she'd never been out of Oregon and she died." Louise didn't know how to act with Anna's sympathetic eyes on her. She stood up abruptly and walked to the window, getting as much space as she could. She stared out at the clear night sky, trying to find something to focus on that wasn't her pain.

"I'm so sorry," Anna responded, and Louise could hear the catch in her voice.

"I know that it's been a long time since she died, but not for me. For me it feels like it was yesterday. I built my life around her, I built myself around her. I just don't know who I am without her." The tears were falling. Louise wiped her face and couldn't help how hollow she felt reliving her loss. "And that day with you, that was the first time I'd felt feelings that strong. Feelings that made me forget." Her words began to come quickly, almost in a panic. "I couldn't stop it, and I shouldn't have kissed you. I know that. I do, but I just..."

Anna stood up from the window seat and moved close to Louise, pulling her into her arms. Louise fell willingly into Anna's embrace, letting herself cry into Anna's soft shirt. Anna rubbed her back softly. She could hear her careful words saying, "Shhh it's okay," into her hair. The feeling of being in Anna's arms, being comforted, being understood, was so soothing. They pulled apart, but Anna didn't let go fully. Instead, she led Louise back to the window seat, inviting her to join. They both fit snugly, Louise with her legs intermingled with Anna's, Anna with her arm over Louise's shoulder, holding her close.

"I'm sorry I judged you. I shouldn't have said anything about your sexuality or pretended like anything that happened was one-sided. I can't imagine going through something so painful. I was so…insensitive," Anna said finally, caressing Louise's hair as they sat intertwined.

"And I'm not innocent in all this," Louise added. Louise looked up at Anna, who smiled in response.

"You're a lot more innocent than I've made you out to be. You have been balancing so many emotions."

Louise was touched just to hear someone witness the things she carried with her. It had been so long since she had talked about Gwen. It was possible she'd never truly admitted, even to herself, all the ways she was hurting.

"I guess this conversation really doesn't bring us up to speed, though, does it?" Louise said.

"No, I guess, not." Anna seemed to hesitate before responding. "What about Clay?"

Louise was still struggling to figure out how to explain her relationship with Clay, past and present.

"The Clay situation is…complicated."

Anna stopped her caress. "I can't keep betraying my brother like this," she said. "I don't want to. It's not fair to him and it's eating me up inside."

Louise could hear the sadness in her voice.

"I know, I don't want that either. I've tried and tried to stay away from you, but…it just isn't working," Louise replied.

"I know."

The truth hung in the air.

"I did try to tell him, and he knows that I'm unhappy and that I don't want a relationship anymore…"

"You did? So, what does that mean?" Anna asked.

"He asked me…really, he kind of begged me, to keep it private until after the trip. It seems like he's under a lot of pressure from your parents and I just feel like I owe him this."

"So, you aren't broken up?" Anna's tone was sad.

"Technically…no."

Anna let out a frustrated sigh.

"I guess it shouldn't even matter. What we've been doing is wrong regardless of if you two have broken up."

"I don't want to get in the way of your relationship with him. I know it hasn't been easy for you both to connect. I can't undo what we've done, and honestly, I wouldn't want to. But I can respect your wishes if you want me to leave." She looked around at their current surroundings. "Or, you know, like stay away from you for the rest of the trip at least."

Anna seemed to think deeply about her response. "You don't wish we hadn't…you know…?"

Louise caressed Anna's cheek and made sure Anna saw what she was feeling. "No, I don't."

Anna leaned in and kissed Louise gently on the lips. The kiss was consolatory and delicate. It made Louise feel yet again like nothing else mattered outside of Anna. When they both pulled away, Louise could see that there were tears in Anna's eyes as well.

"What do you want?" Louise asked, not wanting to accept the inevitability of her potential answer.

Anna wiped her eyes. "I want to have met you at a different time in a different place. Like maybe in New York or Seattle. I could have run into you at a coffee shop."

Louise snuggled back in under Anna's arm. The fantasy was enticing. She allowed herself to let go of their reality and to imagine how it could have been without so many things holding them back.

"If I'd seen you at a coffee shop in Seattle, I wouldn't have been able to resist speaking to you."

"Yeah? Would you have been that bold?"

"I wouldn't have been able to help it," Louise responded.

"If you'd have come up and talked to me, I wouldn't have let you leave without getting your number."

"Is that so? And how long would you have made me wait before you texted me?"

"It would have taken everything in me not to text you the moment you were out of sight."

They sat with this alternate universe a moment.

"Where do you think we would be now if things had been different?" Anna asked.

Louise knew that her next words might rupture the fantasy.

"Maybe I'd be here with you, meeting your parents, instead of with Clay." The words were too much. Louise could feel the fear beginning to take over. She shouldn't have said something so intimate; they had only known each other a few days.

Anna didn't respond right away. Louise was sure she had gone too far.

"No, that would never happen."

Her tone was dark. Louise struggled not to feel hurt by Anna's words.

"I would never subject you to meeting my parents. We would spend Christmas together with friends, or maybe just you and me."

The image of Anna in her apartment, cuddled up with Louise by one of those dilapidated two-foot trees made her feel warm and safe. She pressed in tighter feeling the relief course through her. She closed her eyes and let herself escape into the dream.

"Mmm, that sounds amazing." Louise could feel herself drifting off while Anna continued to softly stroke her head. Louise fell asleep wrapped in the fantasy.

❖

Anna awoke with a searing pain in her back. It was clear from the protests of her body that she had not found a bed last night. She would've been angrier at herself if not for the pressure she could feel down her left side and the swath of curls she was searching through to find the source. Louise had fallen asleep in Anna's arms and her ultra-relaxed looking position suggested she'd been spared the discomfort of a windowsill digging into her back all night.

Typical.

It seemed she was always the one taking the hits. But it wasn't really a hit, was it? Louise lying in her arms was worth all the back pain she could possibly endure. Anna didn't know exactly what time it was, but the sun was streaming in through the window next to her. The steady cadence of Louise's breath could only mean she was still asleep, and while Anna didn't want to wake her, she couldn't quite come up with a reason why she would be holed up here cuddling with her brother's girlfriend.

Last night's revelations had changed Anna's view of Louise. Hearing Louise talk about her first love and the pain she still carried somehow allowed Anna to start letting go of her own anger. It wasn't all as simple as Anna made it out to be. She knew what it was like to be at odds with herself, and to be dealing with layers of complicated feelings. And with the added knowledge that Clay knew on some level that his relationship with Louise would be ending, some of the debilitating guilt had subsided. It wasn't a perfect moral situation, but it was getting better. In this moment of clarity, with Louise in her arms, Anna promised herself that she would no longer add to Louise's weight. Even if she didn't exactly know how to fully manage her own feelings or to properly navigate this situation, she could be happy in the present, and share that with Louise.

Anna's internal debate about whether to wake Louise up or let whoever might find them find them proved unnecessary as she felt Louise begin to stir in her arms. Moments later, Anna watched two puffy sleep eyes peer up at her and slowly shift from fuzzy disorientation into fuzzy happiness.

"Hi," Louise said, her voice raspy with sleep and last night's alcohol.

"Hi," Anna returned. Louise cuddled in closer, and Anna felt relieved that she wasn't, this time at least, nudging Anna again toward emotional chaos.

"Did you sleep okay?"

Anna couldn't help but laugh.

"What?"

"I'm sure *you* did. You weren't the one being used as a pillow!"

"Shit, sorry," Louise responded, seeming to at least profess some kind of shame. Anna continued to stroke Louise's hair.

"It was worth it," Anna said simply.

They enjoyed each other a few moments longer, but it had already become clear they were on borrowed time.

"We should probably sneak back into the bedroom before someone notices," Anna said reluctantly.

"How ridiculous that we chose to fall asleep on a window seat when we had a room with two perfectly good beds down the hall."

"So ridiculous," Anna laughed.

The mess of glossy curls on her chest nodded and a slightly less puffy version of Louise's face reappeared as she slowly pulled herself upright. They gathered their things in unison and snuck out of the library. Anna looked back with her hand on the door and sent a wish that that wouldn't be the end for them. Thankfully, they made it down the hallway and back into the bedroom unseen—a relief, considering their decidedly suspicious-looking sprint-walk.

Once inside, Anna watched Louise sigh happily with the success. She turned to look at Louise, her cheeks slightly pink from the minor exertion of their adventure, her eyes now clear and unbelievably beautiful. A lock of dark hair had fallen over her shoulder to curl, beckoning, around one of her breasts. Neither of them moved.

"What now?" Louise asked.

Anna could see no other option. She strode over to Louise and suddenly Louise's face was in Anna's hands and she was kissing her full lips. She could feel Louise clasping the sides of her hips and everything else was falling away. They were kissing, kissing like they would die if they couldn't.

A knock came at the door. Anna's heart screamed. It was all they could do to separate as the door slowly opened.

"Hey, Belle…" Clay looked between them. "Oh, you're both up?"

Anna could see Clay felt the tension in the room, but she knew he couldn't have seen the kiss based on his reaction.

"Yeah, we, uh, just woke up," Louise said quickly. Anna didn't like the guilty tone she could hear in Louise's voice. Not to mention the guilty feelings she was feeling.

"Okay, well...Belle, your friend Rachel is here for some reason? Mom and Dad are dealing with her so you might want to get down there and save her..."

Anna was shocked by this information. She looked at Louise, whose face was unreadable.

"Okay, let me go figure out what's going on."

She normally would have corrected Clay on his pronoun usage, but it seemed that time was of the essence. As Anna left Louise with Clay in the room they had just been making out in, Anna finally resolved that their borrowed time was over.

Chapter Ten

Walking into her parents' parlor, Anna was met with a scene that looked straight out of some kind of alternate reality. Rachel, with their blueish-green faux-hawk, thick black septum piercing, and head-to-toe leather bodysuit, was sitting quite comfortably across from her pristine and clearly uncomfortable parents.

Anna took a deep breath. The first thing she needed to do was rescue her friend from whatever her parents had already or were about to say that would certainly be, at minimum, offensive. Second, demand, privately, that Rachel tell her what the fuck they were doing here! Had Rachel never heard of a phone?

Rachel noticed Anna enter and rose from their wingback armchair to give Anna the biggest hug that had maybe ever taken place in the Nelson house. As Anna held them, she was hit with just how much Rachel meant to her. Just their smell and their solid arms around her felt like a jolt of power through her system. Rachel was in her corner no matter what, and it never felt so stark as it did in this moment in this place.

Rachel whispered in her ear as they embraced. "I'm sorry to barge in on you, but you wouldn't answer your phone."

Anna grimaced. She pulled away and said to them, "It's okay, I'm so happy to see you."

"Belle, we were just meeting your *friend* who says she was in the area?" The tone from Anna's mother was clear. *Who is this person and why are they in my house!*

"Actually, Dr. Nelson, I use they/them pronouns. And yes, I was in the area and was hoping to see Anna. I apologize for just showing up. I wasn't able to get Anna on the phone, and I didn't want to miss my opportunity."

Anna knew her mother was uncomfortable in more ways than one, but social propriety thankfully stopped her from voicing her contempt out loud.

"Unfortunately, today is a holiday and we have a few family things planned, not to mention some home repairs, so unfortunately," her mother stumbled over the repeated word, "we do not have space right now for another house guest."

Rachel didn't skip a beat.

"Not a problem, Dr. Nelson! Actually, I was just hoping I could steal Anna for a little while this morning to discuss some work-related things. Again, I do apologize for the holiday interruption. I wouldn't be here if it wasn't a very time-sensitive matter."

Anna watched her father roll his eyes.

"Sorry, Mom, I'm going to have to step out for a bit here. Rach, do you have your car?"

"Yup, parked right outside in your Cinderella castle driveway." Rachel gave the room a bright smile.

"Annabelle, today is a family day. This is very inconsiderate to me and your father." Her mother was clearly on her last straw.

"Mom, I'll make it up to you this evening at Josh's Christmas party. It'll be good, you can get some more time with Clay and Louise!" Just saying her name out loud made Anna feel like her feelings were on display to the entire room. Of course, the only person who seemed to notice was Rachel, who gave her a bored look and raised an eyebrow.

"I can't tell you what to do, Annabelle."

Her mother ended the very awkward meeting by nodding to the odd person in her family room and settling Anna with a disappointed look. Her father just moved on to his *Wall Street Journal* with the kind of rudeness that they both could only show to one of Anna's friends.

"Okay, let's go," Anna said as she shepherded Rachel toward the exit.

"It was nice to meet you both!" Rachel called back to Anna's parents, clearly unwilling to mirror their attitudes. When they reached the front door, they almost collided with Louise and Clay coming down the stairs. Anna was quickly pulled right back into Louise's orbit. She looked beautiful, just as Anna had left her.

"So, this must be your brother Clay and...Louise, was it?" Rachel knew exactly what her name was.

"Yeah, Clay, Louise, this is Rachel. Rachel uses they/them pronouns. We're about to head out for a bit."

"Nice to meet you," Louise replied politely. Her tone was kind, but her face showed that she was a bit disoriented by this new person.

"Yes, nice to meet you, Rachel. I've heard a little about you. I'm glad my sister has finally got someone who makes her happy." Clay pulled Louise under his arm in that way that couples do when establishing their superiority to another couple.

Anna said, "Actually, Rachel is—"

"Is not officially invited, as you can imagine," Rachel finished. "But I just couldn't stay away from my Anna." Rachel pulled Anna close in much the same way as Clay, giving her a comical kiss on the side of her head. "You know about that, right...Louise, was it?"

"I'm sorry?" Louise replied, looking suddenly alarmed.

"I was just saying, I imagine you know what it's like to not be able to stay away from a Nelson sibling."

Anna knew Rachel was just being their usual "agent of chaos" and was unaware of the revelations of the past twenty-four hours, but the awkwardness and the intensity was too much in that moment.

"On that note, we're heading out. See you later," Anna said quickly.

"Well, let us know, maybe we'll meet you out?" Clay asked eagerly.

"Uh, yeah sure," Anna responded noncommittally.

"You're coming to Josh's though, right?" Clay added.

Anna looked at Louise, who seemed to be avoiding her eyes at all costs. "Yeah, I should be."

"Well, Rachel, if I don't see you, it was nice to finally meet you."

Rachel went in to hug him. "It was nice meeting you too, Clay." Rachel moved to Louise, giving her the same quick hug, but with a little more scrutiny after. "I hope to see you again, Louise."

Anna grabbed Rachel by the arm and basically dragged them out the front door. Once the door was closed, Rachel stopped and settled on Anna with a look.

"What?" Anna asked.

"Let's get out of earshot before I present a thesis on my answer to 'what,'" Rachel replied.

❖

Anna wasn't used to driving with Rachel due to their mutual reliance on public transportation in New York, so the experience was novel. It made Anna wonder what it would have been like if Rachel had grown up in a place like Trenton. Or better yet, how much better life would have been for Anna if she'd met someone like Rachel when she was younger.

Rachel was clearly taking their sweet time on explaining what they were doing here. Instead, they were blasting a Katy Perry song and making it very hard for Anna to keep her love for Rachel untarnished. When "Teenage Dream" ended, *and only once it ended*, Anna turned the radio down and turned toward Rachel with a look.

"What are you doing here, Rach?"

"Oh, so you want to start there?"

Anna rolled her eyes.

"Before we go into all that, do you have somewhere we can go? Coffee shop, a picnic bench? Anything to get the taste of, no offense, but your family's weird vibes off of us?"

Others might have been offended by the snub, but Anna was just relieved to have someone who agreed with her.

"There's a coffee shop and a bar, but I think the bar is probably closed. Actually, the bar I discovered by a fellow misfit from high school who I sort of reconnected with."

"Well, that's cute! I feel like that story got lost in the tawdry bodice-ripper romance you're insisting on living at the moment."

And there it was, Rachel was not going to resist teasing Anna relentlessly. She decided to ignore it.

"Yeah, I think you'd like him. I actually wish we could go now, just so we wouldn't be seen."

"Well, call him, see if he'll open up for some VIPs."

Anna rolled her eyes. "I don't know about that, but he lives above the place. Maybe I could just check. I don't know what hours he keeps."

"Just tell him a lesser known, but incredibly talented New York artist is passing through and they need a suitable environment to maintain their lived aesthetic. And that they'll tip based on New York City prices."

"I will not say that to him," Anna replied, "but I can check if he's around."

Anna picked up her phone and called George.

"Yo," he answered in a groggy voice.

"Hey, I know this is weird, but are you opening soon?"

"Ummm, no. It's not even noon, I'm still asleep. What are you, some kind of secret wino or something?"

"No, I just have my friend Rachel with me and we wanted to chat somewhere that didn't have a Confederate flag up."

"Well, I'm getting a delivery to the bar in about half an hour. If you bring me coffee and a few pastries from Delilah's, I'll let you use a booth."

"Thanks so much, George, you're a lifesaver."

"Yeah, yeah, leave me alone. I want to enjoy these next few minutes asleep."

He hung up and Anna was again struck with how lucky it was that she rediscovered her friendship with George. He'd proved to be a lifesaver in more ways than one.

"So, where to?" Rachel asked.

"I think I may have found the perfect environment to protect your aesthetic."

❖

"I love the campy post-drag parody of a cis-het sports bar vibe here." Rachel was holding their hands up in a mock camera frame as they assessed the bar. "Not to mention the no name, but then just say what it is—'the bar'—very chic."

It was often difficult to tell when Rachel was joking.

"This must be the friend from New York." George laughed at Rachel's commentary as he approached them. "I'm George."

"And you must be Anna's lavender savior, holding down the queer visibility for the Trenton community." They grinned at him and nodded toward his blue dye job. "Love the hair."

"That's me, just doing what I can for the cause." George engulfed Rachel in a familiar hug. Anna marveled at how different things could be when you are around the right people.

"Okay so, I've gotta go sign for a few orders in the back, but go ahead and grab a booth, help yourself to beverages, and most important where are my pastries and coffee?"

Anna indicated the open pastry box she held in one hand and the coffee tray in the other. George grabbed a doughnut and one of the coffees, threw them a wink, and sauntered to the back of the bar.

"He's pretty dreamy…" Rachel added with their customary eyebrow action.

"He is, if you like that sort of thing," Anna said.

"Ugh, sometimes you lesbians are as bad as the straights with your rigid boxes. Hot is hot." Rachel grabbed another coffee from Anna's tray and headed for a booth.

"Fine! George is attractive. But just a heads up, I'm ninety percent sure he's seeing someone. He hasn't said anything, but he's seemed a little preoccupied."

"I didn't say I wanted to smash. I was just acknowledging beauty where I see it. Speaking of beauty, wow, wow, wow," Rachel exclaimed as they fell into the booth dramatically.

Anna sat down with a bit more purpose.

"I don't know what you are talking about?" Anna replied, hoping Rachel would believe her.

"Uhh, don't play games with me, Annabelle Nelson. I can see by your cagey little face that things have not improved on the Louise front."

Anna could feel her blushing cheeks ruin her attempts to play it cool. Since the morning's near miss with Clay—hell, since she'd met Louise in this exact bar a few days ago—her mind and her heart had been running at a thousand miles per hour. She still couldn't think clearly about what was going on. All she knew was that any thought of Louise had her cycling through a reel of moments and emotions. When she let the good thoughts surface, she was immediately hit with the bad ones. It was exhausting.

"I don't want to talk about that right now. I want to talk about this 'work' thing you allegedly are here to talk about. Like as much as I love you, why are you here?"

At that moment, George appeared from the back room with his coffee and plunked down next to Rachel in the booth.

"Okay, I have some time, catch me up. What are we talking about?" he said.

"Well, I have some news for Anna about her queer creatives platform," Rachel said. "Her site, she may have told you, was days away from shutting down. Server space bills unpaid, apartment rent unpaid, ramen in the cupboard. She was on the brink of utter despair, coming home to lick her wounds."

"Oh my God, Rach, get to the point." While Anna appreciated the lighter tone Rachel brought to her less-than-ideal situation, she was too preoccupied with the situation to let the dramatics go on much longer.

"Well, I didn't want to get your hopes up…" Rachel turned back to focus on Anna. "But as your unpaid PR director, self-titled, I received a call at the office, aka, my pretend office and secretary voice acting"—this was for George's benefit—"that a woman from Vita Investments liked your project. You met her during a pitch meeting weeks ago. Apparently, her old firm wasn't really interested in diversity platforms like yours, but she's going out on her own and she wants to make an investment."

Anna was stunned to hear this. She'd thought it was clear all viable investment avenues had been exhausted. She had pitched her startup to every person she could, even in a desperate moment, some random person in a suit on the subway, and despite generally positive feedback, no one had so much as nibbled when it came to actual dollars.

"Rach, that is incredible news," she said. "But it's too late. I'm in debt, I'm weeks late on payments, and I already took the site down. It's an amazing moment, and if it had been on the table a few months ago, I'd be ecstatic right now, but I've already accepted that it's done."

Rachel balked at her.

"I don't know what virus infected you at your parents' sadist shame dungeon, but I cannot believe my ears. You don't even want to hear what she's offering?"

Rachel was very serious now, and they started to look concerned.

"Sure, I'll hear, even if it is just to see what could have been," Anna replied despondently.

Rachel and George looked at each other with concern.

"I'm not even going to acknowledge your pessimism right now because I'm about to change your life."

Rachel dramatically slammed both hands on the table, seemed to notice it wasn't quite as clean as it could be, and compromised by hovering them slightly above the surface instead.

"She's making a one-point-two-million-dollar investment. Right now, I'm holding a check for one hundred thousand just to help you get through the next month."

They leaned back with a satisfied smirk, hands now behind their head. George was forced to shift slightly to his right to avoid being clipped with an elbow. Anna could not believe the words she just heard.

"What did you just say?"

"I said, one-point-two million dollars. I'm saying that your company is not just saved, it's blowing up! Obviously, there's a bunch of strings attached and hoops to blow through, but right now all you have to do is make a call to this lawyer, say you're in preliminarily, and take the first check."

Anna felt like she couldn't breathe. It was too good to be true.

"This can't be happening. Why is she doing this?"

George looked at her incredulously.

"Don't look a gift horse in the mouth!" he admonished her, clearly also floored by what he was hearing. "This sounds incredible, Anna. Congratulations!"

"Listen, I took a meeting with her in your absence just so I didn't get your hopes up on something fake. Her name is Vita Ventura and all she said was she remembered your pitch and she remembered you. She said she wanted her firm to do more than make money. Something about 'Impact Investing'? She wanted to be able to help her community."

"I honestly don't remember anyone from my meetings with that name."

George rolled his eyes. "Well, I'm not surprised she remembered you!"

Anna blushed. It was always hard to accept her effect on women.

"Yeah, girl, finally that broody, 'I'm so mysterious' vibe is really paying off. I knew you weren't blessed with that face for nothing." Rachel reached across the table to affectionately pinch one of Anna's cheeks.

"Enough!" Anna barked. "I don't want to get this because someone's into me, I want them to care about the project the way I do." Chagrined, Rachel and George stopped teasing.

"Listen. Right now, you just need to take the money, get yourself together, and start making space for our community. Don't worry about the why and how until you get yourself back to New York and get yourself situated again. Which reminds me, you and I have to get back ASAP. She wants to meet with you in two days to go over some of the fine print and get a business plan together. Plus, your rent check was due like forever ago." Anna was hit with the new reality. She was going to have to leave Trenton. Mostly that was a great thing, but suddenly she was transported back to the first few moments of consciousness today. Holding Louise in her arms. What was she going to do about Louise?

"You weren't thinking about holding down queer visibility in Trenton with me, were you?" George asked a little hopefully.

"No, I just, I guess I just wish I had a little more time," Anna said, already feeling the catch in her throat.

"Time? What do you need time for?" George asked.

Anna looked at them and wished she could tell them without explaining.

Rachel got it immediately. "Anna, I mean this is everything you've been working for. This can't be worth missing for a crush?"

The word crush stuck with Anna. Yes, she was being crushed. She was being crushed by guilt and shame and lust and desire, but "crush" was not an adequate word to describe what she was feeling.

"Rach, so much has happened," Anna said and her voice began to break. The strength of her emotion took her by surprise. Anna could feel the utter impossibility of it all.

"Wow, wow, okay, I think maybe I need to be caught up. Last I left this story, there was a mistaken identity incident and then some mild sexual tension. Bring me up to speed?"

Anna put her face in her hands. She was finding it hard to speak.

"I think I'm falling in love with her."

❖

Louise was feeling one thousand different things at once. When she opened her eyes that morning and could feel Anna's warm body enveloping her, she felt safe in a way she hadn't since, well, maybe since before Gwen died. Her mind was calm, her body settled, and all she wanted was to fold herself in closer and let the world cave in around them. She had clarity now, a simple truth: Anna made Louise happy, and she wanted to be happy. Yes, the situation was tenuous. But ultimately it was just that simple. Clay's family, the Nelsons' house, this was all temporary, immaterial. When Louise was with Anna, it all became an irritating sort of background noise that she didn't want to spend any more time than necessary dwelling on. It was more than just their intense attraction, Louise felt a deep connection to Anna. Anna was fiery and tempestuous. She held on to her values even when it was difficult, like with her family. She was brave, being so honest with everyone about her life even at a young age. She was stubborn for sure, but Louise knew that the other side of that was a deep desire to protect. Since Gwen died, Louise learned to protect herself. Maybe being with someone who she trusted, who had these qualities, would be enough to take a risk.

She felt something click into place when they returned to the bedroom and Anna had kissed her. The two of them just fit. Everything felt so natural, so organic. The past years of unexceptional relationships had taught her that a connection like this did not come around every day. She could tell she was already in too deep to pull back. When Clay walked in and almost caught them, she was scared, but not for the same reasons as before. She was scared about what it would do to Anna's relationship with Clay. It was clear to her now that that was more important than anything going on between her and Clay. Family was traumatic for Anna, and having a brother who was there for her could be a game changer. Louise wanted to protect that at all costs. But she knew, as far as her relationship with Clay, that she'd hit a limit—she just wasn't willing to put in all the effort it took to pretend anymore. It was hurting her, it was hurting him, and it was hurting Anna.

The beginning of a very dangerous thought came through.

Maybe there was some way she and Anna could get through this, could have something together.

She hadn't formulated a plan or any next steps, but she was finally allowing herself to dream bigger than the next moment.

Meeting Rachel in the stairwell was…intimidating. She hadn't asked Anna about being in a relationship, but she was pretty sure she was single. Clay had said earlier in the weekend that Anna might have been dating her friend Rachel, but suspecting a partner and seeing the person in the flesh were completely different experiences. First, Rachel was stupidly attractive. They were tall and intense and wearing an incredibly badass jacket. They were exactly the kind of person that was cool in a way that Louise had never been able to pull off. Anna was obviously a heartbreaker, as evidenced by the effect she'd had within three days on basically every person in Trenton, and seeing her with Rachel was humbling. Louise couldn't get over how easily she had become jealous around Anna. This had never been a part of her personality. She fought it, especially after her scene at the bar last night. It was made worse by the fact that she may have actually liked Gina. All of this chaotic emotion made at least one thing clear: Louise was falling so recklessly that she knew there was no way she could get out of this without a broken heart.

But it wasn't clear how Anna was feeling. The connection that Louise saw on the stairwell between Anna and Rachel was intimate. Intimate in a way that Louise had not seen. Intimacy that Louise did not have with maybe anyone, except perhaps her mom.

Don't be stupid again. Louise dashed out of the house.

She wanted not to be a jealous person, she wanted not to feel abandoned by Anna when she chose to run out of the house without even the briefest of explanations, but she wasn't used to this kind of vulnerable. The whole experience had her on her back foot.

"Wow, Rachel was kind of weird, don't you think?" Clay laughed lightheartedly.

Louise didn't answer.

"I mean, you would have thought she'd be with someone a bit more, I don't know…hot?"

It was clear to Louise that she and Clay were looking at the same person and seeing different things. Unfortunately, she couldn't address the comments Clay made about Rachel's appearance over the loud blaring of alarm bells going off in her head.

"What makes you say they're together?" she asked, trying to act casual.

Clay looked at her quizzically.

"I guess I just assumed because Rachel always comes up, they're always texting, and Anna is always Rachel this, Rachel that."

Louise was feeling smaller and smaller by the moment. This whole time, had she been the only one feeling their connection?

"And anyway," Clay said, "I think it was confirmed when I mentioned it." Clay's words felt louder than normal. Louise could feel her stomach roiling.

"I'm, um, I need some air," she said desperately, no longer caring what she looked like to Clay. She pushed past him and rushed through the house and out to the backyard. When she reached the end of the deck, she lengthened her strides and breathed in the fresh, cold air, hoping to ease the overwhelming claustrophobia she was feeling.

Her mind raced as she walked. She felt like an idiot. She was aware deep down that she didn't know anything for sure, but that didn't stop the irrational jealous part of her from cycling through the millions of scenarios that left her feeing foolish and devastated. When she'd walked far enough from the house to no longer feel its looming presence, she called the one person she knew could talk her back from the edge—her mom.

As she waited, she could already feel the tears begin to fall.

"Lou," her mom said, "is everything okay?"

Louise sniffled and then responded. "Mom…I'm…I don't know what to do." Her tears kept falling, but hearing her mom on the other end was already filling her with much-needed comfort.

Louise could hear her mom shuffle the phone and tell someone nearby that she needed to excuse herself.

"Okay, honey, I'm here, what's going on?"

"Mom, I don't want to feel like this again." Her voice broke.

Her mom knew, in a way that only her mom could.

"Oh, honey, I'm so sorry."

Louise sniffled again. "It just feels like all I ever do is hurt. It can't be worth it." She was starting to get angry.

"I know, honey. I know it feels like that right now, but it won't always."

"It never went away with Gwen. It always hurts."

Her mom kept the same soothing tone.

"No, it never stops hurting, but you get used to the pain. And you know, honey, the heart is not a simple thing. It isn't reserved for just one person. It can love in so many different ways. Look at the love you have for medicine, for your friends, look at the love you have for me."

Louise considered her mom's words.

"I promised her I would never love anyone again," Louise said, finally saying the thing that had been festering since the moment she set eyes on Anna.

"Lou, sometimes when we're young or when we're full of emotion like you were when Gwen was sick, we say impossible things. That promise was not something anyone can make. You can't control who you fall in love with, and I think knowing who Gwen was, she wouldn't have wanted that for you."

Louise took in her mom's words and knew deep down that they were true.

"It just feels like I'm betraying her, Mom. What if what I'm feeling, what if it's more. I know it's crazy, it's been so little time, but I just feel like I've already betrayed her."

Louise's mom took a moment to consider her words.

"I don't know what the rules are for how quickly or how deeply you're allowed to feel, but I would have to guess that there aren't actually rules for that. You are a smart, loving, beautiful woman and you shouldn't feel bad for wanting someone."

Louise could feel herself calming down. She let out a small laugh. "God, Mom, I'm sorry for bombarding you with feelings right now. I know you're busy."

"Yes, well, I think coffee with my neighbor can wait when my daughter needs me. Are you feeling better? I can hear some of that life back in your voice."

Louise was feeling better. She took a deep breath.

"I feel a lot better. I wish I could have been there with you for Christmas."

"I do too honey, but don't worry. We'll have other years. Just know I'm saving your gifts for when you're back in Seattle. That's a much easier commute than Virginia!"

Louise sniffled, but she could feel herself calming down. "Just seeing you will be gift enough."

"Okay, okay, enough. I can only miss you so much. So tell me, what's going on with Anna?"

Louise could finally talk without feeling a lump in her chest.

"Without giving you too many details, a lot has happened, and I'm just totally losing myself in her. And I guess the problem now is that I'm not sure how mutual this is. I'm having really strong feelings. Like I want to almost…I know this sounds crazy, but I almost want to try and make something work, like a relationship. But that's crazy right? And then something Clay said, now I'm thinking she's already in a relationship. I know I'm all over the place and this is totally irrational, but this is what I'm dealing with, Mom."

Louise's mom made a "hmm" sound.

"Did she tell you she's in a relationship?"

"Well, no, we didn't really do a lot of talking about things like that. I took your advice, I told her about Gwen, or at least enough of what happened for her to see why I'm all over the place."

"Okay, so it sounds like you don't know for sure if she is in a relationship or what her situation is?"

"Yeah, I guess."

"But your mind has brought you to the worst-case scenario, is that correct?"

"I mean yes, I guess I am very much just guessing."

"Okay, well the first thing you need to do is get your hormones under control and start talking. If you see in this person something special, don't ruin it by getting in your own way. I did not raise you to make decisions based on insecurity!"

"Yes, Mom," Louise responded comically.

"And what about Clay? Have you broken up yet?"

Louise was trying to think of a response that didn't sound like an excuse.

"Honey, I love you no matter what you do, but I can be disappointed. Please treat that boy right. He has been kind to you."

"I know, Mom. I will tell him today," she said with a growing feeling of shame as she heard the disappointment in her mom's voice. She wanted to support Clay and be a good friend, but it was time to deal with the reality of their relationship. She could not continue to let him live in a fantasy. She needed to be honest.

"Okay, honey, are you going to be okay from here?"

"Yeah, Mom, thank you for listening."

"I'm always here, love you, Lou."

"Love you too," she said and hung up the phone.

Louise was still not feeling fully stable about her and Anna, but she was feeling a lot more sure of herself. She knew she was going to tell Anna, and before that she was going to end things officially with Clay. Louise looked up toward the house and prepared herself for her next hard conversation.

❖

Louise closed the Nelsons' back door behind her and followed the sound of irate voices back toward the parlor.

"She does this to shock us," she heard Mr. Nelson say. "I don't feel comfortable with that…person…knowing where we live."

Dr. Nelson chimed in next. "I completely agree. Who knows what she took when she was here? Maybe we should get that spare key back from Anna. She clearly isn't a good judge of character."

"Mom, don't you think that's a little harsh? She, I mean they, seemed fine. Odd, maybe, but fine," Clay responded in a hesitant tone.

The conversation carried on as Louise entered the room.

"That is exactly what I was saying earlier," Mr. Nelson said, clearly disregarding Clay's point. "'They' is not grammatically correct for the singular. What right does this...person...have to change the English language."

Louise couldn't listen any longer.

"Actually, it's colloquially common to use 'they' in the singular," she said coolly. "Like if you don't know the gender of the person you're talking about, you'd automatically say something like 'are they coming' and no one would misunderstand your meaning."

The room went silent and both Nelsons looked over at Louise as if they were seeing her for the first time.

Louise took advantage of the pause in conversation. "Clay, can I please speak to you for a moment?" she asked.

Clay looked back and forth at his parents, who still appeared to be processing Louise's remark. "Yeah, sure, let's go out back."

Louise didn't shy away from the Nelsons' eyes when she said, "Excuse me," before exiting the room.

Once they were both outside and out of earshot, Clay began talking quickly. "I know I know, I was trying to stick up for her, but I was just struggling to find the words." He looked frustrated and angry. "They're just so judgmental all the time, you really got them with that grammar thing. I just wish I'd—"

"Clay," Louise interrupted him, changing the subject with a wave of her hand. "I know I said I could wait, but I can't do this anymore. I want to break up."

Clay stared at her blankly. "Is this because I didn't do more? Because I—" His brow furrowed in remorse.

She interrupted him again. "That's not why, Clay." Louise grabbed his hand and held it. "You are such a beautiful person, and you are someone I love having in my life, but I just don't feel that way about you."

Clay considered her words. "I know that we haven't had the most…passionate relationship, but don't you think we get on well together? I mean, we never fight, we always laugh, right?"

Louise felt the truth of what Clay was saying. "We do get along well, and we are good together…as friends. That may be enough for some people, but I want more." Louise prepared herself for the next part. "And the truth is, I think I might be able to have it with someone else."

Clay's face changed, it was as if he was stuck. "So there's someone else?"

Louise didn't want to lie, but she also didn't want to say more than she needed to. "There could be…" The half-truth sounded stale in Louise's mouth.

"I can't believe this," Clay responded, now looking shocked and hurt.

"Clay, when you really search yourself, when you think about how you feel about me, when you think about how we are together, do you feel a passionate, can't live without kind of love? Or do you feel what I feel? A deep connection, a friend, someone I am so honored to have in my life. Someone who I can't imagine my life without."

"I guess…" he said hesitantly, "I guess I feel more like you feel." Clay nodded in understanding. He was hurt clearly, but he wasn't angry. He seemed almost resolved. "So this is it then? We're done?"

"I don't want it to be it. I don't want to lose you as a friend." Louise could hear the cliché and winced. "I know people say that all the time, but don't you think we're already good friends? I mean, how different would it really even be? I love you, Clay, I just don't want to be in a romantic relationship."

Clay took a seat on the nearby bench. "I guess I just thought…" He slumped down, defeated. "I guess you're right. We're good as friends. I just thought maybe this would be enough."

Louise sat next to him and held his hand. "And it was enough, for a while."

Clay nodded in acceptance. "Okay."

Louise was overwhelmed with how gracious he was being. "Thank you, Clay," she said, pulling him in for a hug. After a moment's hesitation, he returned the embrace and held her tightly. She felt her eyes well up with relief. They were finally on the same page.

"So," he said. "What are we going to do about the rest of this trip?"

She grabbed his hand in hers again and let herself smile.

"Well, I was thinking...friends go to parties together, don't they? I mean we don't need to advertise or anything. We can just let people think whatever and enjoy the rest of our time together without all the added pressure."

Now it was Clay who looked relieved, his face visibly relaxing. "Okay, I really appreciate that. I really REALLY don't want to deal with my parents going on and on about how dumb I was for losing you."

Louise squeezed his hand tighter. "You didn't lose me," she said fiercely.

"I know, but you know how they are."

"Well, they don't seem to like me as much when I speak my mind," she said jokingly.

"I guess there is that," he laughed. Clay took a deep breath and stood, pulling her up. "Okay, let's get out of this place."

"Where should we go?" Louise asked, already feeling like the world had lifted from her shoulders.

"Anywhere but here. Let's just get in the car and drive." All sadness had left his voice and somehow, miraculously, Clay and Louise were back to being what they should have always been, good friends.

Chapter Eleven

"Did you say you might be falling in love with her? Love. After, what was it? Three days? And with your brother's *current* girlfriend?"

Rachel was clearly shocked, which was not an easy feat.

"Rach, please give me a break, just this once. I'm seriously feeling like the worst asshole. I mean, Clay has actually been really trying to, I don't know...be friends?"

"And you, meanwhile, are fucking his girlfriend," George chimed in. His tone was a bit more stern than was typical for George.

Anna looked at him and could sense something was off. Was it judgment? "I'm trying to say it's not like that. It's more.... I'm feeling more. Like I think I want to...date her. I know that's crazy, but I've just never met someone I like this much."

George seemed to notice he had come off harsh and his face relaxed.

"So, three days, is that right? It's been three days and you are dragging your heels on pushing the ejector button on this whole shitty town. No offense," Rachel added quickly, glancing at George. "I mean, we should be in my car, blasting that T. Swizzle and scrolling through Zillow for our new penthouse apartment. I'm thinking Soho?"

"First of all, George doesn't know you well enough to know you aren't being ironic about Taylor Swift, which should already show how reliable their advice is," Anna said pointedly to George. "And second of all, I'm not dragging my feet, exactly. I just want a little more time. I want to talk to her about maybe…what happens next."

George and Rachel looked at each other in a *she can't be serious* way.

"What about Clay?" George asked. He seemed to genuinely care that Clay was going to be hurt by this.

Anna considered a moment. "Maybe there's a way we can sort of minimize the drama, take it slow…I don't know. I'm obviously getting way ahead of myself. I mean this might not even be something she wants. I just know I have to talk to her."

Rachel put an arm around Anna's shoulders and squeezed. "Okay, friend," they said agreeably. "Can we do this clandestine proclamation scene tonight? If I can find a place to crash, we can leave in the morning. As *generous* as your parents have been, I'm pretty sure they have a GPS signal on me to make sure I get out of Trenton ASAP."

"You can stay with me," George said. "I have a guest room."

"You sure you want me in the guest room?" Rachel said, giving him a flirtatious look.

George blushed and almost seemed frazzled.

"Don't take them too seriously," Anna said, giving Rachel a significant glower.

George relaxed slightly but picked at a fingernail with agitation. His palpable anxiety felt odd to Anna and further convinced her that George was holding something, or someone, back from them.

"All right, gang, we have…" George looked at his watch, "four hours till the Christmas party, and since I know y'all aren't busy, grab a mop or a rag. You get to help me clean the bar!"

Rachel looked dubious as they surveyed the less-than-pristine establishment. Anna snorted.

"And if you do a good job, I'll turn on some Taylor Swift B sides." George tossed them each a rag.

"I honestly don't even know what that means," Anna said. But Rachel's face had brightened and they started uselessly scrubbing a table with the dry cloth.

"Come on, Anna Karenina!" they shouted and shoved Anna to her feet.

❖

Driving around Trenton with Clay had been cathartic. Clay was significantly more animated and Louise laughed harder with him than she ever had before. It felt like their relationship was finally settled into a casual intimacy, and Louise couldn't help but think how odd it was not to notice how much better they were as friends.

At one point when they stopped for lunch at Delilah's, he opened up a bit about Anna and how he was feeling hopeful about getting closer to her during this trip. He seemed to be connecting with her and even mentioned being "inspired" by her confidence. This was very different from the cagey, non-committal language he used a few days before. But then again, a lot had changed for everyone. Louise was relieved that she hadn't told him about her and Anna. The breakup had been shockingly painless and it felt like maybe with some time, Clay might be cool about them getting together. Louise knew this was probably a leap, but ending their romantic relationship had only made it easier for her to dream.

It was clear that Clay looked up to Anna. He kept repeating how *brave* he thought she was. Louise couldn't help but agree. Anna seemed completely incapable of being anything but herself no matter what, even when being herself was dangerous. They could all take a page out of that book.

Louise loved having an excuse to talk about Anna. She had to be careful though. She could feel herself come alive when Anna's name came up. It could've been a tell, if Clay was looking for it, but he didn't seem to notice. And the mention of someone else during their breakup also didn't seem to have really registered with him. Was it that he didn't care or was it that he didn't want to know? The ease of their breakup sat oddly with Louise. Had she been walking around empty for that long? And what about Clay—wasn't it strange that he was okay with having so little of her? A few days ago, she was concerned he was going to propose to her. Was everything just so random for him? She wanted to ask but somehow couldn't find the words. Everything seemed a little too fresh to already be doing an autopsy on their relationship.

They got back to the house in time to get ready. Louise didn't see Anna. Talking to her mom helped assuage her prominent feelings of jealousy, but still...she found that she missed Anna. They hadn't exchanged numbers or anything, so she couldn't text and check in. As the minutes without communication ticked by, Louise found herself asking yet again if what was between them was all in her head.

Then her mind went back to the morning, the two of them cuddling in bed, and her stomach did a flip. She was getting excited. Maybe she didn't know where Anna was now, but she knew where she would be and Louise was not going to miss the opportunity to tell her how she felt. To make it known that she wanted the impossible, as crazy as it sounded.

❖

Clay and Louise pulled up the long gravel drive onto a gorgeous looking farm. In front of them stood a massive barn in a classic red, but with some modern twists. The outside boasted a set of floor to ceiling windows that framed rows of startlingly clean industrial beer-making equipment and a gorgeous showroom that led out to a patio with plenty of seating and space. Louise could see the appeal of hanging out at Josh's brewery. She started to think about coming back with Anna when they weren't so buttoned up. There she was, fantasizing about the future again.

Louise imagined that how the place normally looked and how it looked right now must be worlds apart. The craftsman-style tables were draped in crisp, white tablecloths and decorated with dark burgundy bows and table skirts. The event was formal, and it was clear that formal was not open to interpretation. Guests were in suits and dresses. Even Josh had abandoned his usual lumberjack aesthetic and donned an expensive-looking suit. Clay and Louise came in and gave him a hug, thanking him for the invitation.

"Of course, bro. I just wish my parents didn't force me to make it so stuffy." He pulled on his starched collar with irritation. "I would much rather do an ugly sweater version of this, but whatever." He rolled his eyes and scanned the room, waving at guests.

"It is nice to see everyone dressed up though," Clay remarked.

"I guess that's true," Josh said. He gave Louise a bright smile. "Louise, you look fantastic!"

Louise couldn't help but blush. Josh was very charming, and she needed that extra jolt of confidence since she knew she was moments away from seeing Anna again.

"Thank you, you both look pretty handsome yourselves," she said affectionately smoothing an out-of-place hair on the back of Clay's head.

Clay looked at her appreciatively.

"Oh, man, y'all should see Anna and her friend. They look amazing!" Josh said earnestly. "I mean, her friend is a little out there, but super friendly and nice. But Anna looks…. Let me just say I never really thought I could be into a girl in a suit, but damn." Louise felt color rise to her cheeks at the mention of Anna. Just the thought of Anna made her react. The whole thing made her feel totally transparent.

She scanned the room, hoping that she could get herself together before she ran into Anna, but then her breath caught. Anna was across the room, looking at Louise without concern for who might see her staring. She was wearing a black tuxedo jacket with what appeared to be nothing underneath and skinny leather pants. Her standard black-on-black Converse were replaced with pointy boots, and a long gold necklace met in the middle of her chest and then hung straight down, making it hard for Louise's eyes not to travel down too. She stood out as she always did, but in this moment, she looked like a rock star who got lost at somebody's cotillion.

Louise couldn't look away. She imagined someone might be talking to her, but she was no longer able to feign interest. Next to Anna stood Rachel and George, casually laughing about something. Both looked fantastic in their formal wear.

Anna kept looking at Louise like she was the only person in the room. Louise wasn't feeling that same jealous twinge about Rachel anymore. Rachel was looking at her as well, but with interest. Louise began to think of reasons to steal Anna away. Maybe just for a moment. Perhaps she could find somewhere private, somewhere she wouldn't have to hold back from touching all the parts of Anna that she found so tantalizing. Right when she was about to make her move, Anna said something to Rachel and George and started to move to another side of the room. Louise watched, worried that Anna was avoiding her. Was this another game? But then she turned back toward Louise and threw her a look before opening one of the sliding glass doors. She subtly signaled for Louise to follow as she exited the building.

"Excuse me," Louise said absently to Josh and Clay. She did not look back as she followed Anna into the evening air.

Outside, Louise could see Anna walking farther across the grounds toward a nearby wooded area and disappeared into the trees. Louise took off her shoes and carried them, jogging to catch up. Once she was deeper into the trees, she walked a few feet in and looked around. There was silence.

Louise was about to call Anna's name when she felt Anna's body press up against her and hands trail down her hips. Lips were on her neck and she could feel the pounding of her heart as she was again pulled into Anna's rapture.

❖

"I had to touch you," Anna whispered in Louise's ear. "And I couldn't in front of all those people."

Louise turned around and traced Anna's necklace with her fingers, slowly trailing down between Anna's breasts. "We had the same idea," she breathed.

"You look gorgeous." Anna continued her kisses down Louise's neck.

"You look—" Louise said, but Anna decided not to let her finish. She pushed her lips against Louise's, seeking. Louise responded with urgency, pressing her tongue into Anna's mouth. A shock ran through Anna's body.

Anna inched Louise back against a tree and Louise unbuttoned Anna's suit jacket. Anna thought how convenient it was that she was just a few clasps away from giving Louise full access. Louise raked her hands up Anna's stomach and caressed Anna's breasts. Anna's breath caught. She could feel herself becoming wetter with each movement.

"Why do I feel like we're always up against something?" Louise said. "I'm not at all mad about it, by the way!"

Anna let out a small chuckle. "I don't know. I honestly can't help it. When I see you, I want you." The laughter was gone from her voice and she began to kiss Louise passionately. Anna was losing her mind when she heard a loud voice come through the woods.

"Yo, Anna and whoever might be with Anna!" The voice was clearly Rachel's. "You might want to hurry it up out there because Clay is very much looking for a person that may or may not be hearing me at the moment."

Anna put her head against Louise's and let out a frustrated growl.

Louise didn't seem overly concerned. She asked quietly, "So I guess you and Rachel aren't together?"

Anna looked at her with a teasing smile on her face. "We are not. Were you worried?"

Louise went in to kiss Anna and then pulled away right before their lips met. "Maybe…"

Anna growled harder.

"I can hear you making gross sexy sounds, Anna, can you please hurry it up! I sent George to keep Clay distracted, but he can only do so much sports ball chatting."

"Oh my God, Rachel, okay! We are coming." Anna was beyond pissed at her friend. Anna kissed Louise once more, pouring as much feeling as she could into it and hoping that Louise was feeling the same.

They walked out together only to meet a bored looking Rachel.

"Hey, Rachel," Louise said, a blush filling her cheeks.

"Hmmmm," Rachel responded.

"I'll go see what Clay wanted," Louise said, separating from Anna and beginning her trek back to the brewery.

Anna and Rachel watched her go. Then Anna turned to Rachel, finally able to express the fullness of her annoyance.

"What?" Rachel responded. "You want to have a conversation? Have a conversation! This super obvious sneak away to hook up is going to get you caught, my friend. And that girl, she isn't being very careful."

Anna slowly let go of her anger. She looked longingly at the figure that somehow beckoned to her even as it moved farther away. "I know, I just…"

"Couldn't help it, I know," Rachel responded. "Next time you get a shot, tell the girl how you feel, get your cards on the table, and then let's bounce. I really can't deal with another dirty look."

"Okay okay!" Anna said reluctantly. "I'll do it."

❖

Louise came back into the brewery's main showroom floor and searched the space for Clay. She could see the Nelsons and basically everyone she saw earlier at the festival. Gina was across the room, looking devastatingly beautiful in a burgundy dress that showed off her personal trainer body in a way that would have worried Louise if she couldn't still taste Anna on her lips. Gina waved and she waved back. She would get around to saying hi once she found Clay. When she had thoroughly searched the area, she noticed a door behind some of the brewing machinery. The door read "Office" and she figured it was probably just Josh's office. Maybe the two of them were catching up back there. She crossed the space toward the door, turned the knob, and entered the room.

The room was a bit dark, but she could tell there was someone moving around inside. As her eyes adjusted, she realized there was more than one occupant, but she still couldn't quite make sense of what she was seeing. Suddenly, her mind caught up with her eyes and she could see quite clearly exactly who was in the office and what she had just walked in on. Clay was sitting on the desk, his shocked eyes staring directly into Louise's, as George stood in front of him and passionately kissed his neck.

"Clay?" she asked weakly through her shock.

They both pulled apart quickly. George's expression quickly melted upon seeing it was Louise. Clay continued looking at Louise in horror.

"Louise...I was just looking for—"

Louise quickly slammed the door closed behind her. Even in her state of shock, she knew she didn't want anyone else walking in on the situation. George was startled, but he didn't rush to explain or make excuses. Clay was the one scrambling.

Face blazing red, Clay hopped off the desk like it was on fire. "I was just, chatting with George, I couldn't find you.... You ready to go back out there?"

Louise was the one feeling confused now. Did Clay think she didn't see what she just so clearly saw? "Um, Clay, I just saw you making out with George. I think we should take a beat before *going back out there,*" she emphasized.

Clay either did not hear her or did not register what she had said.

"Okay, well, I'll just meet you out there," he said in a voice that was haunted and strange. He strode past her, swiftly opened the office door, and exited without looking back.

Louise was left in the room with George. She looked pleadingly at him, trying to understand what she had just seen, but he was moving toward the exit quickly after Clay.

Louise touched his arm before he could pass her. To his credit, he paused and glanced over.

"What is going on?" she asked him, feeling totally confused and more than a little blindsided.

George looked down and gently moved his arm from under her hand. "I think Clay is going to have to be the one to talk to you about it." He left the room.

So. Clay was making out with George, a guy. It didn't seem like his first time. His face had been in a state of pure bliss, his embrace was passionate. It didn't look like anything Louise had ever experienced from Clay. The whole thing made her head spin.

So, they were both into other people? Not to mention, both into people of the same sex? What were the odds? Or maybe it made a certain kind of sense. Louise didn't have time to analyze the "whys," she just knew that whatever Clay had been hiding was not ready to come out. His whole reaction was so chaotic, so bizarre. She was confused and she was sort of disoriented about how to feel. But most importantly, Clay was her friend, and he was hurt and scared somewhere. She wanted to find him and let him know she wouldn't say anything and that she would be there when he was ready to talk about it.

Once she had her game plan together, she exited the office and rejoined the party. She was moving slowly because she was still feeling the initial shock. She saw Anna across the room and felt incredibly frustrated that she couldn't tell her what she had just seen so that at least someone who understood could help her process. Anna looked at her funny and mouthed "What?" across the room. Louise couldn't even begin to communicate the answer to that question, especially not using lipreading.

It was at that moment that a high-pitched ringing sounded around the room. Josh was tapping one of his champagne glasses with a spoon and calling for a toast.

"Hi, can I get everyone's attention!" he bellowed. The chattering subsided and the room grew silent. Louise could not find Clay in the crowd.

"I just wanted to thank everyone for coming to my annual Christmas party. Y'all know how much I care about Trenton and how much this community has done for me. This brewery, my dream, wouldn't have happened without the love and support of everyone in this room." The room sounded in applause.

Louise finally spotted Clay standing stiffly near Josh and began to shuffle toward him. She was rudely moving people out of the way trying to get to him. She saw him notice her moving toward him and watched as an incredible panic fell over his face once again. He was white as a ghost and was clearly not okay. Louise was trying to think of ways to approach him when suddenly, Clay began to hit his glass as well.

"Hi, everyone," he said in a booming voice that was not his own.

"Thank you, Josh, as usual your party has been amazing." Josh stepped back and seemed to look at him with a bit of concern. "I just wanted to take this opportunity to say something very personal and close to my heart. Louise, can you come up here please?"

Louise had no idea what was going on. Clay was clearly totally out of it. Was he about to come out in front of all these people? Louise was trying to think of ways to stop him. This could not be healthy. She walked up and grabbed his hand affectionately. She would support him through whatever disaster was coming.

She whispered, "Clay, what are you doing?"

Clay turned toward her and looked every part the doting boyfriend.

"Louise, I have a question to ask you."

Louise still could not see where this was going. Then Clay got down on one knee. She could hear gasps and cheers from the partygoers, which melted into a dull roar as her life came crashing to a halt.

What?

"Louise Tanner, will you do me the honor of being my wife?" Clay opened a small blue box with an enormous diamond ring in it and looked up at her with desperate, rabid eyes. What was she supposed to do? This person, her friend, was having a full-on break from reality. The expectant silence engulfed her. She couldn't find her voice. She looked around through blurry vision and could see Anna through the mist. Anna's face was contorted with shock, hurt, anger, all of it. How could she communicate to Anna with her eyes everything that was going on?

Clay began to squeeze her hand desperately. She could see his eyes begin to water and all she could think about in that moment was how much pain he was in. She couldn't abandon him, not now.

She nodded her head slowly, and whispered a faint yes, as the room filled with cheers. Clay got up off the floor and lifted her into a spinning hug. The performance was unnerving. When he put her down, she could see the Nelsons coming toward them both.

"I am so happy you finally manned up and pulled the trigger," Mr. Nelson said, adding his special touch to Louise's living nightmare.

Louise searched the room. She had to find Anna, she had to explain. But she couldn't see her anywhere. She did, however, catch Rachel's eye and there wasn't one humorous drop in the hateful look they were giving her. Louise was concerned she might light up in flames. And then there was George. He was also looking on in horror. He seemed frozen in place, not knowing what to do.

What a mess.

Louise couldn't see a way out. She stood next to her fiancé and tried not to cry.

❖

The moment Anna witnessed Clay getting down on one knee, the world stopped turning. Part of her knew that there was something incongruous about the small things Louise had said about her relationship with Clay, but she never expected that he would be proposing to her that weekend. Just when the shock started to morph into panic, she heard the nail in the coffin of this horrible calamity, she heard Louise say "yes." The cheers from the guests turned up ten decibels and Anna could feel her head ringing with the absurdity. There they were, the perfect couple, embracing and setting off on a life path that inspired literal ecstasy in onlookers. Anna had never felt so stupid.

She knew she needed to be gone from this situation. She needed to be far away from the sights, the smells, the sounds of how deeply she had been deceived. How deeply she had deceived herself. She abruptly turned and strode out the same door she had used just moments ago to seduce Louise. She could feel her own foolishness reverberating with every step. She didn't allow herself to take the same path into the woods, she wasn't quite masochistic enough for that, but she circled around the barn and toward the front path. When she got to Rachel's car, she saw that it was fully boxed in and she remembered that of course she did not have the keys anyway. She thought about texting Rachel, but she just couldn't bring herself to communicate with anyone, even her best friend. Instead, she felt herself begin walking away from Josh's brewery in the only direction she could think of, toward her parents' house. All she needed to know was that she was getting the fuck out of Dodge, and the sooner she got back and got her stuff together, the better.

As she walked, a numbness began to spread through her body. She was finally seeing everything that had happened on this godforsaken trip with an objective, critical eye. It didn't matter what she felt for Louise. It didn't even matter if Louise felt something for Anna. What mattered was that Louise was engaged to her brother. That Louise was always planning on marrying him and that whatever was happening between them was just some distraction, some experiment that did not even register to Louise in her life plan. Who was this person really? Anna had been so sure that they were on the same page. That what was happening between them was unusual and worth…. What? Not worth giving up a PhD husband and 2.5 kids? Not worth giving up the chance to live a "normal," stable, secure life? But make her believe Louise wasn't happy?

Even if Louise wasn't lying about her lack of feelings about Clay, none of that mattered. She was too much of a coward to do anything about it. She was too much of a coward to be honest. Anna's numbness turned abruptly into disgust. Louise was not a safe person to fall for and she needed to do everything in her power to get as far away as possible from Louise and all the pain that came along with her.

Anna was so lost in her own confusion and pain that she did not initially hear the small convertible pull up next to her on the gravel road. When she registered that a car was behind her, she was filled with dread about who would be witnessing this, possibly the worst moment in her life.

"Hey," a familiar voice called from the driver's seat.

Anna turned and saw Gina. She was going slow enough to match Anna's walking pace and she was looking at Anna with caring and knowing eyes.

"Listen, I just want to be alone right now," Anna called back in a shaky voice, not even bothering to stop her moody saunter.

"Hey, I know you're probably really hurting right now, but I don't think you should walk home at night like this on an unlit road."

Anna continued to walk, registering only then that she was walking in almost complete pitch-darkness.

"Let me give you a ride, I promise I won't make you talk to me."

Anna slowed to a stop and considered the offer. If she kept at it on foot, it would take about an hour and a half to cover the ground to her family's house. That would give certain people enough time to catch up, certain people she didn't want to see and who she didn't want to see her.

"Okay." Anna went around to the passenger side and slid into the seat next to Gina. Gina didn't start moving the car right away. She reached over to the passenger seat floor and grabbed a tissue from her purse and handed it to Anna. At first Anna was confused, but then she noticed her eyes were wet with tears she hadn't known she'd shed. Anna wiped her cheeks and turned to look out into the darkness. Gina was true to her word. They drove in silence to the Nelson home. When they stopped in the u-shaped driveway, Gina turned off the car. Anna could see her parents' car was already parked to the side, bringing another wave of dread to the situation. Anna quickly opened the door to get out, hoping to avoid any final words.

"For what it's worth, I do think she cares about you," Gina said. The words felt dislocated from the events of the last hour. Why was she pointing out something so irrelevant at a moment like this?

"Not enough I guess," Anna replied, full of frustrated anger. "Thanks for the ride." Anna shut the car door.

Gina gave her a final look that appeared very much like pity. Anna quickly turned and started to move as far from that look as she could.

❖

As Anna's eyes adjusted to the darkness of the foyer, she could already smell the scent of a cigar coming from her father's study. She wanted so badly to pack her things, text Rachel to work on getting the car out from Josh's lot and leaving town without saying a word. As much as she wanted that, another part of her felt like she owed her parents at least a conversation saying she was leaving. Anna walked toward the study and could see that the door was ajar. She opened the door and saw her father sitting on his armchair with a drink and one of his Cuban cigars.

He looked up when Anna entered, but didn't so much as say hello or invite her in. He looked almost irritated at being disturbed.

"You came back early?" Anna asked.

"Yes, well, I left something and then thought I'd have a celebratory cigar due to your brother's announcement." He took a puff. "I see you felt the need to sneak out?"

He somehow sounded irritated even though he had literally done the same thing. Anna came farther in and decided to just cut to the chase.

"Yeah, I thought I should leave tonight. I've got some important things I need to deal with in the city."

Her father gave a condescending scoff.

"Typical Annabelle." He took another puff and picked up his paper as if to dismiss her. Anna felt her anger start to build.

"What is that supposed to mean?"

He answered without looking at her.

"I'm sure seeing your brother happy couldn't be easy, especially as you continue to squander and waste all that's been given to you. It's fine, go ahead and leave. I'm sure you'll be back in a few months. What was it this time I wonder? Breakup? Arrest? Eviction?"

Anna was seething.

"You know, Dad, you're right. I was having a hard time. But things have turned around and you know, this just might be the last time I'm coming back to this awful family!"

Anna had never yelled like that at her father. Argue yes, but really tell him off, no.

"I guess I thought that someday you'd accept some part of who I am, but clearly that was never going to happen."

Her father put his cigar out and stood up from his chair.

"I am not going to sit here in my own house and be spoken to like this. You can live however you like, Annabelle, but I promise you, I will never accept your decision to be so contrarian. It's pathetic how much you want to be different from your family, how much effort you expend, and for what? We have moved on from you. We do not care what happens to you. We have our son and now his wife."

Hearing those words from her father was somehow the worst part of her night. She was completely demolished. He walked toward the door and dropped his voice to a normal volume.

"I'm leaving and when I get back, you will no longer be here."

With that, he was gone. Anna fell back onto her father's couch as if struck. She had never been so sure that she needed to leave this house and this town immediately, anything to not have to feel this anymore. She reached for her phone and ignored all the streams of texts from Rachel looking for her.

She opened a new text and sent to Rachel

Anna 8:53 p.m.: *Do whatever you need to do to get the car out and meet me in front of my parents' house. We are leaving now.*

Anna received a simple thumbs-up back and went to the guest room and began throwing things into her bag as quickly as possible. Once she had collected everything, she considered leaving a note for her mom, but after thinking about what her father said she decided no one in this house deserved an explanation. She did a final look around and was waiting for a text from Rachel when she heard the door creak open.

Standing in the doorway was the last person in the entire world that she wanted to see. Louise stood before her looking frazzled and upset.

"Anna, please let me explain!"

"I don't want to talk to you. Please just leave!" Anna replied forcefully. Nothing would make what happened okay.

"But if you could just listen, it wasn't what it looked like—"

Anna couldn't help but laugh.

"Wasn't what it looked like? This is such bullshit, Louise. Are you going to stand there and try and convince me that my brother didn't just propose to you in front of everyone in this town…and that you didn't say yes?"

Louise was becoming more and more upset.

"I'm not going to marry him. I just said yes because I didn't want to embarrass him."

Anna grabbed her bag. "You know, at a certain point, if you continue to do things you don't want to do, it becomes who you are. I honestly don't know what I was thinking." She began to raise her voice again. "I just got so wrapped up in you that I ignored the literal words you were saying to me. You didn't break up with my brother, you are serious enough about him that he PROPOSED to you, and whatever this was"—she waved her hands between them—"was not important enough for you to even consider how this whole thing would make me feel."

Louise was crying now and Anna could tell she was struggling to formulate a reply through her tears.

"Anna, please, I'm not…we're not…I think I'm falling in love with you!" The words were desperate. But all they did was fill Anna with so much anger she thought she was going to burst. She heard her phone go off. And saw the text from Rach.

Rachel 9:01 p.m.: *here!*

"I can't believe you would say that to me right now." Anna was shaking.

"It's the truth."

She reached for Anna, but Anna pulled her arm away. Anna couldn't do this a second longer.

"Whatever this is or was, it's over. Don't contact me. All I can say is I hope Clay figures out what an incredible liar you are before it's too late."

Louise covered her face with her hands and began to cry harder. The sight still affected Anna enough that she burst from the room and the house as quickly as possible. She ran across the driveway as fast as she could where she found Rachel waiting. She got into the car quickly, throwing her bag in the front seat. Rachel didn't say a word, but they were looking up toward the house. Anna could see the light was on in the room they shared and there was clearly a shadow at the window.

"Just drive," Anna barked at Rachel.

Rachel put the car in gear and floored it out of there as quickly as their green Prius would take them.

CHAPTER TWELVE

L ouise felt her heart cave in as she watched the car's taillights disappear into the night. How could things have gone so disastrously wrong so quickly? She'd wanted to explain why Clay proposed, why she said yes, she wanted Anna to understand, but it was all impossible to do without outing Clay to his sister. And the truth was, Anna had been right. Louise chose to protect Clay over Anna. Something she'd done consistently. But in the moment, with Clay's desperate eyes in front of her, begging her to save him from himself, she hadn't even considered that saying "Yes" could impact Anna. Of course she cared for Anna. Of course Anna *must* know that, right? Even as she agreed to marry Clay, her boyfriend, in front of a crowd of people…what seemed so crystal clear in the moment now felt preposterous.

Louise, you idiot!

Another ragged sob caught in her throat. Finally, she tore her gaze away from the darkened window, carried herself to the bed, and sat down, dropping her head into her hands. Anna was gone, she was sitting in a house full of Confederate monsters, and she was fake-engaged to a guy she'd been unknowingly "double bearding" with for the last year. At least one thing was clear: Clay's friend credit with her had reached its limit. Nothing would convince her that she needed to stay in this house one night longer.

She looked around the room and felt the emptiness without Anna's belongings. She began collecting her own things and prepared to leave. She wasn't sure where she would go, but it really didn't matter. She was an adult and this social experiment was over. After gathering her toiletries from the bathroom, she turned to leave and saw Anna's Breeders shirt crumpled up in the corner. She must have forgotten it in her haste to leave.

Louise picked it up, suddenly struck with the memory of Anna wearing that shirt, of her own hands underneath it in the alley behind the bar. She brought the shirt to her face to inhale the incredible scent that was Anna. The thought that this was it brought another crescendo of tears. When she finally got herself together, she peeled off her blouse and replaced it with Anna's shirt. The soft fabric draped over her skin and she could almost feel the indents of where Anna's body was just days ago.

A faint knock on the bedroom door snapped her out of the reverie. She sniffled and glanced back at the mirror over the sink, wincing at the pink and puffy reflection half-covered by her curls. Well, she had nothing to hide anymore. She quickly ran a hand through her hair, pushing it back away from her eyes as she tried to both ignore and half-tame the accumulating frizz, and splashed her face with frigid water.

Another soft knock. She walked back through the bedroom and opened the door. Clay stood in the doorway, looking like the smallest, most crumpled person in the universe. Louise let him in and closed the door behind him. They stood in silence. Louise was struggling not to scream. She was so angry and all the empathy she'd had for him just moments ago left her body.

"I'm sorry," he said, looking at her with glossy eyes.

Louise was not altered. She was burning inside.

"I...don't know why I did that."

"You had no right to put me in that position!" she yelled. The silence after was deafening. "I hope it goes without saying that I will not be marrying you."

Clay moved to the bed and sat with his face in his hands.

"I know," he replied sadly.

"And I am done with this pretend relationship. I am not staying here one more night, and I'm not helping you with one more lie."

"Louise, I am so, so sorry. I just…I panicked. I-I didn't know what to do." Clay ventured a glance up at her through teary lashes.

The apology was not enough to quell her rage. "Look, Clay, I wanted to be there for you, I did. I understand what it's like to hide. And if you'd just talked to me! If you told me what was going on, I could have helped you, but now you went and fucked everything up!"

Clay winced at her words. He was already showing discomfort from Louise alluding to his sexuality and what she saw. Louise could see him bristle.

"What I did was wrong, and I get that you're angry, but it can be undone. I mean, you aren't going to marry me. I didn't really ruin your life." He seemed to get a little strength from the thought. "You won't see any of these people again."

Louise was so frustrated. He wasn't understanding how his actions affected everyone. It wasn't just her. It was George, it was Anna, it was Gwen, it was all the people who lived truthfully as queer people while he was so settled on pretending. His actions hurt everyone, and most of all himself.

"Honestly, I can't talk about this right now. I'm leaving." She finished grabbing her belongings and throwing everything into her bags. Clay looked around, only then noticing that the room was completely empty. His eyes went wide.

"Wait, why is Belle's stuff gone? Did she leave?" The pitch of his voice teetered dangerously close to panic. "Did you tell her? Louise, please tell me you didn't tell her."

Louise could feel the tears coming back and she closed her eyes in pain.

"No. I didn't tell her, I would never do that. But if I had, she might still be here."

Clay looked at her confused. "I don't understand?"

Louise looked at him and realized all at once how similar their positions were. How blind they had both been. Her anger began to dull back into a now-familiar misery.

"We're not so different, you and I," she replied. Clay continued to look confused.

"She left because I chose you. Because I chose to protect your secret over being with who I really want." Louise could see the words click into place.

"Her? You and Belle?" Clay didn't sound accusatory, he sounded completely shocked.

"Yes," Louise responded. They looked at each other, as though seeing each other clearly for the first time. Clay was the first to break the spell.

"Well, this is pretty hypocritical!" he said, raising his voice. "I mean I was trying to be cool about you being into someone else, but my sister? What the fuck, Louise, that is so fucked up!" His eyes flashed darkly at her. "So, this whole time you've been cheating on me with my sister? I mean what the fuck, Louise! And here I was talking to you about how close she and I were getting while you two were laughing behind my back!"

Her anger flared back against his accusation. Clay was fully missing the point.

"And what do you call what you were doing with George?" she spat.

Clay went quiet.

"That's not the same thing." He shook his head as if it would make what Louise said untrue.

Louise didn't need to stick around for his denial.

"This isn't going anywhere. I'm leaving."

Clay started to process what this would mean. "What am I going to tell my parents?"

She looked at him and almost felt pity. Almost. "You're good on your feet. You'll figure it out." And she grabbed her bags and left. She walked out the front and started moving toward the direction of town. She needed to get some space before calling a ride share. And anyway, she realized she still wasn't exactly sure where she would go. It was late at night, she didn't have a car, and she was pretty sure there wasn't a hotel in town. Louise cycled through the last week and everything that had happened. Finally, she googled the number for the bar and dialed. A very despondent and irritated voice answered. "Yeah?"

"George, we need to talk, and I need a place to stay."

❖

The sun burst through George's guest room window, forcing Louise to wake from what was a fitful night. She pulled the top sheet closer and let out a long, angry moan of frustration. Nothing that awaited her today felt manageable. Her eyes were still puffy from crying, her clothes were a wrinkled mess in her bag, and the only positive she could see was that her flight back to Seattle left at seven p.m. that evening. Louise hadn't thought about her flight home for days, she was too caught up with Anna, but here it was, the end of the line. She cuddled in, throwing the sheets over her head and hoping to block out the sun. She remembered that she was still wearing Anna's shirt and she hugged it close to herself, already feeling the catch in her throat build. She was about to allow herself to totally indulge her own sadness when she heard a knock on the door. Louise pushed the sheet down and sat up on the futon.

"Come in," she said through a raspy voice.

George came in holding a cup of coffee.

"I don't know how you like it so it's black," he said despondently.

Louise accepted the cup.

"Thank you." George stepped back into the entrance to the room and seemed to linger.

Last night George had agreed to let her stay, but he was working so he didn't come up, and by the time he was done, Louise was too exhausted to speak to him. She was just grateful that he let her stay. With everything that had happened, and with how little she actually knew him, her call was a Hail Mary. The only reason she thought of him was because he was maybe the only other person who knew the whole story, and he was the only person with a phone number searchable by Google, and because he was so kind when she was here with Anna. The memory of their first meeting, a specter already.

"I'm sorry I put you on the spot like that, I just had nowhere to go," Louise said.

"It's fine. I had the room free anyway with Anna and Rachel leaving…." He trailed off almost as if just realizing that Louise might be upset about it.

Louise winced.

"Would it be okay if we talked?" Louise asked carefully.

"Yeah, we can talk. Let's move out to the kitchen if that's okay. I have some breakfast things if you want."

George left and Louise followed shortly behind, putting on some sweatpants but leaving the Breeders shirt on.

They sat at a snug little island with some high chairs, and very quickly the awkwardness settled in.

"You want some toast or a yogurt or something?" George offered, looking anxious.

"No, I'm good."

"So, where do you want to start?" George asked.

Louise didn't know, she also didn't know what right she had to ask.

"I guess I'll start by saying I think you know I saw you and Clay kissing."

George struggled to meet her eyes. "Yeah, I caught that much."

"Okay, well, I think you also know I don't have a lot of room to judge you right now."

George looked relieved. Maybe he thought she was going to blame him.

"I guess what I really want is to say thank you, for letting me stay here, and for not judging me too harshly about everything that happened with Anna."

George shrugged. "It would be pretty messed up if I did."

"Well, let's just agree that we both haven't been the most upstanding lately and maybe call a truce?"

"I think that's fair." George stopped moving around so anxiously and pulled up one of the chairs. Louise didn't know where to go next but George intervened.

"How is Clay?" he asked.

Louise thought about their fight last night and everything she had said to him. That anger, that ire wasn't so strong this morning, and looking at George with his misplaced concern only made her feel worse.

"I'm not sure. I was really mad at him last night and I said some things. I'm not sure we are…friends anymore." Louise tripped over the word friends. This whole conversation was totally weird. Talking to Clay's secret kissing partner? Boyfriend? Who knows what the story was.

"He didn't tell me or he wouldn't really admit to kissing you. I don't want to force you to tell me details, but I would like to know what's going on with him."

George let out a deep sigh. "I'm not really the person who should be saying this…" he said.

"It's not like I don't already know, and considering I've been sleeping with his sister, I'm not too eager to make trouble for him or anything."

George considered her words a moment.

"I don't know what to tell you. I don't really know what was going on myself." He let out a sigh.

"Clay and I were always sort of nice to each other but never really friends. Sometimes when he would come in town and Josh wasn't available, he would come hang at the bar with me. A few months ago, he was visiting for the weekend, and we were chatting and he ended up being the last person here. He was helping me clean up and we were laughing and just hanging I guess, and then he kissed me. I didn't make a big thing and he sort of freaked and left." George looked sadly on as he continued.

"So then I just sort of figured he was having some struggles and I left it at that. But he came by a few days later and apologized for freaking out. He said he just wanted to be friends and we left it sort of awkward, but then he would text me when he was abroad. Little things, memes, funny things, and I don't know, I just sort of liked him." George started to look a little dreamy. "I didn't know he had a serious girlfriend."

Louise gave him an assuring nod.

"He told me he was going to be in town for Christmas and then I ran into him. Looking back, I probably had a crush on him at that point. I didn't understand why I was so excited to see him. I met you, I had no idea who you were. He didn't stop by or try to see me, but he kept texting me and joking with me. Then that night you came in with him, Anna put it together for me. I felt awful."

George truly looked like he had been carrying the weight of the world.

"I can't really blame you, can I? You didn't know. Not to mention, me and Anna."

George again seemed to be relieved to hear the sentiment repeated.

"I knew the situation was sticky so I really tried to back off. I wasn't replying to his texts that night and he was sort of off. He drank way too much and tried to talk to me after you left and I was pretty harsh with him. I said he needed to stop playing with me. I'm sure the alcohol didn't help, but he was super upset and Josh took him home and I was just sort of confused."

"That makes a lot of sense. I would have been confused as well."

"I know I have a lot to be mad at him for right now, but I just…I know he puts a lot of pressure on himself, and I just know what it feels like to be confused."

"You and me both," Louise added sadly.

George looked at Louise knowingly.

"I'm sorry I gave you a hard time about Anna. I just had a lot of things going on and I couldn't figure out who I was mad at. I guess mostly I should have been mad at him."

Louise considered his words.

"Well, if it helps at all I think I got mad at him enough for the both of us." Louise began to feel bad as she thought about how confused Clay had been.

"I told him about me and Anna," she said simply.

"How did he take it?"

"Not well," Louise replied. "This whole thing is such a mess."

"And the proposal? Was any of that real?"

Louise gave George a look that made it clear how ridiculous that question was.

"We had already broken up. It was a totally bonkers thing for him to do. I honestly cannot believe he put me in that position."

"I can," George replied sadly. "I think he just wanted to be normal and when you saw us, he saw his whole fantasy slipping away."

"How can you defend him about that? He hurt you too."

George nodded. "He did, and I'm hurt, and I'm not defending him, but I can't say I don't understand wanting to be normal."

Louise was taken aback by what a wonderful friend George was. Even in his own pain, he could see the good in Clay.

"So, what are you going to do about Clay?" Louise asked.

"What are you going to do about Anna?" George shot back.

Louise was reeling from the question. "I'm leaving for Seattle. Obviously my fake relationship with Clay is over and he's going to have to pick up his own mess."

"That doesn't answer my question. What about Anna?" Her name cut through Louise. What could she do about Anna? Not what she wanted, she had lost her chance.

"She's gone. And before she left, she made it clear she's not interested."

George looked at her sympathetically.

"Now you answer the question."

"I...don't know. I care about him, but he's not in a good place. I feel like even if all of the drama he caused ended, he still wouldn't be in a place to treat me well. I mean, he can't even treat himself well."

Louise could see a deep wisdom in George's words, but she could also see the part of him that hadn't quite given up.

"But I do think you're wrong about Anna," George interjected.

"Which part?"

"That she isn't interested."

"I think if you had seen her and heard what she said to me, you wouldn't be saying that."

"Well, I think if you had heard what she said about you yesterday before Josh's party, you wouldn't either." George gave her a knowing look. "You have to understand, Anna is a product of her environment. She's used to having people treat her badly, lie to her. Anyone would, growing up with parents like that. It's easier for her to believe you don't care about her than that you do."

"How do you know so much about her?"

"I don't. I just know what it was like growing up in this town around people like her parents and not fitting into the mold they shove you into. I'm just saying, just because she acts like she hates you, it doesn't mean she really hates you, know what I mean?"

Louise laid her head on the counter and covered it with her arms.

"Ugh, this is all so fucked up," she said in a muffled voice through her arms.

George came to her side of the table and wrapped her in his arms.

"You and me both," he said with a sigh.

They finished what breakfast they could stomach, and Louise hung around planning her route to the airport. George agreed to take her at two p.m. and she had hours of painful soul-searching to do until then.

Louise opened her phone, wanting to send a text to Anna using the number she got from George. She began to write.

Louise 9:46 a.m.: *I'm sorry for*

Then she deleted it. Nothing felt adequate. There was nothing she hadn't already said. A text came in from Clay.

Clay 9:47 a.m.: *I'm sorry about how I reacted yesterday. Can we talk?*

Louise considered her reply.

Louise 9:47 a.m.: *I don't want to fight anymore.*

Clay 9:48 a.m.: *Me neither. I have thought a lot about what you said, about Anna and I'm not mad. I shouldn't have reacted like that.*

Clay 9:48 a.m.: *Can I come to where you are and explain? I want to make it right. I don't want to lose you as my friend.*

Louise could feel her hard shell soften.

Louise 9:49 a.m.: *I'm not the only person who deserves an apology*

She added a pin showing where she was.

Clay 9:49 a.m.: *You are with George?*

Louise 9:49 a.m.: *Yes, is that a problem?*

There was a delay in his response and then the three dots, then they disappeared, then three more.

Clay 9:52 a.m.: *Do you think he would talk to me?*

Louise 9:52 a.m.: *Why don't you ask him?*

She let him stew a bit. After a few minutes, he responded.

Clay 9:54 a.m.: *He said I can come over. Be there in 15!*

Louise wondered how many more heart-to-hearts she could fit in today.

❖

Louise could hear the door open and muffled voices coming from the other room. She had been drafting her text to Anna for the longest time and she was still getting nowhere. She got up from the futon and went out to see Clay holding flowers and George standing a safe distance away with his arms crossed. They stopped speaking when she walked in. Clay turned to Louise and attempted to hand her the flowers.

"Are you sure those are for me?" she asked, feeling protective of George in this moment.

Clay looked down. "I want to apologize to both of you."

Louise and George exchanged looks.

"Louise, is there any way I could talk to you alone for a mome—"

"Anything you want to say, you can say in front of George. I don't want any more half-truths."

Clay looked back and forth between them and sighed in acceptance. "Okay."

He first turned toward Louise. "I'm sorry for proposing to you yesterday. It was so cowardly, and I just made such a mess of your life...and my own. I don't know what I expected, but I thought you would hate me if you knew."

Louise didn't want to push Clay, but she hated that he was still not saying the words. She could see that George was feeling the hurt too.

"If I knew what, Clay?"

Clay seemed to beg her with his eyes to let it go, but she stood firm. He didn't have to broadcast it, but he should show the two of them the decency of acknowledging it.

"I...have been having feelings...for...George." Clay looked at George with so much sadness. George listened but didn't say anything.

"I'm sorry, George, that I've been so confusing, and that I didn't tell you I had a girlfriend...I just didn't expect this and I thought it would go away."

"Did it?" George asked patiently.

Clay looked at Louise questioningly. She gave him a reassuring look.

"It didn't. It's, umm...only gotten worse."

"You really hurt me yesterday. And this whole week really," George said flatly.

"I did. I hurt a lot of people," Clay replied, and looked down.

"Okay," Louise said. She was reminded again why she cared about Clay so much. He was a kind and gentle person and so much of him reminded her of Anna. Seeing him here like this, she wondered if her attraction to him might have somehow been about Anna too, in some weird, cosmic way. Something about Anna made her think about everything more magically. Even their apologies, he took so much responsibility, maybe too much. "I forgive you. I know this isn't easy, questioning your sexuality, and I want to be your friend. But you have to promise me, no more impulsive proposals."

Clay let out a reluctant laugh. "I promise, no more socially-pressured forced marriage."

George was still standing with his arms crossed.

Clay looked at him hesitantly. "How about you? Can you forgive me?"

Louise could read the conflict all over George's face.

"I don't know, Clay. I'm not mad at you, but I don't know what this is or…" George seemed to be at a loss for words.

Clay began to respond. "I know I haven't treated you well, and I know I'm not yet comfortable with talking about what I'm feeling, but I would like to be your friend. Talking to you, hanging out, has made me so happy these last few months."

George responded carefully. "I've really liked talking to you too, but I'm out. I live in Trenton. I don't have the luxury of flying under the radar. Honestly, I'm not even sure we could be friends publicly without someone suspecting, and it seems like you aren't ready for all that."

Clay considered what George said. "I might not be totally ready for everyone to know that I might be…not straight…or something." Clay stumbled through the words, but then gained some momentum. "But I am ready to be your friend and all that comes with it. I know it feels like I'm pulling a one-eighty here, but I just feel like I've lost so much in the last twenty-four hours. Louise, you, and even my sister. I really loved having her back, and now it feels like I lost her too."

This was the next subject for them to tackle, and Louise was already feeling the sadness settle in.

George considered a moment. "I need some time to think about it," he said finally.

Clay looked sad hearing the words. "I can accept that."

A calm passed through the group. Clay had started to suck out the poison.

"So, Louise...you and Belle are...?" Clay asked carefully.

"We aren't anything. At least not anymore." She knew he deserved more of an explanation than that. "I lied to you too, Clay, I'm so sorry."

"I didn't even know you were into women," he said.

"Well, I think you and I left a few things undiscussed. I've always been more into the person rather than the gender."

"I get that," Clay responded with a new level of legitimacy. "So, how long have you been...I don't even know what to call your relationship with Belle. How did it even happen?"

"Remember when you picked me up at the bar?"

"Yeah."

"That's where we met. I didn't know she was your sister, and I was having some second thoughts about coming to meet your parents." It was weird saying it out loud, almost if they were talking about other people who were in a relationship.

"We just sort of...clicked, and I thought I wouldn't see her again. Then there she was in your house being introduced as your sister." Louise could remember the shock and fear she felt in that moment. It was all so meaningless now. "I tried my best to do the right thing, to put a stop to whatever it was between us, but the more time I spent with her, the more time I wanted to spend with her. I should have ended things with you, but you had so many people pushing you in so many directions and when you asked me to just hold on for the week, I felt I owed you that much."

Clay listened with kindness in his eyes.

"I just felt so connected to her, and I think, or I thought she might have felt the same way. I don't know, it sounds crazy, but maybe we could have seen each other after some time passed. But when you proposed, she just totally shut down. She said I lied to her, and I guess in a way she's right. But it doesn't matter now. She doesn't want anything to do with me."

Clay didn't react right away. It was a lot to process. "So, while I was questioning my sexuality and trying to hide how I was feeling by committing more to you, you were falling for my sister?"

"I think that's the short of it."

Louise waited for Clay to react, get mad at her, something but instead, Clay burst out laughing. The tension broke and Louise couldn't help but laugh as well. George joined in too.

"Is this more hilarious or more tragic?" Clay asked.

"Both, I think," Louise replied.

"So, what now?" George asked as the three of them started to calm down.

"Well," Clay said, "I took care of the most important things first, making sure you two were okay and hoping you both wouldn't hate me."

Both George and Louise were already totally melted by Clay, but hearing that they were most important, sealed the deal on his forgiveness.

"The next thing I have to do is a bit more difficult. I told my parents you went somewhere else last night because of a fight we had, which is true, but I think I need to come clean about all of it."

Louise reached for Clay. "I'm sorry I was so mean last night. I didn't mean to say you needed to tell your parents everything. I don't want to force you to come out."

"Yeah," George added. "If you're not in a place to accept it in yourself, that is totally okay, and there is no rule that says you have to come out to your parents right away. You saw how they treated Anna. It's really reasonable to not want to deal with that right now."

Clay shook his head. "But isn't that exactly why I should? I mean look at how brave and honest Anna has been all these years.

I never stuck up for her. I never even called her. And here I am in the same situation and all I do is hide."

Louise rubbed his back.

"Anna is brave, but she's a different person than you. This needs to be on your own terms, not because of me or Anna or anything. This has been a super stressful time and you should put your energy into other things...like maybe exploring this for a bit. You can be private about it without lying or having fake relationships," Louise said, the last part playfully.

"I'll think about it," Clay responded. "But I do need to tell them the wedding is off, and that I'm not taking their shit anymore. Not just for myself but for Anna too. I know I could be mad at her, but I'm not. She seriously endures so much, and I owe her one on this."

"I'm sure she would appreciate that," George said supportively.

"And I also want to talk to Anna. I feel like we can come back from this. I hope she can forgive me for not being there all these years. I know I can't fix that right away, but I want to try."

Louise wished forgiveness was possible for her as well.

Clay let out a deep sigh. "Well, I guess now is as good a time as any?" He got up to leave.

"Do you want support?" George asked.

Clay smiled affectionately. "I don't think I can ask that of you after everything."

George looked at his watch. It was almost two p.m.

"I'm about to take Louise to the airport, but what if we drove you over there and waited for you to have the conversation? When you finish, we could drive her to the airport, then I don't know, get food? Not like a date or anything! I just feel like you could use a friend, and honestly, I could use one today too."

Clay's smile was contagious. "I would like that. Louise, are you okay with that?"

She considered the plan. "That's fine as long as I don't have to come in."

"Okay," George said. "Let's do this!"

❖

Anna woke up in her completely empty apartment. She had put most of her stuff in a storage unit when she thought she was going to lose it, but with the sudden influx of cash she was able to contact her property owner and put a stop to the end of her lease. Luckily, she did have her mattress since it didn't fit in storage. Rachel agreed to stay with her out of solidarity even though they had their own apartment across town. Anna didn't want to go there because Rachel had roommates and the idea of having to talk with another person other than Rachel made her nauseous.

Anna felt bruised and battered. She didn't want to get up; she didn't want to do anything. She knew she had to find the energy somewhere since there were so many tasks she needed to accomplish to get herself back online. She was already able to pay her back bills for server space and she had a meeting scheduled for that afternoon to meet with the investor and sign some documents, but that was mostly handled by Rachel. Everything was coming together, and she was finally out of Trenton. Anna no longer had to endure the abuse of her parents, the discomfort of being in her hometown, and most of all, she didn't have to think about Louise.

But she did think about her. Against all her best efforts, Louise was constantly on her mind. Anna wondered how she was, she wondered what she would think of everything that had happened with her job, she even wondered what Louise would think of her apartment. These thoughts made her angry. She wanted Louise out of her head. For all Anna knew, Louise could be her sister-in-law in six months. The thought truly made her ill.

Anna pulled herself up and walked over to Rachel who was hooking up a router.

"Hey, bitch, just trying to get internet so we can prep for the meeting today."

"Thank you," Anna said. She realized that Rachel had shown up for her in every possible way over the last few days...and honestly, always. She hadn't been very kind yesterday.

"Thanks for everything, Rach." She said it with as much sincerity as she had.

Rachel stopped their tinkering and looked at Anna. "You would do the same for me."

Once everything was hooked up, Anna got her computer out and started getting numbers together for the meeting. Rachel went out for coffee and came back a short time later. One of the advantages of living above a coffee shop!

They both worked quietly for a while, but Anna kept being derailed by thoughts of Louise. She couldn't let what happened go. She was angry, she was sad, she felt like she couldn't truly let herself be back in New York. She shut her computer, frustrated.

"So, are you ready to talk now?" Rachel asked, no-nonsense as usual.

"I don't know what there is to talk about," she said childishly, moving to her bedroom to get out of the conversation. Rachel followed.

"Okay, how about the fact that the girl you can't stop obsessing about totally eighty-sixed you in front of everyone and now you're walking around here like a zombie. And to be clear, zombie is putting it kindly."

"*Was* obsessing. Past tense," Anna shot back.

"Okay, fine, we can pretend your feelings just magically went away."

Anna scrolled through her phone trying to make sure Rachel knew she wasn't listening.

"I just wanted to say I'm sorry," Rachel said seriously. "That was awful, and you don't deserve to be anyone's secret. And you definitely don't deserve to be hurting like this."

Anna began to tear up again. The truth was, she had been willing to be Louise's secret. What did that say about her, that she could so easily settle for a few stolen moments? Finally, she put her phone down and looked at her friend. Rachel sat on the bed next to her and wrapped her in their arms. Anna hugged them tight and let the tears fall.

"Shhh," Rachel said. "It's going to be okay."

"It just really hurts," Anna said through her tears.

"I know, and I know that you can't see this now, but it will get better. This is the hardest part."

The words weren't helpful, but Anna was grateful to have someone who loved her that much there with her. Anna was able to settle into a feeling of peace in Rachel's arms.

"I guess I'm going to have to pull it together here, aren't I?"

"Only for a few hours," Rachel replied. "Then you can let yourself fall apart again. I'll be here."

Anna was overwhelmed with love. She could do this. She could survive one more day, and once it was over, she could start trying to forget Louise again.

Chapter Thirteen

L ouise and George sat outside the Nelsons' home anxiously
waiting for Clay to come back out. They didn't even feel
comfortable in the driveway, so they'd parked about two hundred
feet away from the property, making sure they wouldn't be pulled
into whatever drama ensued. A song played faintly on the radio
as they both sat in thought. So much had happened and was still
happening. Louise was getting closer and closer to leaving Trenton
and she just didn't know what to do with all these feelings she
was having. She knew it wasn't going to go away with a flight to
Seattle.

"You're thinking about her, aren't you?" George asked.

Louise let out a sigh. "Always," she replied.

"I'm sorry it didn't work out between you two. With all things
considered, you seemed to really make her happy."

"She made me happy too. It was the happiest I've been in a
long time."

George nodded. "I'm proud of him," George said, changing
the subject and giving Louise some relief.

Louise smiled. "Me too."

"I'm glad you didn't pressure him to come out. He might have
done it just to be forgiven."

Louise shrugged. "No one should ever put pressure on
someone to come out."

George nodded.

"So, what are you going to do about your crush?" Louise asked.

"I don't know, I guess I'm going to see how this friendship goes and then maybe with time…" George got a faraway look.

Louise was envious. She wanted George and Clay to be happy; she just wished they all could have figured this out sooner. Maybe Anna wouldn't have left and who knows, maybe she would be planning a trip to New York to visit her.

Clay came out the front door and walked toward them. George started the car, ready to make a run for it. Clay was walking fast, clearly on a mission to get the fuck out of there. He jumped in and quickly turned toward George.

"Drive!" he exclaimed.

George peeled out. Clay was quiet for a while in the passenger seat, clearly recovering from whatever fresh horror had just happened.

"How was it?" Louise asked softly, hoping for the best.

"It was a disaster," he responded, but his tone wasn't sad, he seemed almost…happy?

"Is everything okay?" George asked.

"Everything is amazing," Clay responded, smiling from ear to ear. "I told them we broke up. When they started blaming me and yelling at me, I told them it was for the best. And then I told them I'm pursuing my professorship in England and that I didn't care what they thought. They both exploded and I told them if this is how they're going to react to my life choices, I'll be getting some space from them going forward."

"That's amazing!" Louise said.

"And then, right on schedule, they started blaming Anna and her 'influence.' And I told them she's the best person I know and that they treat her like shit. I told them I would never set foot in that house again if they continue to speak about her that way. When they didn't take me seriously, I told them to fuck off and walked out the door. And here I am."

Louise was totally shocked.

"It wasn't the most eloquent I've ever been, but I think I got my point across."

"Why do you seem so happy?" George asked, confused.

"I guess I just feel like I'm free. I don't care what they think. And honestly, I'm glad I didn't come out or whatever. They haven't earned the right to know more about me."

Louise agreed. This was a process, and right now, Clay just needed people who loved him around him.

Clay rolled down the window and stuck his head out. He began to scream a celebratory "Wooooo!" that startled both George and Louise.

"Okay, so I also have another idea," Clay said, keeping that same energy.

"I think that I've done all I can do at this point to fix my life. I think now it's time to switch roles." Clay turned in his chair and looked directly at Louise.

"What?" she asked.

"You're into my sister, right?" The question was serious.

"Clay, I don't want to go there."

"Just answer," he pushed. "I owe her a lot and I just want to make sure your intentions are good here." He said the comment humorously, but the irony wasn't lost on Louise.

"Yes, I have feelings for her," she said quickly. She was getting angry just thinking about it.

"Okay, so what are you going to do about it?" he asked almost as a challenge.

"Nothing. I'm leaving. She made it very clear she doesn't want to be with me."

Clay rolled his eyes.

"It all doesn't matter. I have a flight in a few hours."

"Yeah, I thought about that and then I was like… Do you have to get on that flight? I mean you have a few more days before you have to be back at the hospital. Maybe you have another chance here?"

Louise was getting more and more angry. "Clay, it isn't that simple. She doesn't want to see me. I've already tried. I sent her texts all afternoon. I even left her a voice message. She's done with me. I think on the last text she blocked my number."

"What do you think, George?" Clay asked.

George considered a moment. "Normally, I would say it's always best to respect someone's wishes, but…" He let the word linger.

Louise was clearly getting ganged up on right now. "But what?" she asked.

"But I'm like ninety-nine percent sure she's super into you too and I kind of feel like if you don't say something now, you'll both regret it forever."

Louise scoffed at the thought. "I don't think you guys understand. I told her how I felt, she knows. What more can I do?"

"Louise, she had just watched you accept a proposal from her brother. She just spent the last week getting shit on by her parents. She wasn't in a place to hear you. Sometimes you have to say these things more than once."

Louise shook her head. She didn't want to let in the possibility that she still had a chance. "It's more than that. She thinks I'm a coward. She thinks I'm too scared to be with her."

Clay jumped in. "Okay, so she thinks you're a coward, show her you're not! Fight for her. Prove to her you aren't afraid to be with her." Clay said it so passionately, but Louise could feel the sadness behind his voice. His own regrets.

"Okay, let's say I did want to try. Let's say I had nothing to lose, which I don't. I don't know where she is! She won't answer her calls."

Clay and George looked at each other.

"What?" she asked.

George replied, "Well, I've been trying also, and Clay too. She isn't responding to any of us, but I did get a response from Rachel."

"What did they say?" Louise asked, already assuming it wasn't good.

"Well, at first they were really protective and pretty pissed at you." But I was able to clear a few things up with them and they say that they'd be willing to talk to you and hear what you have to say. They said if they felt like you were full of shit they would 'avenge Anna's honor to the death'—direct quote—but that if there is a chance you were 'worthy,' they might help."

Louise was floored. This was her chance, a small window.

"So, what do you want to do?" Clay asked.

Louise didn't need time to think about it. "I guess I'm missing my flight," she responded. "How long would it take to drive to New York?"

"Eight hours," George responded. "And don't worry about me, I can get coverage for the bar."

"Are you sure? You don't have to come. I can rent a car or..."

"No, I want to come," George said confidently. "If I made the wrong call in helping you with my friend, I want to be there to get what's due to me."

"I'm coming too," Clay chimed in. "I want to talk to her, say I'm sorry, and I want to come out to my sister. I think if anyone would understand it'd be her."

Louise couldn't believe her luck. After all of the melodrama between them, she had ended up with two incredible friendships.

"Okay, now for the hard part," she said, already dreading the call.

George handed his phone to her and showed him Rachel's profile in his phone. "New York Hottie" was the name he selected.

"They put it in," he said with a shrug.

Louise took a deep breath and made the call.

❖

Anna and Rachel walked out of the swanky midtown investment firm that had just changed Anna's life. The meeting went amazingly. She signed the contract, with a few adjustments. She was looking at a six-figure salary, office space, money to hire a team, the works. It was a dream come true.

"You killed it!" Rachel said, holding Anna's shoulders like a boxer.

"All thanks to you!" Anna added, again floored by how integral Rachel had been to all of this happening.

"Let's go get a drink to celebrate!" they said ecstatically.

"Yeah, okay, Cubbyhole?"

"Let's do it."

They made their way to the West Village and got a spot at one of their favorite New York bars.

Once they both ordered their respective drinks, they toasted to a new chapter in their lives.

Anna tried to match Rachel's energy, she tried to focus on the good that was happening, but she couldn't help the lonely feeling that was creeping up inside her. Everything was a little worse now that Louise had come into her life. Anna thought how weird it was that a few days ago she didn't know to miss Louise. It felt like she had lost her best friend. No one had gotten this close since maybe meeting Rachel. She knew it was for the best that it was over, but it was almost as if her heart was going through withdrawal. It hadn't been very long, but Anna wasn't used to having something permeate all parts of her life like this. Maybe it was partially because of her family. She was so isolated when she was there, and their words, no matter how hard she fought them, their words seeped through. Maybe being in that darkness made Louise's light that much stronger. Anna was reminded of her dimple when she smiled. Such a small thing, but the sadness it brought on was debilitating.

"You okay?" Rachel asked. They already knew she wasn't, that was clear. Trying to hide it was useless.

"I just can't seem to let her go. I want to, but I can't."

Rachel seemed to consider their words.

"Well, maybe you aren't ready to give up?" Rachel asked.

"Excuse me?"

"I'm just saying, I've never seen you this…invested. Maybe it's worth having a second look?"

"Ummm, you were there? She literally got engaged to my brother right after hooking up with me. Does that sound like someone I shouldn't give up on?"

Rachel took a sip. "I guess I just wonder what was going on from her point of view. Like she clearly was into you, maybe there's more to the story?"

Anna was floored. "I'm sure there is, but I just think the best thing for me is to cut the whole thing off and move on. There are people who are available that I should be with. Even just looking at the last year, I know I've been going from person to person, never really getting close. Maybe I'm ready for something more substantial, someone I can grow with. This whole Louise thing was doomed from the start. I should be with someone else, someone single, someone who hasn't dated a member of my family!"

Anna looked at her friend, continuing to be confused by their total reversal. On the car ride to New York, Rachel was seconds from casting a curse on Louise.

"Okay, but let me ask you this. You met this chick and against all odds and against all your better judgment, you fell for her, right?"

"Yeah, Rach, I don't need a play by play."

"Okay, but just bear with me a second. So then you decide it's all a big mistake because why again?"

"Because she got engaged to my brother, in front of everyone."

"Okay, but, and correct if I'm wrong, she told you afterward that she wasn't going to marry him, she just couldn't embarrass him."

"What's your point?"

"I guess I'm just saying what if that was true and she ended her engagement?"

"The engagement was just the last straw. I didn't like sneaking around, I didn't like any of it. And when the moment came to make a choice to either hurt him or hurt me, she chose to hurt me."

"After everything your parents put you through, that makes sense. You wouldn't want to be with yet another person who pushes you to the sidelines. I guess I just want you to be happy, and it seemed for a moment there that she might be able to do that."

Anna sighed. "Yeah, maybe." Anna sipped her drink and looked around at the patrons for the first time. She wasn't looking forward to dating again anytime soon, but she did feel changed by the last week.

Rachel was looking at their phone and smiling.

"Who was that?" Anna asked, getting curious about who could make Rachel smile like that.

"Well, actually I did want to tell you," Rachel replied mischievously. "Before everything exploded at that party I kind of met someone..."

Anna was totally shocked. "In Trenton? Who?"

Rachel gave Anna a playful nudge.

"You would be surprised what one can find in some of these 'rural communities,'" they said with air quotes.

"Who?" Anna pushed.

Rachel showed Anna their phone. The text name was "Red Silk Fox" and in the text thread there were a few selfies of none other than Gina Perez.

"No!" Anna exclaimed.

"Yes," Rachel replied, smiling fully now. "She's super-hot. We were flirting that night and we've been texting ever since."

This was so typical. Of course, the only other person in Trenton Anna hooked up with would be interested in her best friend.

"She told me y'all have a history, but it sounds pretty ancient. Also, I figured you were a bit tunnel vision about Louise anyway."

"She's great, you should totally go for it," Anna responded, happy it was someone she liked.

"We'll see," Rachel said, pretending to play it cool.

Anna tried her best to let go of her angst and focus on all the good that had come into her life, including the happiness of her friend. She enjoyed the rest of her night the best she could and she went back to her apartment, this time alone.

❖

Anna looked around her new-old apartment. She had just finished arranging all her furniture back to how it was. She reflected on the incredible speed with which things could happen when you had money and were willing to pay movers. The whole experience of being displaced and then suddenly having financial stability was giving her whiplash, and the full day she had spent alone setting up her space had taken its toll. She was hurting and all she could think about was Louise. Rachel's words had broken through her anger. Things were more complicated than Anna had tried to make them seem. Part of her wished she could go back in time and at least listen to Louise. It most likely wouldn't have mattered, but then she would know for sure that they couldn't work. Now it felt like this unfinished piece of herself that she couldn't stop running her finger over.

She heard a knock on the door. This was unusual. She wasn't expecting anyone and there was a downstairs buzzer before you got to her apartment door. Then again, it wasn't uncommon for someone to get in while the door was unlocked for someone else in the building. She got to the door and looked through the peephole. Her heart stopped. Louise was on the other side. More knocking.

"Anna, I know you're in there. Can we please talk?"

Anna was trapped. She had just been fantasizing about having this conversation, but she didn't expect for it to be happening right then. She looked through the peephole again and noticed it wasn't just Louise. Standing farther back, almost out of sight, were Clay and George.

"Shit," Anna said under her breath. A million things were running through her head. Was Clay here to confront her? Why would Louise be here with her fiancé? Was she going to try to push Anna into lying? She decided right then and there she wouldn't do it.

"What are you doing here, Louise?"

"I'm here to talk to you."

"How do you know where I live?"

Then Anna heard another voice she recognized. "Sorry, Anna, that's my b."

"Rachel, what the fuck?" Anna was incredibly confused now.

"I know I'm overstepping, but I just think you should hear her out."

Anna was beyond irritated. Rachel was not in the habit of overstepping her boundaries, so everything about the situation confused her. She did the only thing she could do—she turned the lock and undid the chain. She opened the door slightly and walked back into her living room. Louise followed, but everyone else stayed out in the hallway.

"Are you all coming in?" Anna asked the group.

Clay responded. "I think we're going to give you both a second first."

"Just come in. You can hang in the other room." Anna escorted everyone through the very small apartment. All three of them scampered in and quickly stole away in the half den/New York version of a second bedroom with Rachel whispering a reluctant "sorry" and closing the door behind them.

Anna and Louise were alone. Anna couldn't believe she was seeing Louise here in her apartment.

"I like your place," Louise said. "It's very you."

Anna looked around and saw all the shabby chic furniture and thrifted items.

"I guess it is," she replied. "What are you doing here, Louise?"

Louise stopped fiddling. "I'm not giving up."

The words were enticing to Anna, but her defenses were still up. "Louise, this whole thing between us has been a mistake."

"I don't believe you truly think that."

"Well, I do." Anna could feel her resolve starting to break. "This was never going to work."

"Why?" Louise looked stern.

Where to even begin. "Because you're engaged to my brother. Because we live in totally different places. Because I'm a complete mess and I have no idea what I'm doing. Because no matter how much I want to understand all you went through with Gwen, I can't be with someone who is scared to take a risk with me."

Louise seemed to gather her thoughts. "You're right. I've been scared. I've been so scared that you were going to hurt me and I'd do anything not to hurt again. But here I am, hurting. Since the moment I met you, it's as if I've been woken from sleep. I'm here in front of you, telling you I want to try, telling you I want to try something totally impossible. What could possibly hurt me more, Anna?"

The words struck Anna hard. "What about Clay? What did you tell him?"

"Clay and I are over, and the truth is we've been over longer than we were willing to admit. I don't want to tell you everything that's going on with him, but suffice it to say he knows how I feel about you and he's here to support both of us."

Anna was shocked. "But why?"

"You can ask him yourself, but before you do, am I too late? Do you feel even the smallest amount of what I feel for you?" Louise's beautiful brown eyes looked up at her.

Anna didn't know what to say. The information had all come so fast. She was so resolved that it was impossible for the two of them to work, but here was Louise, standing in front of her saying they could.

"So, you want to be with me?" Anna asked, hearing a break in her own voice.

Louise had tears in her eyes as she let out a chuckle. "Yes, that's what I've been saying!"

Anna couldn't think of any other reason to resist. She had already used up all of her energy a week ago. Before Anna could think of the words, she kissed Louise. Louise pulled Anna in closer and Anna could finally feel the weight she had been carrying around start to lift.

"Is that a yes?" Louise asked, kissing Anna softly on the lips and caressing the back of her hair.

"I don't remember the question," Anna said honestly. Anna could feel Louise's smile against her. Louise pulled away for a moment and she began to look almost sad.

"Are you okay?" Anna asked, holding her cheek with her hand.

"I just...I was trying so hard to accept that I couldn't have you. Being here like this it just..."

"I know," Anna said, kissing her again.

They could hear the door open from the den and slowly pulled away.

Just because Clay was okay with it doesn't mean he wanted to see it.

"Sorry to interrupt," Clay said reluctantly. "We were trying not to listen in there, but we kind of got the gist and I was just hoping I could add something."

Anna looked at her brother, still feeling the guilt pouring in. She still felt like she had something to apologize for, because of course she did.

"Clay," Anna said. "I was so shitty and you really never deserved it."

Clay held his hand up to stop her. "Listen, Belle, Louise didn't tell you the whole story out of respect for my privacy, but I haven't been perfect either."

George and Rachel joined them in the main room.

"I let Mom and Dad talk to you like you were nothing. I should have stepped in. I should have helped."

Anna tried to interrupt, to tell him it wasn't his fault, but he held up his hand again.

"Hang on, I have to get this out. I think the reason I didn't say anything is because I was scared that if I stuck up for you, they would look too hard at me. That they would see that I'm not... straight...either."

Anna couldn't believe what she was hearing. "What?"

"Yeah, I think I've known for a long time that I was different, but it wasn't until recently," Clay looked at George, who looked back with an encouraging smile, "that I really started to deal with it."

Anna looked between George and Clay.

"You two?" she asked, indicating toward George. "I knew there was something up with you!"

"But you see," Clay went on, "Louise found out, at Josh's Christmas party. She saw me, she saw us...kissing. And I freaked and that's why I proposed. She didn't choose me over you, Anna. She chose to protect me, she chose to help her friend who was freaking out."

Anna felt it all click into place. "And you couldn't tell me because you didn't want to out Clay."

Louise reached for Anna's hand and held it.

"I'm sorry I misjudged you for the hundredth time," Anna added, feeling ashamed.

"Don't be," Louise said, kissing Anna gently on the hand. "I saw your family this past week. I can see how it would be hard to trust anyone."

Anna touched Louise's cheek. Anna was starting to feel again truly seen by Louise.

"And that's another thing," Clay added. "I'm done with them. I told them Louise and I are over, and I told them I'm not going to let them treat you the way they do anymore. I actually told them to fuck off, if you can believe it!"

Anna laughed. "Honestly, I don't."

Anna crossed the room and swallowed her brother in a hug. He held her tightly, and she could feel all the stress and all the toxic shit their parents had put them through leaving their bodies. The healing wouldn't be easy, and it wouldn't be instantaneous, but they could help each other. They separated and Anna looked at her friends. She was lucky to have so many people who cared about her. They were all the family she needed.

"Ahem..." Rachel said, fake-clearing their throat. "On that note, let's all go out for some pho or something. George, Clay? You are coming with me."

She grabbed them by their arms and started moving them toward the door.

"So, I guess we're not joining?" Anna asked, not at all wanting to.

"I think you both have more to talk about," Rachel responded with a wink. Then they were out.

Anna went to the door and did up the locks. "I don't think we need them walking back in here," she said with a smile.

Louise was close behind her and quickly pinned her to the door. "No, we don't."

She kissed Anna softly against the door, moving her hands all over. Louise pulled away long enough to say in her ear, "I've wanted you alone for so long I don't even know where to start."

Anna pushed Louise back and toward the bedroom, kissing her everywhere she could see skin.

"I want you in my bed," she said forcefully.

"We've never been in a bed together, have we?" Louise pulled away and began stripping articles of clothing off, one by one.

"No, we haven't, or at least not together."

Louise was in her thong and bra and pulling off Anna's clothes when she paused.

"What does that mean?" she asked skeptically.

In between kisses, Anna said, "The day before we all went to the bar for post-Christmas fest, after we made out in the maze…"

Louise was breathing hard. "What about it?"

"Well, I was so turned on, I couldn't think, and I lay down in your bed while you were gone…" Anna could hear how the words were turning Louise on. Louise had gotten Anna's shirt off and was working on the buttons of her jeans.

"And?" Louise asked, barely making out the words as Anna began kissing her breasts.

"And I could smell you on the sheets, I was so wet…" The words made Louise moan. Anna moved her hand inside Louise's underwear and moved through her wet folds.

"I came so hard thinking about you watching me." She pushed her fingers inside Louise, who groaned, letting Anna know she was already close. Louise pushed Anna onto the bed and straddled her, making sure that Anna's fingers never left from inside her. She began to fuck herself on Anna's fingers while she caressed Anna's breasts.

"God, that's so…hot…" she said through panting breaths.

"All I could think about," Anna continued, feeling herself getting closer without even being touched, "was how that night when you went to bed, you would have my come on your sheets."

The words sent Louise over the edge. She expelled a scream as she orgasmed. Anna thrust harder, wanting to be closer. Louise collapsed onto Anna, lying across her torso as her breath came out belabored and satiated.

"That was so good," she finally said, languidly leaving kisses on Anna's face and neck. Anna was fully satisfied. Feeling Louise's release was enough. She had never orgasmed without direct contact, but she had been so close.

They rested, but not for long. Pretty soon they were both naked and Louise was able to touch and kiss every part of Anna's body, leaving them both totally worn out, tangled in the sheets. By the time they woke up from their post-sex nap, it was nighttime. They ordered pizza and continued to explore and tease until finally Louise proclaimed that she was so tired she couldn't take even one more touch. They lay together intertwined and at peace.

"So, what are we going to do now?" Anna asked, suddenly remembering that Louise didn't live in New York, and she didn't live in Seattle.

But Louise wasn't bothered. She cuddled in closer and held Anna tightly. "We'll make it work," she said, already half overtaken with sleep.

Anna found that she wasn't scared. They would make it work. For now, that moment was enough.

THE END.

About the Author

Spencer Greene is a fiction writer who lives in Washington, DC. When she's not writing, she's making music or riding her bike around the city. She is an avid reader and loves queer media, especially the bad stuff.

Books Available from Bold Strokes Books

Lucky in Lace by Melissa Brayden. Straitlaced stationery store owner Juliette Jennings's predictable life unravels when a sexy lingerie shop and its alluring owner move in next door. (978-1-63679-434-1)

Made for Her by Carsen Taite. Neal Walsh is a newly made member of the Mancuso crime family, but will her undeniable attraction to Anastasia Petrov, the wife of her boss's sworn enemy, be the ultimate test of her loyalty? (978-1-63679-265-1)

Off the Menu by Alaina Erdell. Reality TV sensation *Restaurant Redo* and its gorgeous host Erin Rasmussen will arrive to film in chef Taylor Mobley's kitchen. As the cameras roll, will they make the jump from enemies to lovers? (978-1-63679-295-8)

Pack of Her Own by Elena Abbott. When things heat up in a small town, steamy secrets are revealed between Alpha werewolf Wren Carne and her human mate, Natalie Donovan. (978-1-63679-370-2)

Return to McCall by Patricia Evans. Lily isn't looking for romance—not until she meets Alex, the gorgeous Cuban dance instructor at La Haven, a newly opened lesbian retreat. (978-1-63679-386-3)

So It Went Like This by C. Spencer. A candid and deeply personal exploration of fate, chosen family, and the vulnerability intrinsic in life's uncertainties. (978-1-63555-971-2)

Stolen Kiss by Spencer Greene. Anna and Louise share a stolen kiss, only to discover that Louise is dating Anna's brother. Surely, one kiss can't change everything...Can it? (978-1-63679-364-1)

The Fall Line by Kelly Wacker. When Jordan Burroughs arrives in the Deep South to paint a local endangered aquatic flower, she doesn't expect to become friends with a mischievous gin-drinking ghost who complicates her budding romance and leads her to an awful discovery and danger. (978-1-63679-205-7)

To Meet Again by Kadyan. When the stark reality of WW II separates cabaret singer Evelyn and Australian doctor Joan in Singapore, they must overcome all odds to find one another again. (978-1-63679-398-6)

Before She Was Mine by Emma L McGeown. When Dani and Lucy are thrust together to sort out their children's playground squabble, sparks fly leaving both of them willing to risk it all for each other. 978-1-63679-315-3)

Chasing Cypress by Ana Hartnett Reichardt. Maggie Hyde wants to find a partner to settle down with and help her run the family farm, but instead she ends up chasing Cypress. Olivia Cypress. 978-1-63679-323-8)

Dark Truths by Sandra Barret. When Jade's ex-girlfriend and vampire maker barges back into her life, can Jade satisfy her ex's demands, keep Beth safe, and keep everyone's secrets...secret? 978-1-63679-369-6)

Desires Unleashed by Renee Roman. Kell Murphy and Taylor Simpson didn't go looking for love, but as they explore their desires unleashed, their hearts lead them on an unexpected journey. 978-1-63679-327-6)

Maybe, Probably by Amanda Radley. Set against the backdrop of a viral pandemic, Gina and Eleanor are about to discover that loving another person is complicated when you're desperately searching for yourself. 978-1-63679-284-2)

The One by C.A. Popovich. Jody Acosta doesn't know what makes her more furious, that the wealthy Bergeron family refuses to be held accountable for her father's wrongful death, or that she can't ignore her knee-weakening attraction to Nicole Bergeron. 978-1-63679-318-4)

The Speed of Slow Changes by Sander Santiago. As Al and Lucas navigate the ups and downs of their polyamorous relationship, only one thing is certain: romance has never been so crowded. 978-1-63679-329-0)

Tides of Love by Kimberly Cooper Griffin. Falling in love is the last thing on either of their minds, but when Mikayla and Gem meet, sparks of possibility begin to shine, revealing a future neither expected. 978-1-63679-319-1)

Catch by Kris Bryant. Convincing the wife of the star quarterback to walk away from her family was never in offensive coordinator Sutton McCoy's game plan. But standing on the sidelines when a second chance at true love comes her way proves all but impossible. (978-1-63679-276-7)

Hearts in the Wind by MJ Williamz. Beth and Evelyn seem destined to remain mortal enemies but are about to discover that in matters of the heart, sometimes you must cast your fortunes to the wind. (978-1-63679-288-0)

Hero Complex by Jesse J. Thoma. Bronte, Athena, and their unlikely friends must work together to defeat Bronte's arch nemesis. The fate of love, humanity, and the world might depend on it. No pressure. (978-1-63679-280-4)

Hotel Fantasy by Piper Jordan. Molly Taylor has a fantasy in mind that only Lexi can fulfill. However, convincing her to participate could prove challenging. (978-1-63679-207-1)

Last New Beginning by Krystina Rivers. Can commercial broker Skye Kohl and contractor Bailey Kaczmarek overcome their pride and work together while the tension between them boils over into a love that could soothe both of their hearts? (978-1-63679-261-3)

Love and Lattes by Karis Walsh. Cat café owner Bonnie and wedding planner Taryn join forces to get rescue cats into forever homes—discovering their own forever along the way. (978-1-63679-290-3)

Repatriate by Jaime Maddox. Ally Hamilton's new job as a home health aide takes an unexpected twist when she discovers a fortune in stolen artwork and must repatriate the masterpieces and avoid the wrath of the violent man who stole them. (978-1-63679-303-0)

The Hues of Me and You by Morgan Lee Miller. Arlette Adair and Brooke Dawson almost fell in love in college. Years later, they unexpectedly run into each other and come face-to-face with their unresolved past. (978-1-63679-229-3)

A Haven for the Wanderer by Jenny Frame. When Griffin Harris comes to Rosebrook village, the love she finds with Bronte de Lacey creates safe haven and she finally finds her place in the world. But will she run again when their love is tested? (978-1-63679-291-0)

A Spark in the Air by Dena Blake. Internet executive Crystal Tucker is sure Wi-Fi could really help small-town residents, even if it means putting an internet café out of business, but her instant attraction to the owner's daughter, Janie Elliott, makes moving ahead with her plans complicated. (978-1-63679-293-4)

Between Takes by CJ Birch. Simone Lavoie is convinced her new job as an intimacy coordinator will give her a fresh perspective. Instead, problems on set and her growing attraction to actress Evelyn Harper only add to her worries. (978-1-63679-309-2)

Camp Lost and Found by Georgia Beers. Nobody knows better than Cassidy and Frankie that life doesn't always give you what you want. But sometimes, if you're lucky, life gives you exactly what you need. (978-1-63679-263-7)

Felix Navidad by 'Nathan Burgoine. After the wedding of a good friend, instead of Felix's Hawaii Christmas treat to himself, ice rain strands him in Ontario with fellow wedding-guest—and handsome ex of said friend—Kevin in a small cabin for the holiday Felix definitely didn't plan on. (978-1-63679-411-2)

Fire, Water, and Rock by Alaina Erdell. As Jess and Clare reveal more about themselves, and their hot summer fling tips over into true love, they must confront their pasts before they can contemplate a future together. (978-1-63679-274-3)

Lines of Love by Brey Willows. When even the Muse of Love doesn't believe in forever, we're all in trouble. (978-1-63555-458-8)

Manny Porter and The Yuletide Murder by D.C. Robeline. Manny only has the holiday season to discover who killed prominent research scientist Phillip Nikolaidis before the judicial system condemns an innocent man to lethal injection. (978-1-63679-313-9)

Only This Summer by Radclyffe. A fling with Lily promises to be exactly what Chase is looking for—short-term, hot as a forest fire, and one Chase can extinguish whenever she wants. After all, it's only one summer. (978-1-63679-390-0)

Picture-Perfect Christmas by Charlotte Greene. Two former rivals compete to capture the essence of their small mountain town at Christmas, all the while fighting old and new feelings. (978-1-63679-311-5)

Playing Love's Refrain by Lesley Davis. Drew Dawes had shied away from the world of music until Wren Banderas gave her a reason to play their love's refrain. (978-1-63679-286-6)

Profile by Jackie D. The scales of justice are weighted against FBI agents Cassidy Wolf and Alex Derby. Loyalty and love may be the only advantage they have. (978-1-63679-282-8)

Almost Perfect by Tagan Shepard. A shared love of queer TV brings Olivia and Riley together, but can they keep their real-life love as picture perfect as their on-screen counterparts? (978-1-63679-322-1)

Corpus Calvin by David Swatling. Cloverkist Inn may be haunted, but a ghost materializes from Jason Dekker's past and Calvin's canine instinct kicks in to protect a young boy from mortal danger. (978-1-62639-428-5)

Craving Cassie by Skye Rowan. Siobhan Carney and Cassie Townsend share an instant attraction, but are they brave enough to give up everything they have ever known to be together? (978-1-63679-062-6)

Drifting by Lyn Hemphill. When Tess jumps into the ocean after Jet, she thinks she's saving her life. Of course, she can't possibly know Jet is actually a mermaid desperate to fix her mistake before she causes her clan's demise. (978-1-63679-242-2)

Enigma by Suzie Clarke. Polly has taken an oath to protect and serve her country, but when the spy she's tasked with hunting becomes the love of her life, will she be the one to betray her country? (978-1-63555-999-6)

Finding Fault by Annie McDonald. Can environmental activist Dr. Evie O'Halloran and government investigator Merritt Shepherd set aside their conflicting ideas about saving the planet and risk their hearts enough to save their love? (978-1-63679-257-6)

Hot Keys by R.E. Ward. In 1920s New York City, Betty May Dewitt and her best friend, Jack Norval, are determined to make their Tin Pan Alley dreams come true and discover they will have to fight—not only for their hearts and dreams, but for their lives. (978-1-63679-259-0)

Securing Ava by Anne Shade. Private investigator Paige Richards takes a case to locate and bring back runaway heiress Ava Prescott. But ignoring her attraction may prove impossible when their hearts and lives are at stake. (978-1-63679-297-2)

The Amaranthine Law by Gun Brooke. Tristan Kelly is being hunted for who she is and her incomprehensible past, and despite her overwhelming feelings for Olivia Bryce, she has to reject her to keep her safe. (978-1-63679-235-4)

The Forever Factor by Melissa Brayden. When Bethany and Reid confront their past, they give new meaning to letting go, forgiveness, and a future worth fighting for. (978-1-63679-357-3)

The Frenemy Zone by Yolanda Wallace. Ollie Smith-Nakamura thinks relocating from San Francisco to her dad's rural hometown is the worst idea in the world, but after she meets her new classmate Ariel Hall, she might have a change of heart. (978-1-63679-249-1)